The Good Physician

Also by Kent Harrington:

Dark Ride (1996)

Dia de los Muertos (1997)

The American Boys (2000)

The Tattooed Muse (2001)

Red Jungle (2005)

The Good Physician

Kent Harrington

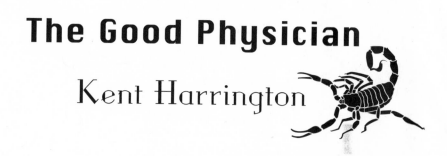

20 08

Dennis McMillan Publications

FIRST EDITION
Published April 2008

Dustjacket and interior artwork by
Carol Collier.

ISBN 978-0-939767-60-1

DENNIS MCMILLAN PUBLICATIONS
4460 N. HACIENDA DEL SOL (GUEST HOUSE)
TUCSON, AZ 85718   TEL. (520)-529-6636
EMAIL: DENNISMCMILLAN@AOL.COM
WEBSITE: HTTP://DENNISMCMILLAN.COM

For a good physician, James R. McCurdy, M.D.

But I've a rendezvous with Death
At midnight in some flaming town,
When Spring trips north again this year,
And I to my pledged word am true,
I shall not fail that rendezvous.

—— *I have a rendezvous with Death,*
                    Allen Seeger

The Good Physician

1

They could hear it coming, a plane approaching from the west. It flew low; first over the beach, its dark silhouette trailing across the white sand, then past the high dunes, and then past the windsock at the end of the runway. They could hear when it finally touched down.

Someone said it was the mail plane back from the Gulf run. They were mostly older turboprops that called the airport home: Fokkers, DC-7's and Brazilian Bandeirantes. The airport was primitive. It sat alone on the desert near Cabo San Lucas. Nothing much to the place but a few dismal hangers, the stained tarmac, and men who knew a lot about planes and flying them.

Jimmy Hidalgo, the owner of one of the cargo companies, had been saying that the runway at San Javier, where the doctor and his friends were going, was tricky. It was too short, he explained. You had to drop in very quickly as soon as you cleared the mountain.

"And on the way out it's worse; you have to clear the date grove," he said. He glanced at his son, who was talking to the German girl, Marita, who'd come with the doctor and Alfredo from Mexico City for the weekend.

Dr. Collin Reeves looked at the old DC-5 on the tarmac. His father flew and owned a plane, so the doctor had grown up with talk of airplanes and difficult landings. The plane that was to take them to San Javier was far too old to still be in service. He understood now why the man at their hotel in Cabo San Lucas had suggested driving to San Javier, rather than risk flying in.

They were drinking coffee in the hangar and watching the dawn break outside, suddenly, the way it does in the desert. The cargo boys had arrived for work, and the place seemed more like an airport now.

The owner told them that he'd bought his DC-5 from a Dutch mining company two years before in Ecuador. According to Hidalgo, it had been built in 1935 and seen action with the Marines at Guadalcanal—"and been shot at by Japanese gentlemen that didn't like her." Hidalgo had found her abandoned in an Amazon boom town where, he said, everyone was digging for gold, covered in muck, and drunk. He'd always wanted a DC-5, and bought her from the Dutch owners, who were using her for parts.

He loved the plane, he told them. "Sometimes you love things you shouldn't love, doctor," Hidalgo said. "But that's life. I've spent more restoring her than she'll ever make me." Collin's friend Alfredo, a painter, said that had to be the definition of love, and they all laughed.

A mail pilot stopped by the hangar to report that visibility was poor over the coast between Loreto and Cabo. The doctor listened as the two professionals talked about the weather. Hidalgo bit his lip. He nodded twice when he heard the word "fog," his expression serious. Before he left, the mail pilot turned to the doctor and said that conditions were actually pretty good for the end of March, when things could be quite bumpy.

The pilot gave them a fey smile, as if he understood something Collin didn't. Then he wished them all *buena suerte* and rode his bicycle back across the tarmac, the morning sunlight making the airport's old hangars seem somehow beautiful and ugly at the same time.

Collin had asked why Hidalgo wasn't flying them. Hidalgo explained that he wasn't allowed to fly because he'd had a bad crash up at San Quintin in a Fokker 27 the year before. His right leg and foot had been badly burnt before he was pulled from the wreck. He'd been lucky to survive it, he said.

"So when you take off at San Javier, the date palms end right up under you, doctor—just a *few* feet under you. You could pick the fruit as you go by! The trick is to clear the date palms."

Collin understood that it was probably dangerous to take off from San Javier, and that Hidalgo missed doing it.

"Are you a pilot, doctor? You seem to know something about it."

"No, but my father is," Collin said.

"Then he would understand. I finally ran out of luck at San Quintin in that Fokker," Hidalgo said, before his mechanic interrupted him.

Everyone runs out of luck some place, Collin thought. *It was just a question of where. Everyone gets their San Quintin.*

The mechanic started the DC-5's engines in the cold. Each one turned over slowly so you could see the propeller shudder-rotate, cough black exhaust and then finally go strong. The sound was thrilling once they got going. The plane was definitely too old, Collin thought again, watching the mechanic. But this was Mexico, and there were no rules about things like that. If there were, no one paid them any attention. Everything had two or three lives here, before it was finally allowed to die.

Collin watched as the mechanic popped out of the cabin, listening carefully to the engines for any sign of trouble. The ground crew began loading a crazy assortment of cargo to be dropped off at various airstrips along the way: a horse, some scuba gear for a hotel in Loreto, and a motley assortment of luggage.

"Of course, sometimes there are accidents at San Javier," Hidalgo said over the sound of the engines. "Usually pilots from Texas or Arizona who aren't familiar. It's only fair that we charge more to land at San Javier. At least we've done it before," he said, laughing. Then he went outside. Collin noticed how big Hidalgo was, walking with his cane, limping, his right leg shot, to check the plane himself.

They flew with the rear hatch open and no thought of personal safety, the cargo door long ago removed for convenience' sake. They landed thirty minutes later at a desert airstrip, seemingly in the middle of nowhere.

A rancher and a young boy came and helped take the horse off the plane, leading it off on a makeshift ramp. Then they'd taken off again, the rancher waving at them as if he'd met them all.

The doctor, standing near the open cargo door, waved back feeling like they were on the edge of a lonely, beautiful world, the last ones left. *Sometimes you fall in love with things you shouldn't.*

They flew over the mountain, and then he saw the date palms and the dirt landing strip of San Javier below, stained dark by the March rain, all looking like a painting. They dropped hard, as Hidalgo had said they would, just as soon as they cleared the mountain. The nylon netting—kept for bundling large cargo— slid at the doctor, and he had to turn away from the open cargo door to brace himself against it.

Hidalgo's son throttled the engines back and landed the plane expertly, *mano-a-mano*, just as he'd been taught. When they'd landed, the son, big and handsome like his father, shook everyone's hand and promised he'd come for them that Sunday at noon, unless the weather got bad. The pilot shook the German girl's hand twice. While their luggage was loaded into the taxi, they all watched the son take off and clear the wall of date palms by a good six feet.

On the way to the *pensión* they'd agreed that the son was a good pilot and that his father had done a good job with him. The German girl didn't say anything, but she'd watched, too. She was just quiet, Collin thought, in that way that made you know she was paying close attention to everything.

• • •

Dr. Collin Reeves' specialty was tropical diseases—parasitology, his card said. They were the diseases travelers feared most, some tiny invertebrate that had penetrated the unsuspecting patient's defenses and gotten down to its nasty god-given biology, thriving while their host suffered. As one of his professors had been fond of saying: "If you have one, you've probably got several."

He was listed as a "go-to" doctor by the U.S. Embassy in Mexico City, where he saw American tourists—either at their hotels, which he preferred, or at his combination office and apartment downtown, not far from the *Zócalo*.

Several doctors were on the list, but he was the only young American. He was boyishly handsome; being a doctor still seemed secondary to his obvious youth. He'd played basketball as an undergraduate, so was naturally commanding. His patients seemed to feel better in the hands of a tall man.

He'd fallen in love with Mexico and with painting it and was paying the price, something he wasn't yet aware of. If anyone had told him that he was a bohemian in the making, he would have laughed.

His parents, very well-to-do, had despaired completely when he hadn't come home after medical school. They'd expected a successful physician, not what they thought he'd become: a hand-to-mouth backwater doctor, throwing his life away in various slums.

His father, a prominent San Francisco surgeon, had announced the previous Thanksgiving that his son had failed to live up to his promise. It seemed to slip out of his father's mouth without his being able to stop it. It was a shock. Collin had thought, sitting at the table, that it all sounded true. He couldn't really deny it.

Yet it wasn't right to say it like that, in front of people Collin had known his whole life. He hadn't tried to defend himself. He couldn't. Everyone at the table was quiet for a moment; it was out of character for his father to speak that way. His younger sister managed to change the subject.

They'd gone on from there, but the damage had been done. His parents had expected a wedding at their country club, a pretty young blonde wife, and grandchildren they could spoil. They'd gotten none of it. They were angry at him now, because he hadn't lived up to his end of the contract.

After two years in the intelligence service, he regretted joining. They hadn't used him for much, kept undercover as a go-to doctor first in Kuwait, then in Mexico. But he could do little about it, other than quit and go home, and he couldn't face that.

He didn't miss the States at all; that was the truth. Part of him loved the backwater existence: the tramping without a clear destination, playing the rôle of a country doctor to the hilt. He couldn't explain it, really. He was angry at his parents, especially his father, but he couldn't explain exactly why, other than he hated his father's arrogance, which his father thought—in his stupid way—was how he was supposed to be a father. Collin had learned to hate arrogance of any kind.

After graduating from medical school, rather than go back home to San Francisco, he'd gone to study, on scholarship, at the University of London's famous school of tropical diseases. Then he'd gone to Brazil, where he'd volunteered for a program treating poor people in the *fávelas*. Later he'd joined *Médecins Sans Frontières*, confronting strange and frightening diseases in various African *bidonvilles*.

He made no money. In fact, sometimes he had to borrow it just to go on. He enjoyed living from day to day in the bush with no one to answer to. It was the first time he'd felt free and done whatever the hell he wanted.

He had a certain quiet confidence that worked for him. While other doctors gave up, or wouldn't go that extra mile, afraid for their own safety, he always had. He was always certain he could beat whatever was thrown at him. The more filthy and dark the hut, the better he liked it. He hated the diseases he fought and took the misery they brought his patients personally. They were the enemies of *his* State. He believed in Science's power to do good. He was inspired by the power of human intelligence and believed in it. It was his religion.

He had been recruited in Africa where scouts were attracted by his having gone native, a talent the agency sought for their clandestine service. The fact that he was a brilliant young doctor hadn't been very important. They simply needed doctors—brilliant or otherwise—for those moments when they couldn't call a "civilian" doctor.

Someone called Bill came to see him after 9/11, while he was working in Nairobi. Collin wanted to do his bit to help fight the terrorists, and he'd agreed to go to Virginia to see some people in a company called "International Recruiting Services." He was hoping to be sent to Afghanistan.

The agency had lied to him. They'd promised him he'd be in the front lines of the war on terror; instead, they'd sent him to Kuwait for a year to be at the beck and call of some local Emir who was the Embassy's darling. The man's greatest fear was that his live-in Russian prostitutes were going to give him some horrific disease, or kill him outright when they were drunk.

"You check good. Take all the time you need. You check *every-thing, young man*," his master said to him over the phone whenever he expected a new girl. Collin would be called to his white marble palace in the desert, built by the Bechtel Corporation. He would be forced to wait like any other flunky in the Emir's pay, in an enormous foyer chilled by air-conditioning and staffed by young Filipino girls in uniform, who seemed never to speak to anyone. His Emir would appear suddenly with his retinue of bodyguards, shake his hand perfunctorily, and politely remind him to check her for *everything* one more time, in case Collin hadn't understood before. They'd all wait for the limousine carrying yet another diffident and breathtaking 18-year-old from Belarus whose visa said "administration services." The girls were changed frequently, for safety's sake.

Collin realized one day while shaving that he'd become an on-call brothel doctor. It had shocked him at first; he'd graduated at the top of his class at medical school. He would certainly have been more valuable to his country doing real medical work somewhere in the front lines of the War On Terror—but he'd had to get used to it. His Emir was important to his bosses at the Embassy, and that was that.

The rest of the time he was free to play golf in one of the hottest places on earth. He'd spent hours alone with a caddy from China who couldn't speak a word of English. He'd come close to going mad.

His service in Mexico had been no less boring. He believed he deserved revenge on the system, and took it by leaving the city at every opportunity to paint, something he'd discovered he loved. He no longer thought much about the War On Terror. No one seemed to notice when he was gone.

2

They took the taxi from the runway to a rustic *pensión* near the church. The room, when Collin opened the door, smelled of the sea and the ancient timbers used to build the place years before. He had gotten a room on the desert side. Its one small window offered a good view of a treeless mountain, almost blue, scarred by jeep tracks that seemed to wander aimlessly across the mountain's face like scars.

He found a bark scorpion in the shower and killed it with a newspaper. Its amber-colored body scrambled on the tiles to avoid the blows; then suddenly it was dead. As he cleaned up for breakfast he wondered where else they were hiding.

He thought about the German girl while he put his things away. He couldn't help it. He'd always liked women too much: not just the sex, which he enjoyed, but their company. He loved the company of women. He loved them for being mercurial and taciturn at times, the very things that most men he knew disliked.

He met his friends for breakfast on the *pensión's* second floor balcony, under a green market umbrella with a view of the oasis. In the distance the doctor could see the tops of the date palms sway from the weight of the pickers, some shirtless, who were already up in the trees, harvesting the fruit before it got too hot. Everything was done in the town before it got too warm, their waiter told them. Children, he joked, were all conceived at dawn, or after midnight.

9

After breakfast they'd all gone out to paint. The doctor wanted to work alone; he thought he wasn't as good a painter as the others. They were professional artists, and he considered himself a rank amateur. He'd stayed out of the oasis, where his friends all wanted to be, or in front of the town's famous church. It was better if he were alone, he'd told himself, not getting in their way, taking up a valuable position that rightfully belonged to the professionals.

Instead, he'd wandered down a dirt track running by the back of the *pensión*. The dirt road became very rough and rutted as he walked towards the sea. He carried a cheap backpack that he'd bought in the market at *San Angel* in Mexico City. It carried his portable easel, paper, his watercolors, and a bottle of iced tea he'd bought in the town.

He walked for a kilometer or so and found nothing of interest. The heat, building suddenly after eleven, pressed down on him almost like a weight. The intense sunlight started to rob the landscape of its hard, clean edges. He was going to give up and go back, because all he'd seen was the strange landscape with its hulking barrel cacti and the odd signs of civilization: a rusted and defiled car and an unfinished building's foundation sprouting steel rods, oddly surreal in the middle of nowhere. But he kept going, enjoying the walking, the feeling of being completely alone, not wanting to waste the morning.

He stopped finally at an abandoned one-story adobe rancho sitting by itself. *Someone's homestead?* He couldn't tell for sure, but it had that feel. From the look of it, whoever had built it had abandoned it years ago. Its roof had been smashed in; its adobe walls, once whitewashed, were pocked now by the weather, big brown patches of mud showing through the lye. He knew right away that he wanted to paint the place, to render its lonely deserted dignity, the worn face of someone's dream all gone wrong. He unpacked his things and worked standing in the sun, adding a few shadows, like people standing inside the rancho.

He got a good painting out of it because he worked fast: all impressions, no explanations, no over-thinking or consciously trying. He'd left a lot of white from the paper showing, which gave the rancho's blistered lye walls a stark quality that excited him. The week before he'd had to tell a patient of his, an engineer, that he was going to die and that there was nothing he could do for him. It had stuck with him, the sadness of it all, because he'd gotten to know the fellow, personally. And now a little of that moment was forever in the painting, too: the rancho vulnerable, deserted, left to face the desert alone, no illusions about failure or hope. He decided it was truly stoic, and painted it that way.

He drank his tea, which had gotten warm, and carefully rolled up the painting by one o'clock. He was slightly sunburnt around his arms and the back of his neck, but he felt satisfied in a new way he couldn't explain with words. It was as if the act of painting were some kind of catharsis that for a moment had purged him of everything he'd been through lately. He felt good heading back with it to the *pensión*. It was a small, still-wet victory tucked into his backpack when he walked up the stairs eager to show it, but also afraid to.

At lunch, everyone in the party was impressed with what he'd done. The German girl, Marita, looked but said nothing. She painted in oil, and his was a very small watercolor. He assumed she would dismiss it as sophomoric. Alfredo told him he should abandon his "straight" life and become an artist and stop screwing around with medicine and science, because he had real talent. It was the first time he'd ever said that. He seemed to mean it.

Alfredo had propped up the doctor's painting in the center of the table without asking him, so they could all see it. They were all intellectuals, and it was intimidating but exciting, too. By then the painting was completely dry and looked pretty damn good. He'd gotten the sky, too, Collin thought—the dry empty-beauty and the blue nothingness in it.

At lunch they talked about Goya and his paintings of the French invasion of Spain. There was a white tablecloth, and the doctor, without wanting to, started looking at the plates and people's faces, the sweat on the water glasses as the others spoke, making a kind of music as it was in Spanish. The others talked about what was happening in America, which everyone hated now and he was tired of defending, after the awful photos from Iraq. He composed a still life in his head as they inveighed against his country.

They assumed he was against the war because he seemed sensitive and was a doctor. He wasn't sure anymore what he felt. He'd joined the intelligence service to fight terrorism. They'd sent him to Kuwait, and he'd run pap tests on whores. When he'd complained about it, they'd accused him of not being a team player. His artist friends had no idea he was an intelligence officer and had believed in the war.

Twice he looked at the German girl and wondered what she was thinking, and why she looked so good without obviously trying to. Maybe it was the bright light in her hair when she sat down, or the fact that she was bra-less, or because she was quite intelligent. He just looked at her beauty as he would at a very good painting, a Sargent maybe, and got lost in it.

After lunch they were all a little drunk because they'd drunk wine. They all met at the pool to read and do nothing but lie around the verge and wait for the late afternoon; it was too bright to paint during the heat of the day.

He'd been pretending to read a paperback by the side of the pool, but in fact had been looking at the girl. She was wearing a two-piece orange bathing suit. He watched her boost herself out of the water. Her body glistened wet, the curve of her ass womanly. Her shoulders were very straight. The sun in her short blonde hair sparkled so you could see all the different colors of blonde in it. The doctor had an overwhelming desire to make love to her, a full blast of lust. It was like when he'd seen the island in the Gulf from the plane, and wondered how it might be to go ashore and explore.

The girl had sat next to him in Alfredo's beat-up Volvo for the drive to the airport. When she'd jumped into the car, she was wearing a peasant blouse and cutoffs. No luggage, just all her stuff in one of those cheap plastic market bags that the poor carry. Everything seemed to be spilling out: her painting stuff, food, a bottle of wine, and mostly her youth. She bought a bathing suit at the airport in Cabo. She'd smelled, because she didn't have a shower in her studio. She'd smelled like clay and turpentine and woman. He was a little overwhelmed by her, by her goddess-girlness.

He was hopelessly attracted to her physically, and now by the pool, he was suddenly tired of trying to play it cool. He wanted her to notice him in that way men want women to notice them. He was always decisive with women; it worked because he was handsome. He had been lucky in that regard.

He decided, putting the book down, that he was going to flirt with her. Try and get her away from the others, if he could, and take it from there. He had a plan. Like the painting he'd done that morning. He'd had a plan from the moment he'd come across the rancho, not to over-think it, but just to get it down.

He felt the concrete's heat on his ass immediately when he sat down next to her. The heat seemed to go all the way up his spine and to warm his crotch. The heat of the concrete made his sexual fantasy somehow more tangible. Looking at her while he'd pretended to read, he'd been afraid he'd get an erection and embarrass himself, like he had once in high school.

"How do you live," he asked her, "without a job, I mean?"

"From day to day," she said. "My mother sends me a little money. It's just enough for the studio and tortillas. . . . She's a judge. In Hamburg." Like so many Europeans, she spoke English almost perfectly. He thought her accent charming.

She was twenty-five. She lived in Mexico City where she had some kind of studio space which, according to his friend Alfredo, had to be seen to be believed. She was a painter's painter, Alfredo had told him. "She has all her sheets to the wind," he'd said. He supposed Alfredo had been her lover at some point.

Apparently it was rough living. No water, a dangerous neighborhood. She thrived on it, she told him. The neighborhood toughs were all in love with her, she claimed; he believed it, too. Her small body was so alive-looking.

Alfredo had lent her the money to come painting with them, as she was broke all the time. Collin's friend Alfredo came from a *very* rich family and never had to worry about money. Alfredo was kind to her, even after they'd broken up, checked on her to make sure she had food and a little cash. He was old-fashioned that way, a gentleman.

"That must be difficult," the doctor said to her. "No potable water, I mean."

"Yes, it's difficult," she said. "You can't wash dishes with tequila."

She smiled. She was wearing the big sunglasses that had come back into fashion; the doctor remembered them from his childhood.

She slipped her dark glasses up and took notice of him now, not as a member of the group, but as Collin, the man who was obviously pursuing her. He could see into her eyes. They were like the *pensión's* pool; very, very clear and light blue. Her intelligence zigzagged there at the very back of them. She gave him an "Okay, I get it" look.

Later, when she was in bed with him, in that room that smelled like the Gulf of California, he was amazed by just how physically strong she was. She was kind of a beast, really. They'd made the wooden bed move on the tile floor. She asked him to do something he'd never done before and he liked that, the danger of what they did. The adventure of it.

The clinical approach to sex taken in medical school had almost ruined it for him. Sometimes while making love, though, he'd see the old-fashioned medical drawings of coitus from the 19th century texts that med students had passed around for laughs, and those drawings and their stark, lyrical beauty had recaptured the romantic tenderness and intimacy of it all for him.

She seemed hungry for everything, where he was more careful and always had been. She was all about the Right Now, it seemed: the pleasure of painting, the pleasure of legs-in-the-air screwing, drinking at lunch, dope smoking, blowing him in a hammock on the deck overlooking the oasis, where they could be caught by a maid or a passerby.

He watched the tops of the palm trees while she went down on him. He'd struggled against the orgasm like a man who doesn't want to get off an escalator—going up, the palm trees blurry now in the sun. Then orgasm. The mind and body suddenly pushed together. A wash of sunlight and sweat on his face. A small delirium. Her fatuous smile.

He'd slipped off the verge into the pool.

"You have a job?" she'd asked. She was interested, he could tell. She said she liked the painting he'd done. She said it had a "male quality," but didn't explain what she meant by that. He'd decided right then, feeling the cool water around him, that he was going to do everything he could to get her into bed. He watched her wet her knees, dipping water out from the pool. "Alfredo says you're a doctor, and you work for the U.S. Embassy."

"Yes. I'm a doctor," he'd said. She'd broken out laughing and said something in German that he didn't understand, but that must have been something like "Oh shit!" She jumped into the pool and stood next to him in the water. Sometimes you can feel another person's body without actually touching it. He'd felt hers then because she stood very close, the unseen tendrils of energy moving around them like the light in the water.

"And I thought you were just another down-and-out American painter," she'd said. "I meet them all the time at parties at Alfredo's house. They always want to borrow money!"

He got what he wanted that night, and then some. Love making, tile sounds. The sound of her voice when she came filled the candlelit room. Very good.

Later, she'd told him she couldn't sell any of her paintings. She wasn't going to give up, she said, but he'd heard the desperation in her voice. She said he couldn't understand; he had a straight job and didn't live like she had to live, like an artist. It stung a little because it was true. He'd been a kind of voyeur, watching his friends be artists. Alfredo kept telling him it was a dangerous occupation, but he hadn't really understood that until he saw the fear in Marita's eyes. For some reason he thought of the old pilot and his kind of bravery, the silent get-up-and-do-it kind. He thought maybe the German girl had it, too.

"People like you—straight people—will never understand us," she'd told him in bed. "Not in a million years."

He didn't try to answer her back; it hadn't seemed right.

3

Nothing is worse than an old spy, Alex Law thought. He'd been an intelligence officer for over twenty-five years and he really didn't trust *anyone* now—governments, religion, most people, even himself. That was the problem: alcoholics can't even trust themselves. That was the final irony; he had now to spy on himself, to look into his own heart and see things without anyone noticing that he was watching.

He'd been a bad man in many ways. He'd cheated on his wife. He'd drunk too much and been out of touch with his family. And he had done things he wasn't proud of in the name of God and country. These were the truths. Now his job—in the attempt to better himself—was to sift through his past to find the truth about his life.

He'd carried with him a weapon of personal destruction for most of his adult life, a WPD. Buried in his subconscious, ready to go off and wipe out all decency and self-respect and right thinking. That weapon had made him effective at his job; that was the horrible truth, too. He'd been effective because he'd been more than a little crazy.

You get to a certain age, and a lot of things don't matter any more, he thought. It was early in the morning. He'd ordered coffee to be sent up and he was sitting, watching the Acapulco skyline from his little house at the Villa Vera. He had the one in the very back that his father had always gotten for them when he'd been a kid.

It was the same one that Elizabeth Taylor and Richard Burton had lived in once. It was the best one, the biggest one at the hotel and the most private. He loved it; if he could, he'd have lived the rest of his life there.

He looked down at the beach, a few miles down the hill. He'd had his first sexual experience down there at fifteen, on a yacht with the daughter of the *Pan Bimbo* empire. She was the older woman; she was seventeen. He smiled, remembering it.

The waiter in his starched white coat came around the corner, checking first that it was all right, calling ahead to announce himself as he wheeled the room service cart up the path. Alex Law, the CIA's station chief in Mexico—head of the agency's largest post in Latin America—waved the waiter through with a quick smile.

He didn't look the part of spymaster. He had planned the overthrow of Hugo Chavez, which had gone badly, but otherwise he'd done well here. Chavez's resilience had been unexpected. But because of that failure, the higher-ups now viewed him as no longer up to the job at hand. It would be only a matter of time before he would be replaced; that was the cost of failure.

The young waiter and he talked for a moment about the weather, which was going to be perfect again. They'd come for their anniversary, Alex told the young man. Twenty-six years today, he said. The young man congratulated him and said he hoped to be as lucky. He said that he was getting married soon and had great expectations for married life. He was all of twenty, Alex thought.

"The important thing is to be nice . . . no, kind," Alex said in Spanish. "If you do that, it will be all right, no matter what else you do wrong. Never say anything you'll regret. That's what I've learned." The boy looked at him a moment and nodded, taking it in.

"You know what I mean?" Alex said.

"Yes. I know. Something hurtful, once said. . . . You can never take it back," the waiter said.

"Right," Alex said. "That's it. The trick is never to say it."

His wife, Helen, was standing in the window watching him. He wondered, waving to her, what she really thought of him.

The waiter left. Helen wouldn't come out until he'd gone. She was a very beautiful woman, even now, but she was always careful that way, a little shy. When he'd been such a whore, she'd been always proper, a good wife—until he'd gone too far, and then she'd struck back and hurt him, the way only a woman can. And then she'd walked out and taken life, as he'd known it for twenty years, with her.

"Is it clear?" she said from the door.

"All clear," Alex said. He poured coffee for the both of them.

She was wearing a bathrobe with the Villa Vera's blue logo. They'd made love in the morning, and it had been very beautiful. The coolness of the room, the knowing her that way, and what she liked, and making sure that it was good. The falling asleep again with her.

"Why is it so perfect here, Alex?" she said, looking out. The little pool had a few orange bougainvillea leaves floating on the water. She held the big French-style coffee cup with two hands.

"I guess because it's Acapulco and it's the Villa Vera in winter, which is perfect. And you're here with me," he said.

She smiled. "No. I mean the *place*, this spot. The quiet. If I were a writer, I'd come here. I'd only work here."

"Well, you'd have to be a successful writer," Alex said.

"I would be. Terribly. I should have been something like that."

"We all should have been something else, right?" She knew what he did, and they never talked about it. Her father had been in the game, too; she considered spying the family business.

"Are we going to make it, Alex? This time."

"Yes."

19

They'd been separated for five years. It was a long time. He'd tried to get her back several times. Each time, she'd said that she wouldn't come back until he stopped drinking. He kept lying and she kept refusing until one day he did the unthinkable and checked himself into a place in Napa. He called her from there and had the doctors call her from there.

She'd shown up the day he was leaving, which he hadn't expected—and he'd cried. He'd been to a lot of frightening places and he'd done a lot of frightening things, and he'd never once cried. He hated it when men did, but he'd cried that day when he saw her standing there. Cried like a baby. She was the only thing he'd ever really wanted, even when he was with other women and the WPD's were going off and he was in hell.

"It's never too late," he said.

"Are you going to be a good boy, Alex? Do you promise me?"

"I promise. Cross my heart," he said.

"I'm not pretty the way I was. I know how you like pretty women. I know that. I'm not stupid. I'm going to be fifty soon. You know that. Can you accept that? Because I don't want to be one of those sad women wearing mini skirts and getting operations. I won't do that. Not even for you, Alex."

". . .Don't care about that. Just care about you," he said, and he meant it. All that super-model culture that was being shoved down the world's throat was dead to him now. He'd crawled out the other side of something, and was free.

"What is it with men, anyway?" she said. She tousled his hair. "You're getting gray, too, you know. I'm glad. Maybe it will slow you down. Your problem was, you were too handsome. My girlfriends told me that—that you were, and it wouldn't be good for me."

"Was I?" he said. "I'm going to go to the gym and work out. . . . And get my bottom lifted. Brazilian butt lift."

She laughed. She didn't look her age. She'd been his opposite, eating right, never drinking. She put her feet in his lap. He looked every bit of his age.

"So we have a deal, Alex?"

"We have a deal," he said.

"Okay. I'll move in with you."

"Thank you. I've bought out the Victoria's Secret catalog. It's all waiting for you. . . . Just kidding."

"You want to take a swim? Remember, we used to when the kids were gone to the beach. I always liked that."

"Okay." He watched her stand up. She took her robe off and, naked, walked across the verge to the steps of the pool. He bit his lip. He was a lucky man.

"God, you look like a wolf," she said, the water moving up her flat waist.

"I can't help it." He took his robe off and followed her. The water was neither warm nor cold. They swam to a ledge at the deep end. He was happy holding her, kissing her, the feel of her wet hair on his shoulder with one of the papery bougainvillea petals caught in it. He hadn't felt happy in so long that it was a little frightening. Being an old spy, he couldn't trust even himself. But he was going to try, he thought. He was going to try to trust himself to be happy.

When they were drying off, his cell phone rang. It was the embassy. He listened for a long time. Twice, Helen tried to kiss him. They were going to order more breakfast, then go shopping for furniture for the house he'd bought in the city.

"Yes. Okay. I'll see him. Have them send someone. In, say, an hour." He saw her girlish smile leave her face. The job—if he told the truth—had always been a problem. He never really wanted to admit it. The job, in fact, had given him the excuse he'd needed to be a bastard to her.

"I've got to go out. Work. For an hour or so."

"Here."

"Yes. I promise I'll be back for lunch."

21

"Alex. It isn't . . . I mean . . . I'll kill you if you have some little. . . ."

"No. It's not that. I swear."

She looked at him a long time; in the past, he'd been capable of that.

"Okay. National security, then?" she said.

"Yes."

"I hope it's important," she said.

"It might be. It was Butch on the phone."

"He's always been a bad influence on you, Alex. You two are always getting into trouble."

"He's got a girlfriend now," Alex said. "He's changed. Keeps regular hours."

"Poor woman. If you're not back by lunchtime, I'm taking up with that cute waiter. I'll order everything off the menu, too."

"Deal," he said.

He was dressed for the Villa Vera and not for the main jail that served Acapulco. Like all jails he'd ever been in, it was noisy. But like all things Mexican, the jail had the feeling that it wasn't what it appeared. The inmates ran the place, and the guards were just cooperating with the strange status quo.

Alex took out his glasses. The liaison from the Mexican intelligence service was a slight young man, nervous because he was dealing with Alex, who was a somebody.

Alex opened the file that was sitting on the wooden table of the little room near the entrance. He was relieved that he didn't have to go see the prisoner in the general population; there was something pathetic about seeing men in cages, even if the cages were better than American ones.

The file contained the man's passport, Indonesian, and a brief description of his crime. He'd murdered two young women in a brothel the previous Saturday. Alex flipped through pictures of the crime scene, immediately hating the man. He read through the charges, but they gave no explanation for the violence.

The man had been arrested with less than fifty dollars in his possession. He was a sailor on a cruise ship and the file concluded with the fact that he was a Muslim. His ship had sailed. The man had insisted that he had important information that he would discuss only with someone from the American embassy, information he claimed was critical to the safety of Americans.

Alex pulled his glasses off and closed the file.

"Do you want to see him now?" the young man asked.

"Yes," Alex said. "Does he speak English? It doesn't say here."

"Yes. He speaks some English," said the young officer, whose English was perfect.

The young man left Alex alone in the small room. He looked at the dirty green walls, then at his watch. It was just ten-thirty. He worried about getting back to the hotel. He looked at his cell phone. His daughter had called from New York while he'd been studying the file. He saw her number.

The door opened and a short Asian man in his forties came into the room shackled, still dressed in the clothes he'd been arrested in. Two unarmed guards led him to a chair directly across from Alex. The prisoner's chains clinked as he walked around the table, taking small steps.

He glanced at Alex as he sat down. He looked frightened and exhausted.

"I'll see him alone," Alex said.

"You're sure?" the young man asked from the doorway.

"What's he going to do to me, shackled like that?"

The young man spoke to the guards, and they all left the room. Alex took his reading glasses and laid them on the file. He said nothing for a moment.

"What your name?" the prisoner asked.

"Tom. My name is Tom," Alex said.

"You American from the embassy?"

"Yes."

"How do I know that?" The man said. He put his hands on the table.

"You don't," Alex said.

"I have to be sure," the man said. "I want to see something that says that you're from the American embassy." The man had black hair that was very dirty and matted and a mustache above a cruel mouth. Something about his full lips looked almost like a woman's. He looked like what he was, Alex thought: a low life, probably a butcher. And now he was frightened, because he'd been caught.

"Well, it's been a pleasure. We really have to do this more often." Alex stood up, dropped his glasses in their case, and headed for the door.

"Okay," the man said. "Okay."

Alex waited a moment, then sat down again.

"What is it you wanted to tell us?" Alex said.

"I have a problem," the man said. He turned for a moment and looked at the door. Alex could see the young intelligence officer's face in the little window. He was keeping a close eye on them.

"Yes. I can see that."

"I'm innocent," the man said.

"I'm sure you are," Alex said. "I'm sure you are."

"They have death penalty here, Tom?"

"No. But I'm not sure if that's a good thing or not, from your point of view. You have no money, you see. Everything costs money here. Even your food."

"I need lawyer. I got no money. Nothing."

"I'm sorry for your troubles, but you really must tell me why you wanted to see someone from our embassy."

The man rubbed the side of his cheek with his shackled hands. Alex saw a small red stain on his shirt pocket.

"I didn't kill those girls," he said.

24

Alex looked at his watch. It was almost eleven. He felt himself get angry; perhaps it was the room, or the disgusting man, or his own anxiety. *You're an asshole,* he thought to himself, who will probably ruin everything you ever loved. Maybe they can write that on your tombstone. *Asshole.*

"Listen, my friend. I'm about to get up and leave this place, and that's going to be the end of it. I don't give a shit whether you are innocent or guilty. Do you understand? Not one shit. That isn't why I'm sitting here. And now that I think you have something important to say, I may make your life even more difficult. Do you understand *that?* If you want my help, you'll tell me what it is you have to say, *now.* Is that clear?"

"I heard something, Tom." the man said.

"What?"

"Something on the ship, Tom. . . ."

4

It was 1:30 P.M., and the cafeteria at the embassy, crowded and noisy earlier, was starting to empty. They were standing in line with their trays, the sun streaming through big transom windows.

"You're sure?" she asked.

Kwana Jones and he were about the same age, so Collin felt he could be himself. She was a little younger, maybe 25 or 26. Black people had that effect on him, as if they could see through his class's bourgeois pretense. She was the person in charge of the list, calling the doctors and referring them to patients on behalf of the embassy. And she'd been kind to him when he'd first arrived, when most had been indifferent.

"You're pregnant," he said. "Yes, I'm sure."

"You're sure, sure?" she asked again. "I'll pay for this." Jones saw that Collin was reaching for his wallet; she produced a bill first and paid the woman behind the register.

They carried their lunch trays to an empty table in the back, under the windows. Kwana walked with a real grace. She was tall, as he was, and he enjoyed watching her move.

Collin wondered why she didn't have a trace of African-American idiom. She spoke English like an English teacher. She probably hid it, he thought, in order to get on in the world. He knew that she'd grown up poor. She sounded like any young American professional woman, except she was black and trim

26

and pretty—if not beautiful, then very close to it. She had a nice smile that told you that she was probably kind and naïve—except when you looked into her eyes. Something in the eyes disabused you of that. She may have fixed the English to pass, but the ghetto she'd grown up in was stamped in her eyes. There was a hurt part somewhere at the core.

He wondered who the boyfriend was. Someone here at the embassy, he imagined. He was going to be a father, whether he was ready to be or not.

They sat down. She was wearing a white sweater with a big tall collar, and it made her brown skin look that much more beautiful. He'd asked her out when he'd first arrived, but she'd said she was seeing someone and turned him down. He remembered the rejection very well; he didn't get them that often. He wondered if it would have been his child now if fate had had it another way.

He unloaded her tray for her and put both trays on an adjoining empty table. When he turned back, he saw that she was crying. She quickly wiped the tears away with a napkin. He was a little shocked.

"Can't have that. What is it? Can't be the food? You haven't tried it yet," he said, trying to make a joke.

She smiled and reached over and held his hand, which he hadn't expected either. She'd been so formal; warm, but a little formal, always a little distant, too.

"Thank you," she said.

He looked into her eyes, seeing a very complicated look there.

"Well, you paid for lunch," Collin said.

"I didn't want to believe that little plastic stick thing," she said.

"I don't blame you. . . . I was glad to do it." He'd run the test for her at the American hospital where he had privileges.

"Are you going to tell me who the lucky young man is?" he asked.

"No," she said.

"Okay. Does he know?"

"No."

"I see," Collin said.

"He's not young, either," she said.

"I see. You are going to tell him, though?"

"I don't know. . . . He's white."

She hadn't touched her food. He picked up his sandwich and took a bite. He was hungry and getting a little uncomfortable. He couldn't put on his doctor's face; he had one especially designed for these kinds of talks, but he knew it would be wrong to put it on. She was talking to him like a friend, and it dawned on him that she didn't have anyone to talk to.

One of Kwana's colleagues from the State Department, an older white woman, passed with a friend; they stopped at their table and said hello to Jones. Kwana introduced Collin and they were impressed, thinking that they were an item. She didn't mention the doctor part.

"We should have gone out. When you asked. And maybe I wouldn't have all these problems right now," she said after they left.

"You couldn't blame me for trying," he said.

"I thought you were cute. For a white boy," she said. "All the girls here think you are. They all want to get deathly ill so that you can hover over them, if you know what I mean."

She started to work on the soup in front of her. She opened the package of crackers on the side and ate one. She was thinking, looking at the soup. "He works here. I'm not in love with him," she said. "He's in love with me."

"Of course he is. Look at you," Collin said. "Is it the age thing?" He decided to engage. He forced himself *not* to act like a doctor.

"Yes. I suppose so."

"Does he *really* love you? Then it might not matter so much. Or is it something else?"

"Yes. But I don't think I can have a baby with a white man. No, that sounds stupid. I mean, it was hard enough being black. Why would you do that to a child? You know what, everyone, black and white, they make these kids feel bad. I've seen it. They want something from them. You know what I mean? Some kind of allegiance. It's . . . sad, because they don't have it to give."

"No, not really. I mean, I don't *really* understand. They're just children, aren't they? Why do they have to fly a race flag?" he said.

". . .There's something else. I have to tell someone. Will you . . . I don't want you to think less of me. I like you. I don't have a lot of friends here. Here at work, at the embassy."

It seemed odd that she was picking him to confide in. He was white. He was a man. He hadn't really known her that well. She was the woman who called him to refer patients. It was true they spoke often, but they weren't really friends. Not really.

"Of course not," he said.

"I dated him because of who he is. I mean, I needed a favor. My mother was in New Orleans, all my family. This person. He's . . . Let's just say, he was able to do things most people can't do. He got them out, all of them. Right away. I knew he could. Or at least, I thought he could."

"I see."

"I was attracted to him in a strange way before that. I can't even explain it. We were going out. Nothing serious. I liked him. He beat some guy up in a restaurant who insulted me. Some college boy half his age, calling me a bitch. He was nice. But I knew it couldn't go anywhere. I think he's almost sixty. He won't tell me for sure. It's a mess, isn't it? He helped me. I was the one who seduced *him*. I felt grateful, like I owed him something. After I saw what people went through there . . . he got them out. One

29

phone call. Can you understand? I didn't think he'd fall in love with me. I thought he'd see it for what it was. I don't know what I thought. I was grateful, but that's all."

"You'd better eat something," Collin said. He reached over and touched her hand. It was cold. She picked up her spoon.

"Am I a bad person, doctor? . . .Was that wrong?"

"No," he said.

"Now we'll never be able to date. You know too much about me." She laughed. And he laughed, too. But he was afraid for her.

She ate for a while, and they talked about the embassy, the people they knew. He told her about some of the funny tourists he'd been treating lately, the woman who wanted to hire him to travel with her.

Then she stopped him and asked him if he would help, if she wanted to get rid of it—if she could have it done at the American hospital. He told her she could, but it wasn't covered and she would have to pay something. She nodded.

He looked out the window on the opposite wall then and into the blue afternoon sky. It seemed endless and sure of itself. Before he left, she hugged him. She said she would call him and let him know what she had decided.

5

Alex's assistant used her thumb to indicate that the caller was important. That was their code. If it was a thumbs down, he didn't usually take the call. She'd raised her thumb up, *twice*. Alex went to the phone and picked up. She mouthed the word *Homeland* from outside his door.

"It's John Burns. We've got a problem, Alex," the voice on the telephone said. Alex recognized it.

"Yes . . . well, there are a lot of problems in the world," Alex said. He wasn't really paying attention to the conversation; rather, he was thinking about his wife and what she'd told him that morning.

She'd come down to breakfast just before the car from the embassy drove into their grand driveway. He'd watched it from the window as it slid in, and then the chase car behind it, with their Coldwater, Inc.-supplied Russian rent-a-thugs. She'd come in, walked by and kissed him, sat down and told him as she poured her coffee.

She'd tried to sound matter of fact, but he could tell she was upset. Since that moment, it had felt to him as if he were plummeting through space—he'd barely been able to concentrate.

She'd found something on her breast—probably nothing, she assured him. She asked him to get her a doctor from the list at the embassy.

31

"We had a wonderful weekend," she said, trying to change the subject right away. "Can we go back soon?"

He had tried to ask her a question, but she'd waved him off saying that it was probably nothing. He should go to work and not worry.

"Yes—but in your part of the world, Alex. We've got a warning about Mexico," the man said. "Not much more."

"Yes. I'm listening." Alex forced himself to listen, now.

The man from Homeland Security had worked for Alex in the 1980s, in Central America. The man on the phone had run Llopango Airport in El Salvador for him. He'd done a good job making sure the Contras got their dope out, but he was a mean authoritarian type who liked to degrade his underlings, and Alex had never liked him. He'd left the Agency and started a consulting business, but it had failed and he had been on the verge of bankruptcy when 9/11 happened, ironically saving him from losing everything.

"Something we picked up. There are hundreds of these a month, it seems, all over the world. I thought I'd give you a call myself so there's no screw-up about you not hearing from us. I'd heard you were head man. Things here are still—well, *confused*, situation normal, all fucked up. Just an unsubstantiated reference in a phone call from Saudi Arabia. They mentioned Mexico City several times over the course of a week. We thought it odd. They never talk about Mexico City, and then all of a sudden they mentioned it twice. These are bad guys—that, we *are* sure of."

"Thanks," Alex said. "I owe you one for calling me directly, John." He didn't say anything about the prisoner he'd interviewed. He'd learned not to trust the other agencies. He'd heard nothing but bad things about the new Homeland Security Department; like the FBI, they were considered publicity-hungry hacks, and old timers at the Company kept them at arm's length.

"Like I said, if we chased all of these random conversations down, we'd never get anything done . . . assholes are everywhere. Of course, if you hear anything, you'll tell me."

"Right. Assholes everywhere. Of course I will," Alex said. "I'll look into it. Thanks, John." He didn't even bother playing the how-are-you-and-the-kids game. He was too preoccupied.

He rang off. Alex put down the phone.

He looked out on the city. It had always intimidated him. Mexico City was a daunting place, where *anything* could happen. It had been his very first posting, more than twenty years before. The city was cleaner-looking then, elegant still, but the years of pollution were starting to paint everything, making even new buildings look seedy.

His boss then had shaken his hand and said, "Welcome to Mexico City, kid. No one hits the ground running here, if you know what I mean. Don't drink the water."

The man's advice still held. Alex buzzed his secretary and asked if they had any doctors on the list who could see his wife today. Someone who wasn't a quack, he told her. She suggested Dr. Collin Reeves. She had met him at a party and was looking for an excuse to meet him again. She said she'd have the liaison officer at State call him.

"He doesn't drink, does he?" Alex asked her. He recognized the name. It wasn't his real name. He'd asked for clandestine to make sure there was a capable CIA doctor on the list, as soon as he'd taken over as head of station; Alex remembered the name.

"I don't know, sir."

"Most of them do," Alex said. "Backwater doctors. But I suppose he'll do."

"I think he's too young to be all that," she said. "And he's very handsome. He's only been out of medical school a few years. I'd call him if I were sick."

"I'm sure you would, Ms. Fong. I take it he's *soothing?* Call him, then," Alex said. "As long as he doesn't drink and owns a suit, I suppose he'll do. I want him to see my wife as soon as possible. Today, if you can find him. Try all the bars around here."

The girl laughed. He'd been kind to her, and she liked him. Not many people in the embassy liked him, and he knew it; but then, they never had. He'd always been too different, too well-connected. His father had been second in command of the CIA at one point in the '60s, and people somehow held that against him. He was used to it. The world had always held him at arm's length, as it does some people.

He went back into his office and tried to call his wife, but she'd gone out. He had no bars on his cell phone; it angered him. And then he realized what he was really angry at.

Fong came in behind him.

"Sir? That was the liaison person. He doesn't answer his phone—Reeves. Should I have her call someone else?"

"All right. Someone else then," Alex said. "Will you get Butch for me? He should be back by now."

• • •

Butch Nickels opened the small cabin door. He'd flown by helicopter up the coast to the cruise ship's stop at Puerto Vallarta. He'd brought an agent from the FBI's field office in the embassy to front for him. The story they gave the captain was that they were after a fugitive wanted in America.

They had the name of the man who'd shared a cabin with the prisoner in Acapulco. He was called Setiawan Datuk.

Butch closed the door to the cabin. A Chinese kid, maybe only seventeen or eighteen, sat on his bunk reading a Chinese porno magazine.

"I'm looking for Datuk," Butch said. The kid made a face like he didn't speak English. Butch motioned for the kid to get out. The kid seemed to not understand.

"Get the fuck out," Butch said. The cabin was tiny and it

smelled of cooped-up men. It hadn't really been cleaned well in years. Unlike the upper decks, which were elegant, the lower decks were grim windowless cells.

He walked over, yanked the kid up out of his bed and tossed him out of the cabin. Then he went through it. He found nothing of interest.

Setiawan Datuk—or whatever his real name was—had left the boat in Mazatlan, the captain had told him. The captain had never met the man and said he wouldn't know him from Adam. Butch tracked down one of the main stewards, who said that Datuk had been a good worker and had left unexpectedly at Mazatlan.

6

The doctor's apartment was near the main plaza—the *Zócalo*, one of the oldest neighborhoods in the city. It was a warren of dreary streets with hoary stone government buildings from the nineteenth century, some with wide arcades where criminals and beggars lurked in a kind of paper-strewn demi-hell. It was a grimy, crowded place with the close unhealthy feel of a souk, made worse by the city's bad pollution. It was just the place for a backwater doctor, which was why they'd chosen it for him.

The stores near his apartment reflected the surreal hodge-podge of the city's cultures: from the intensely Catholic, where a black Jesus hung from a blinking cross, to the narrow open stalls selling CD's and blasting Latin rap music with only the traffic's hubbub for a melody. It was the kind of intensely crowded neighborhood you'd expect some foreigner on the way down to have chosen; someone who might have a drinking problem, or perhaps was hiding from the police back home. It was the most anonymous set of streets he'd ever seen.

The doctor had hung a few of his watercolors around to break the horrible drabness of his apartment (there were strange stains on the wall, as if motor oil had been splashed around). It had worked; the apartment had the feel of an atelier now, as the paintings, all unframed, were simply tacked to the wall wherever he'd felt like putting one up. He could pretend, at least, that he was an artist and this was his studio.

He dreaded the place and tried to be there as little as possible. The doorbell had to be the worst of it, though; it had gone off twice now.

The buzzer went off again, but he ignored it, hoping whoever it was would simply give up and go away. He certainly wasn't expecting anyone, and it was unsafe to open the door to strangers in Mexico City. He'd asked for a pistol, but they'd refused to give him one; they told him he'd probably end up being shot with his own gun. Better he try to talk his way out of a problem, his watchdogs had advised.

He'd been up late the night before, treating an American family for food poisoning at the Ritz Carlton in the *Zona Rosa*. The family, from Kansas, had all gotten terribly ill and were dehydrated and frightened by the time he got to the hotel. Even the richest people become pathetic when their strength goes. Poor people were used to life's unexpected assaults, but not the rich. The father—some kind of nails-for-breakfast executive with Merrill Lynch—told him he'd never been sick a day in his life before coming to Mexico and swore he'd never take another vacation outside of the United States. He'd run off to the bathroom, and Collin had tried to talk to the wife.

"What kind of country is this?" she'd asked him angrily. Her girls had fallen asleep on the couch behind her. "My children are sick." He wanted to shake her and tell her that what they were experiencing was nothing compared to what he'd seen. He was running out of patience with American tourists.

"One without clean water," Collin said, trying to mind his manners. All he could give them were the standard remedies: 7-Up, crackers and Lomotil. He told them to rest. He woke the girls up and checked their vitals, more to show the mother that he wasn't unfeeling.

He put his coffee down and glanced towards the still-dark

narrow hallway of the flat. He could hear the traffic on the *Boulevard Mateo*, which always prohibited sleeping late.

He'd lie in bed and wonder what the hell he was still doing here. Why hadn't he quit the agency? He wanted to put his finger on the reason. *Why?*

The horrid front door buzzer went off a fourth time. Whoever it was didn't plan on going away. He went to answer, wondering what he planned to do if it was one of the gangs who were specializing in home invasions. He steeled himself a moment, then pulled open the door.

"Masa'a Alkair," the old man said in Arabic.

"Masa'a Alkair," Collin replied, relieved when he recognized his neighbor. *"Alingli'zia.* Please."

The man, named Madani, owned a hotel across the street. He switched to English, obviously upset. "You come hotel . . . see young lady. High fever."

The man was being pelted by the rain, his thin cotton shirt stained by it. He had a birth mark below his right eye, the color of black olives. He was 70 or so and seemed completely out of place in Mexico City. His people had all been desert people; to the doctor, he seemed very far from home.

The old man held a Syrian passport, but he was, in fact, Bedouin by birth. He owned the small, third-class Hotel Gobi. The Gobi had three floors; the guidebooks called it "tourist class." It had a small restaurant with a few oilcloth-covered tables that served North African fare. The dining room had a view of the *Zócalo*, and was clean but without any personality at all. There was one fly-specked picture on the wall—of the Matterhorn.

The place was frequented by the neighborhood's Arab shopkeepers. There was a mosque a few blocks away where the men worshipped. The restaurant was a meeting place, after Friday prayers, for a group of old rheumy-eyed men who smoked and played with worry beads, and talked about the past as if it were all going to come back tomorrow and be glorious.

"High fever. You better come now," Madani said. Excited, he slipped into Arabic again. Collin caught the Arabic word for "guest." He had learned oil-field Arabic in Kuwait. He'd tried to keep it up with the old man, who was patient and a good teacher and always wanted to speak in Arabic when he came to eat at the restaurant. He was the one person Collin had gotten to know in the neighborhood, and he liked him.

Madani wore what he always wore, regardless of the weather: thin cotton pants, clean white shirt, and black open-toed rubber sandals. He was using a plastic shopping bag to keep the rain from hitting him in the face. Like all desert people, he seemed to treat the rain as a great mystery, never using an umbrella.

The doctor made him come inside. He switched on the light in the small corridor. Water puddled around the old man's sandals, pooling on the wood floor. The doctor listened to a story about a sick guest at the hotel. He didn't want to go, and he was trying desperately to think of an excuse not to—but he was a good doctor and couldn't, in the end, refuse his friend, who seemed truly upset. It was clear from the way the old man was talking that the woman had no money and wouldn't see a doctor on her own. Madani assured him that she was very ill and needed to see him.

"Let me find a coat," Collin said finally. "I'll be right with you."

"A thousand blessings on you," Madani said when he saw Collin come back into the hallway carrying his doctor's bag.

It was the young woman's hair Collin noticed first; he'd never seen hair blacker, or more lush-looking and beautiful. "Have you been in the South . . . perhaps Tehuantepec?" he asked her. She was a great beauty; it had stunned him when he'd first walked into the room. He'd expected an older woman, for some reason.

He withdrew the thermometer from the woman's lips quickly and wiped it with an alcohol-doused towelette. He'd been making a one-sided conversation with her while they waited for a reading, their eyes locking for a moment. It was the doctor who looked away first. She had beautiful green eyes, and they'd startled him with their intensity.

The girl had been silent and watchful. Because she was indeed ill, she was thankful that a doctor had come to see her. She hadn't smiled when they met. They'd shaken hands perfunctorily, Madani standing behind him. When he saw he'd done his job, the old man had left them.

Collin walked towards the window of the hotel room so he could read the thermometer. The room smelled of a woman's perfume and the hotel itself. It was a bit stifling.

The perfume was the one luxury she still allowed herself. There was a small cheap-looking suitcase in the corner and not much else. She was traveling very light, and she seemed to be completely alone; the old man hadn't mentioned a companion or husband.

He wanted to look at her again but forced himself not to. He thought it a bit odd only because she didn't strike him as the typical young person backpacking her way across Mexico. She was young enough, but something about her was different, older than her years.

He shook the thermometer back down. She was running a fever. She couldn't be more than twenty-five or -six at the most. Her name, she said, was Dolores Reyes: an American, she'd told him, from Chicago. He assumed she was a Latin, although at first he thought she was an Arab. She spoke English with a British accent. He supposed she'd married an American called Reyes.

"Yes. How did you know?" she said from the edge of the bed. He didn't look at her, but kept his eyes trained on the thermometer for a moment.

"Water is terrible the further south you go," he said.

She had noticed the doctor's eyes were blue, like the sky on the bus ride from Veracruz to Mexico City. She'd ridden in the back of the bus. Everything about the country seemed strange and slightly hostile. She'd slept on the bus and had vivid dreams about Baghdad, about her husband and son. She'd dreamt about her apartment, with its views of the city and the river. In the dream, a white curtain was blowing just off the balcony of their bedroom—a sheer white curtain that moved in the breeze like a poem. No sound, just the curtain moving in the breeze. It was sheer enough to see the sky behind it.

In the dreams, she was often getting dressed for Mass. Her own mother and father were Arab Christians. In those days—when she'd been a child—no one thought much about all that. But she'd liked to go to church as a child, to smell the incense and kneel and pray to God, who she thought was like her grandfather she'd never known. He'd been killed in the Six-Day War.

Sunlight was suddenly injected into the room. It hit the doctor's face and changed it as he stood by the window, making him all the more handsome. It was the first time she'd allowed herself to notice a man that way since she'd left Iraq.

"How long have you been ill?" he asked. "You have a temperature of 102. That's not good. We have to get that down."

"Three days . . . I think," she said. "What day is it?"

"Wednesday," Collin said.

"Yes, three days," she said.

The doctor seemed so young. She wondered how young. Old enough to be a doctor, at least. *Old enough to know things about life and death.* Her husband had been fifteen years older than her when she married him.

She noticed the doctor's hands as he put the thermometer down. He had long slender fingers that went with his face. She thought about him, about his maleness. What he thought of her looks. She was wearing a scruffy red robe; she'd found it in the closet and hated that she was wearing it. *He must think I'm a frump. Sick frump. I was pretty once.* She saw the sunlight strike the mercury from where she sat in bed.

41

"Is it serious?" she asked. She had turned 26 that week and never thought about death. Like most people, she'd thought about dying, missing out, but not about *death*, that shimmering timeless void. Eternity's song. She'd seen violent death since the war started, as most had. She'd lost her child, but that was about grief, not about death. It had been about the separation of a mother and her child. She'd felt pain of a kind she hadn't known existed—a complete violation, like a rape.

The grief had changed her. She was very beautiful. Her beauty was full-on, even now that she was sick. But since her son's death, she couldn't see it. Her beauty had disappeared to her, been erased by her grief.

Now the possibility of her own death lurked in the twinkling of the shaft of silver mercury. The doctor's smell. His coat was wet; she glanced at it where the rain had darkened the shoulders. You can tell so much from a man's coat, she thought. His was slightly worn. A short English trench, black. Her father had worn one like it in London, where the family had moved after she was born. She caught a whiff of it now.

The fever was making her light-headed, but also oddly perspicacious. She'd been in bed two days, and finally the hotelier's wife had called for a doctor because she'd stopped eating. She had very black hair and pale skin and green eyes. Everyone noticed her even when she tried to dress down; men noticed her even when she did her best to look ordinary. But it had always been that way, since she'd been a child.

The doctor thought she was one of the most beautiful women he'd ever seen. He'd seen pretty girls—the German girl, for example—but never one like this. Perhaps it was her illness that set it off perfectly. He'd once walked in Kew Gardens when he'd been a student and spotted one of those rare tropical plants that seemed vulnerable to the English winter but somehow thrived under glass. Her beauty seemed like that, thriving even here in this squalid little hotel room in a squalid city.

"It depends what you call serious," Collin said, stepping away from the window. He smiled. It was reassuring, but there was a hint of something else—something approaching, if not concern, then the clinician's educated precaution.

He'd been well educated. It was the one thing he owned completely, his education. He seemed far too young for it. In fact his owning it, at his young age, put people off.

"A delay in my journey . . . I'm on my way back to Chicago," she said.

"Well, you've got to be tested," he said. He brought a wooden chair and sat near her bed. "For parasites. You've probably picked some up. We can fix that, but you'll have to go to hospital. It's not uncommon in Mexico."

"Do I?" she said. She thought she sounded childish. That he had taken possession of the situation so suddenly, in just a few moments, surprised her; she wanted it back. Since her son had died, she'd taken hold of something, something so deep and profound about herself that holding it was sometimes over-whelming. It was a thing she was forced to carry, like women she'd seen in Africa or here in Mexico, wood or water jars piled on their heads. The same look in their eyes, the look women who are simply trying to survive get, a kind of lonely, half-frightened stare of acceptance. It was a look she'd seen only in women who were not necessarily alone, but very lonely.

"Yes. I'm afraid so." He said. "There's an American hospital. It won't take long. . . . I'll drive you. I have a car."

"I've no money for hospital," she said quickly.

"Your family should know what's going on," the doctor said. He glanced towards the door. Someone was walking by in the hallway. They heard a door close.

"My family has no money for that, either. Of course, I will pay you for the visit," she said. This seemed to throw him. "I'm sorry," she said. She didn't know why she said she was sorry, but it made taking possession of the situation easier. "I'll just get on with it," she said.

"Are you British? I went to school in London," Collin said.

"No. American," she said. "But I studied in England too."

He looked at her a moment. She couldn't tell exactly what kind of look it was: a doctor's look, or simply a man's. She guessed the latter.

Her hand moved to the top of her robe. There was an attraction; it jarred her and made what she'd been carrying—her son's death—slip out of her hands unexpectedly. She scrambled to pick it up. *How dare you*, she thought. *How dare you.* And then her anger seemed silly. He was just a man. A doctor who'd come to help her, a stranger.

"Well, you won't be able to get on with it, if you're sick. You may have amoebic dysentery. Dehydration is the problem. Electrolytes out of whack. You're probably dehydrated right now," he said, slipping easily into doctor mode. "It's serious; you must treat it. And I can't rule out other parasites. That's why I need the tests." He was standing now in the tiny bathroom, cleaning off the thermometer in the sink, talking to her over his shoulder as the water ran. She could hear the water running.

She touched her face; it was very warm and had been that way for days. They kept telling her you couldn't drink the water here. At least there *was* water. In Baghdad there had been no water in her flat for months. She'd sat in the flat for days alone, frozen with fear, like an animal. She and her husband had been married for three years. She'd loved him. She'd expected to grow old with him. She wasn't a virgin when they'd married. She wished she could have given him that. She'd lied about that. Had he known? She expected he had.

She'd grown up in England, and things there for young women were so different. Her husband had been very devout. Her father had introduced them. He seemed very foreign, and she'd fallen in love with that part of him.

She looked at the doctor. She had a sudden desire to tell him her real name. To explain everything to him, because he seemed kind and would understand everything that had happened to her since her son's death.

Would he understand? He was talking now about the hospital; was he ignoring her, as women are so often ignored by men? She was used to it. It was one of the things she'd grown used to now, pretending to acquiesce. Since her son had been killed, she was ignored. Her city was full of ignored women with no future. *To live without a sense of future is a kind of death*, she thought. *Is that all death is, then? A futureless time. . . .*

He came out of the bathroom. She watched him shove his thermometer into a clear plastic case and put it in his doctor's bag.

'How much do I owe you?" She decided she wouldn't go to the hospital. She got up off the bed and moved toward her purse. She looked very thin.

She had four hundred dollars in cash. It was to last until she reached her destination.

He had to catch her when she fainted. He was right; it was the dehydration, of course.

He drove her to the American hospital in the *Zona Rosa* and had her admitted for tests. She was too fragile and weak to really object, although he thought that she was secretly angry at him for interfering. He had quietly arranged to pick up the cost of her stay, as it was obvious she had only refused to go to a hospital because she had no money. He put her down as an American tourist. He and the nurse at the hospital looked for her passport in her few things, but they hadn't found it.

7

Sorry—I know it's early, but we have a referral for you. It's Carol," the voice said over the phone. It was a different woman from the embassy, who sometimes called him if Kwana didn't.

"Where are they staying?" Collin asked.

"They're at a private residence."

"What's their complaint?"

"The usual," she said. "Someone from the embassy will pick you up. They'd like you to go to the corner and wait."

"Okay," he said, and rolled over in bed. "Usually I go to them."

"This is a VIP," she said. "They have a driver. You'll love it. Half an hour, then?"

"Fine. . . . How do I know—" She'd hung up before he'd finished the questions.

He showered and got dressed. It was six in the morning when he slipped on his watch. He walked to the corner, and a white van pulled up almost immediately. A man in a suit got out and opened the rear door for him.

"You'll have to put this on," he said.

"Excuse me?"

The man handed him a black nylon hood.

"I don't understand," Collin said.

"Just put it on, dude," the man said. "Orders."

46

Butch Nickels' face was a little frightening. A cold toughness was stamped on it, becoming more and more obvious with age—he was fifty-seven now. Any cop in any city in the world would recognize that look. It belonged to someone who had been working the streets.

And yet he was the kind of man who made people feel oddly safe. He was wearing a gray suit and white shirt and thin red tie, and his gray hair was cut very short. He'd worn it that way since he'd played football at Notre Dame. He looked—Collin thought when he walked into the room—like a composite of all the PE teachers he'd ever had.

"Your patient is in the guest house. My name is Nickels— Butch. You can call me Butch," he said. "I hate sir. Just never call me sir, kid."

"All right, I better go see," Collin said. "You said he was hurt?"

"Not yet," Butch said. "Wait a minute."

Nickels was past retirement age, but he'd been called back into service—with many other old hands—after 9/11. He was second in the embassy to someone called Alex Law, who was head of station. Collin hadn't met Law, but he'd heard of him from one of the old-school trainers who'd taught some of the tradecraft courses designed for Mexico. Collin had heard that the two men had been working together since the war in Vietnam, and the last thing anyone in the Embassy wanted to do was to screw with them. He'd heard that Law didn't suffer fools, that he was a reformed alcoholic, and that his family was one of the richest in America.

"But you said he was hurt," Collin said. "I need to know."

"He jumped out a third story window in Cuernavaca. He's hurt, all right," Nickels said. He seemed to be glad about it.

Collin stood up, a little shocked by his tone. It was reflexive. His whole experience in the agency had been benign. Because he was a doctor, he'd been spared much contact with men like Nickels, what the old guard called knuckle draggers.

"Sit down . . . doctor," Butch said. "You look like you jumped out a window yourself."

"I don't understand," Collin said.

Nickels looked at his watch. ". . .Give it a few more minutes."

There was a silence.

"He's not . . . not an American?" Collin asked, needing to talk.

Nickels picked up a *Time* magazine with a picture of Spielberg on the cover. He flipped through it quickly, indifferently.

"No. No, of course not. Listen, I haven't been sleeping well, Doc," Nickels said, not bothering to look up. "The hours, I guess. Could you give me something for it? Valium, I bet, right?"

The safe house was immaculate, a huge and walled-off-from-the-street affair with canary yellow walls, which had faded over the years. Like so many of the agency's safe houses, it had been in service since the cold war. People coming and going, but no one really living there. A Mexican caretaker, who would live there without knowing who exactly owned the place, kept it clean and ready. Months of inactivity, and then suddenly it would be electric, the caretaker replaced with the people who ran safe houses when they were hot.

Two guards came into the living room, young, obviously U.S. military hard-jaw types. One of them nodded a hello to Collin as he passed. They were about the same age.

"What do you think? Valium, doc?" Butch asked again, ignoring them.

"I'm sorry?"

". . .I can't sleep. Late nights, no schedule lately. New girlfriend. Have to take her out all the time."

Collin was getting frustrated. There was an injured man and he thought he should be attending to him. That was his job, after all. That's what he was here for; what his cover was for. A doctor who could treat people when other doctors couldn't be called.

Nickels returned to his magazine, flipping through to the end.

"I liked that *New World*. Did you see that picture?" Butch asked

"No," Collin said.

"Damn good picture. Saw it last night. Took my girl. Okay. Let's go see your patient," he said suddenly.

They went out of the living room and through the kitchen. A cook was preparing food, a Filipino man. He didn't bother to look up as they passed him. They went out the door to the garden and toward a small separate guesthouse. The pool furniture looked brand new.

The hallway was dark. Two men in blue jeans with automatic weapons leaned against the wall outside the bedroom.

"Wait here a moment, will you, Doc?" Nickels stepped into the bedroom for a moment. Collin saw, when the door opened, that the room had several men in it. The door closed before he could get a better look. He nodded nervously to the guards.

"You a doctor?" one of them asked.

"Yes," Collin said.

"Personally, I wouldn't have called you," the man said. "But that's just me. I hope the motherfucker dies."

The door to the bedroom opened suddenly. Two men in suits pushed past the doctor, and then Nickels ushered him into the room.

"Are you Collin?" a thin, good-looking man asked.

"Yes, sir." Nickels and the good-looking man, whom Collin had never met before, stood next to a man lying on the bed. The person on the bed was hooded and shackled. He seemed to be asleep, or at least unconscious, because he was supine and wasn't moving.

"My name is Alex Law. I'm the head of station," the good-looking man said. He approached the doctor, and they shook hands. The man who'd introduced himself had blond hair that was going gray in places. He was handsome and thin and seemed almost fragile compared to Nickels and the other men who had pushed past him. Law had piercing blue eyes that were looking at him now in a way that Collin didn't ever remember being looked at before.

"Yes, sir. Pleased to meet you."

"They tell me you're a pretty good doctor," Law said.

"I try, sir."

"You don't seem to be around much when the embassy calls."

"I . . . I was. I had some days off lately."

"Can you keep this son of a bitch alive? It's important he doesn't die. At least, not right now," Law said.

"Yes, sir. I understand."

"Butch will be here all the time. If he wakes up, I want you to let him know immediately. Butch is the boss here. Whatever he says goes. If you need anything, you tell him and he'll see you get it," Law said.

"I have two patients at the hospital. Can I leave to check on them?" Collin asked. "It wouldn't look good if I didn't check in."

"Call someone else on the list and have them fill in for you. Someone will be outside all the time, if you need them," Law said. He was already moving toward the door. "If the prisoner asks *you* any questions, don't answer. Nothing. He speaks English, they say."

"Can I remove the hood?" Collin asked.

"Only if you have to. The Delta guys gave him some Demerol. But he'll come around," Butch said.

"Meperidine, you mean?" Collin said.

"Whatever," Nickels said. "You're the fucking doctor."

"I should know what they gave him," Collin said. "It's important."

"And I should know where Bin Laden is, too. But I don't," Nickels said.

Then Law and Nickels were both gone, and he was alone in the room with the prisoner. Collin immediately pulled the hood off the man's head. He was young, and he'd obviously been badly beaten.

"They're getting younger all the time," Butch said, looking back at the guest house. "You think that kid knows his asshole from his elbow?"

"Probably," Alex said. "I asked for him."

"Why?"

"He finished top of his class at Tulane," Alex said. "This may boil down to keeping one asshole alive for an extra five minutes."

"No shit. He looks like he's in high school. A fucking Doogie Howser," Butch said.

They walked past the pool, and Alex turned and looked at his friend.

"We're completely alone on this," Alex said. "No one in Virginia wants to believe there's an *al Qaeda* cell here in Mexico. But I think there is. I think that guy on the ship came and delivered some kind of bomb, maybe, or perhaps money," Alex said. "The guy in Acapulco said he thought he'd seen wires and tools, that kind of thing. He'd heard Datuk talk about a bomb, anyway."

"Well, he didn't have it with him," Butch said. He thought they had a good chance of making the guy talk, and that he would tell them where the bomb was, if there was one. In fact, he was sure of it.

"They said it was unlikely to be a very serious cell, if it existed at all. They're overwhelmed with Iraq," Alex said.

"You told them we heard it from our friends at Homeland, too?"

"They never understood Mexico," Alex said, interrupting him.

"Don't see it, you mean?" Butch said. "That it's our underbelly?"

"Right. Even in the old days. The Russians had their biggest network here in this city, and they never really got that," Alex said.

"It's a question of breaking into one cell and then out from there," Butch said in a matter-of-fact way. "That guy from the boat, Datuk, has a contact. That's all we need; it was the same with the Viet Cong."

"Yeah, but you know there could be five, six different cells. By the time we get there, we could be too late," Alex said.

They'd come back into the house and were sitting in the living room. Alex had ordered a drink. He'd started drinking again after Helen had told him about finding a lump.

"I think we have to persuade that fellow upstairs to talk. I'm thinking it *is* a bomb. Maybe they'll use it here—or take it north?" Alex said.

"Yeah . . . leave it to me," Butch said.

"The doctor is going to have to cooperate," Alex said. "But he will. You have to make him understand how it is, sometimes."

"Maybe he's not right for this, Alex. Let's get one of those old drunks on the list."

"You weren't right for this either, once," Alex said.

"He's a pencil-neck, Alex."

"Stop being so generous," Alex said, and smiled.

• • •

Collin held the hood for a moment, then put it down. He thought of the famous picture from Abu Ghraib, the one of the man standing on the box. The hood wasn't too different. It was nylon and soft to the touch. He put it down next to his patient.

He's my patient. They'll have to understand that. He'll need some kind of medical record if he's here long.

He took off his coat and laid it over a chair. If it was meperidine, it wouldn't be long until the pain from the fall woke him up. He heard the door open behind him and turned.

"Is he breathing, Doc?" Nickels asked.

"He's still asleep. If it was meperidine . . . Demerol, then it won't be long. It's an old drug family, not very useful for pain, really. Kind of a dinosaur drug . . . I think he's broken his ankles. I'll need X-rays to be sure. But they're very swollen," Collin said.

"Really? Is that so," Butch said, coming towards him. "Well, live and learn."

Collin watched Nickels go into the bathroom. He heard the shower go on. He heard the shower curtain rings roll over the metal pole. For some reason, the sound of it made him flinch.

"Would you tell those fellows in the hall to come in here. . . ?" Butch stuck his head out of the bathroom. He had the cold water running in the shower. "We're going to need a hand to get him in the shower. I need to talk to him."

Collin didn't move. "I don't understand," he said.

Nickels smiled at him. He came out and took his coat off.

"Nap time's over, kid."

8

Collin pulled back the curtain. The sky was deep blue and clear, no smog at all. He stared out a moment. *Better not to think.* He turned and looked at his patient.

"You're out of the worst of it," he said. "The doctors here think you can leave tomorrow. I just spoke with one of them."

"Where were you?" Dolores asked.

"Emergency . . . a case out of the city," he said. The young woman looked at him. "I've spoken to Madani; he has your old room for you. He likes you. Says you're *muy simpatica*. It will be easy to look in on you there. You won't be able to travel for a few days. Maybe a week." He brought a chair by the bed and sat down.

". . . All this. It must have cost a fortune," she said. "I've been here for three days."

"Yes, well, you were very sick . . . don't worry about it. You're a guest of the American government."

"I don't understand."

"I'm on the list," he explained. "At the embassy. I can put Americans in here at no cost if need be, if they're patients of mine. I've put you down as indigent. It means you won't be billed. It's entirely free. I hope you don't mind."

"I see," she said.

"I'll have to give them your passport. The number. But that's it."

54

"It was stolen . . . on the bus. While I was asleep," she said. She had a lunch tray in front of her, and he noticed that she'd eaten.

"Why am I not surprised?" he said. "We can get another issued from here. I'll let the embassy know."

"I was sick on the bus. Perhaps it's in my suitcase," she said.

"You can look when you get back to the hotel," he said. "Don't worry."

"Thank you," she said. "You've been very kind."

There was an awkward silence.

"It's what you pay your taxes for," he said finally, trying to make a joke of it. "Would you like to have dinner . . . before you leave?"

She was surprised and she wasn't surprised. She hadn't been married that long, and she still remembered what it was like to be single—to be a single woman and attractive.

Her husband had been nervous, too, when he first asked her out. It had been in London. She thought she was going to marry an Englishman; she would have bet on it. The Arab men she knew all seemed so old-fashioned, so formal. Or worse, they were the kind who were afraid of women, especially women like her who had been educated. She was an architect, just finishing up her degree when they met.

"Yes of course," she said. "I owe you dinner, at least."

"I know a French place. I think you'll like it. They're *really* French. A man and his wife run it," Collin said.

"That would be nice," she said.

"Were you on vacation?" he asked.

"Yes . . . vacation," she said. She looked down at the tray.

"I hope it wasn't ruined by the illness."

"Well, I suppose it may have been," she said finally.

He wanted to make her smile. She was even more beautiful when she smiled.

"Have you called your family?" he asked.

"No, not yet. I didn't want to worry them," she said.

He thought that odd. People and their families were odd these days; half of his friends didn't even talk to theirs. He supposed his relationship to his family was old-fashioned now. There was great tension in his relationship with his mother and father, but certainly no break.

"Here," he fished out his cell phone. "You can call now, if you like. They must be worried about you."

She deliberated a moment, then took the phone from him. "Are you sure?"

"Yes. Please."

She took his cell phone and dialed a number in the States. He got up and walked out to the hallway to arrange her bill.

• • •

The embassy called his cell phone while he was driving Dolores back to the Gobi. It was the same woman who'd called two days before, with the same message. They had a VIP patient, she said. They would pick him up at his apartment in an hour.

He tried to seem unchanged by the call, but it was difficult. He immediately felt as if the car had gotten smaller. She noticed and pretended not to. They drove on a while, listening to the radio.

"I've decided to stay a few days longer," she said finally.

"Really?"

"Yes. I want to see the archeological museum. I told my family I would stay a few extra days."

"Probably the right thing," he said. "Perhaps we could go together. I've never been."

A taxi cut him off and disappeared around the corner. He swore under his breath, which surprised him.

"Why are the building fronts tiled, do you think?" she asked.

He turned to look at her. They were passing directly in front of the *Zócalo*. It had rained and the *Zócalo* was wet. Tourists under umbrellas were looking at the relief map of the Aztec capital as it had been the day Cortez came to the city and changed it all forever.

"I don't know why," he said.

"I like it very much," she said. She was looking out the window, and he saw her smiling for only the second time since they'd met.

"There's Sanborns, then. You have to see it. Tiled all over," he said. "It's a chain really, but they have the colonial motif and it's nice. I go there with friends sometimes, for the coffee."

"Do they serve dinner?"

"I think so. But I can take you for coffee. There's no rule that we can't do two things. Now that you're staying on, there will be time," he said.

"But your work," she said.

"Well, you're a patient, aren't you?" He smiled at her.

Something changed on her face, warmed up. The distance between them that had been so obvious, which he'd been working to bridge, suddenly shortened. He'd thought it was the illness; now he realized that something else was making her sad.

He'd guessed, as they'd driven along with the radio playing, that she was getting over someone: a boyfriend, some love affair that had gone wrong. It was as if suddenly they could be friends. Or at least speak like friends, like man and woman perhaps. He hoped so. He didn't know why, other than the obvious fact that she was quite beautiful, but he wanted to get to know her. He felt protective.

"London is so different," she said, breaking the silence. Then they started to talk in a normal way for the first time. He was very glad she was staying on.

• • •

He was driven to an apartment outside the city, on the road

to Cuernavaca. He was going to resign. He'd decided that the moment he'd seen Nickels drag the prisoner into the shower. He'd protested and he'd been told to leave the room if he couldn't take it. He'd thought of going to the embassy and reporting the whole thing to the ambassador without letting him know that he himself was an intelligence officer. He supposed he could simply go as a doctor on the list. But he'd been warned that compromising the agency was a criminal offense, and he was frightened of being accused of something like that.

He'd learned in training that there were legal channels where he could lodge concerns, but as a covert operative, he had no immediate contact with his superiors in the U.S. He couldn't very well go to the head of station to complain about the head's best friend. The best thing to do was simply to quit. He certainly couldn't be part of what he'd seen at the safe house. He decided to do it now.

"You won't believe this place we're going," the driver said as they pulled off the highway.

Collin looked out the SUV's window. Popocatepetl, the volcano, loomed in the distance. Global warming was exposing bits of the volcano's side that had never been seen before.

The ceiling in the foyer was thirty feet high. The Laws were renovating a colonial mansion. It had a center courtyard with a beautiful *Bellas Artes* fountain. Workmen were painting the living room's coffered ceiling. Law's cover was as the embassy's trade attaché. Since the killing of the head of station in Greece in the '70s, the agency had worked harder to protect its in-country station chiefs. Because of Law's family background, the local press believed him to be nothing more than a wealthy banker with interests in the capital, who made frequent visits to the U.S. embassy.

"This was Porfirio Diaz's first Presidential residence," Law explained to him. "He didn't like the palace on the *Zócalo*. Of course, *Los Pinos* didn't exist, then. . . . I wanted you to examine my wife," Law said, casually. "She thought she felt something the other day." Law looked at the doctor, then. He'd been watching the workmen on their ladders. "She's upstairs. I don't trust these quacks in the city. . . . It's probably nothing. One of your colleagues on the list came out. Helen sent him packing. Just went right back up the stairs when she saw him."

Collin realized that Law was afraid that it *was* something. He'd been a doctor long enough to recognize that look. He'd seen every kind of man give that look. It was a frightened, shot-out-of-a-cannon look. His boss, who'd seemed so imperious the last time they'd met, had that look now. Law was stone scared.

"How do you do, Mrs. Law?" Collin said.

The bedroom was huge. A purple duvet on the bed was striking, because the walls were painted gold. Tall, thin colonial windows gave a view of the garden.

Law's wife was a beautiful older woman, and Collin was nervous at the idea of examining his boss's wife's breast. Somehow it seemed all *too* much.

He tried to smile and put her at ease. He put his doctor bag down on the floor.

"Can I sit down here, doctor?" she asked. "I'm afraid I was hiding, until I saw you. You looked kind. Are you kind?"

"Yes," he said. She looked him in the eye.

She sat next to an 18th-century mirror and dressing table. He could see her great beauty in the mirror. She put her hands on her knees. She was wearing a black velour gym suit and white Nike shoes that looked brand new.

"Do you like the room? I made them finish the bedroom first. There's so much to do. The place is really too big, but Alex loves it. I spend all my time in antique stores, it seems. I love Mexico. Don't you?"

59

"My bedroom isn't as nice as yours," he said, and smiled into the mirror. She was watching him.

"My husband tells me you aren't a quack. Of course Alex is terrified," she said.

She pulled down the zipper of her sweat suit. She'd been working out, she said. He could see the glistening sweat on her neck and on her chest. She was like a movie star even now—in her late forties, he guessed.

She took the jacket off. "I'll undo this. . . . I'm not afraid. I felt it when we got back from Acapulco. That morning. I felt it a week ago. I thought it would go away. Of course it hasn't," she said, looking into his face.

He saw her expression change as he squeezed her breast. He felt the lump immediately. He moved to her other breast without saying anything.

"But that one is okay," she said.

"I had a professor once tell me that you can be a Catholic and still ride a motorcycle," he said. "It took me a moment to get it. I'm really thick. Really sometimes I'm quite stupid."

"You mean you can have two lumps. That *would* scare me," she said

"It just means we should always check," he said.

"I see." This time she sounded serious.

He pulled his hands away. He made a point of turning away and picking up his bag while she put her bra on. He heard the zipper to her jacket.

"I think it's best if you go back to the States," Collin said. He turned around and faced her when she was zipped up.

"You felt it, too?"

"I'm afraid I did. That doesn't mean . . . It could mean a lot of things. But you have to have someone look at it. I think it would be better if you went home. It's just that here . . . well . . . they make more mistakes. I would feel more comfortable sending you home to the States," he said. "As soon as possible."

"I see. Would you like some coffee, doctor?"

"Yes, actually, I would," he said.

"Alex won't like it. He needs me here. All this work to do. We've only done a few rooms." She looked around the bedroom.

Then she smiled. Her composure had left her for a moment, but she regained it and was the official's wife again. He wondered if she knew what her husband did. She must, of course.

"Oh God, I hate telling Alex. He's so sensitive. He's not going to take it well. You see, we were separated, and now. . . . But you don't want to hear about two ancient people. You're *so* young. What's it like to be young here now? Is it fun? We were young in Portugal and Paris, and then in Asia. We had a lot of fun," she said. "I miss that *looseness* of youth. Before it all piles up on you—well?" She took his arm. "No lumps, then . . . you can tell me. I'm good with secrets."

"You have to be nice to him, Alex. He's *my* doctor now," Helen said. She touched Collin on the shoulder, kissed her husband, and said she wanted to go make reservations for a flight home. She told Alex to call her sister, because she didn't want to be the one to tell her. "She's a crier," Helen said, turning to Collin. "The only one in the family."

"Well, it's a bit of a shock," Alex said. She'd left them to have coffee alone.

"She should go to someone in the States as soon as possible," Collin said.

"You felt it, then. You're sure?" Alex said.

"Yes, sir," Collin looked down at the coffee cup.

They were in an old dining room off the kitchen. It hadn't been touched. A rough-looking colonial bookcase ran up one wall. The other had a window with a view of the fountain and what must have been horse stalls, a whole row of them across the huge patio. A magnificent bougainvillea hedge ran down the front of the stable.

The maid had placed a silver coffee service on the white lace tablecloth in front of them.

"Damn," Alex said. "Damn. Well, of course. She'll go tonight. Damn it."

"Sir. I have to talk to you about what happened the other night."

"I heard. You shouldn't have left," Alex said.

"He ordered me to leave, sir."

"Did he? Can't pay attention to Butch when he's in one of his moods," Alex said.

"That's not all, sir. I'm afraid that . . . can I speak here?"

"Yes. Don't be too sharp, though, if you know what I mean. People can always be listening in."

"It wasn't acceptable, sir. I'm a doctor."

"What?"

"His behavior, sir. In regard to the . . . guest."

"Is that all?" Alex said.

"I'm sorry?"

"Is that all? You object to his behavior towards our guest?"

"Yes. I'm a doctor."

"I *know* that," Alex said.

"There are . . . standards of behavior. I've taken an oath."

"Have you, then? Right. Of course. I admire your sincerity," Law said, pouring them coffee.

"Then you understand if I were to tell you that I have to. . . that I can't. Can't work with that person. In fact, I'm thinking of leaving our company."

"You can't do that," Alex said.

"Why not?"

"Well . . . because. It just wouldn't do. That's why. Certainly not right now," Alex said. He poured milk for both of them. "Anyway, you took an oath; you just told me. If I recall, it says you shall do no harm. Doesn't it? If you were to leave now, you might help the competition. They're up to something—here in

México. We're trying to figure out what the hell it is. And I need you, someone I can trust."

Collin watched his boss pour the milk carefully into his cup.

"Listen, our business . . . it's never pretty. We don't wear white coats and wash our hands in pretty sinks and stay clean, but we save lives, nonetheless. Think of us as white blood cells who wear suits. We're supposed to surround something nasty and kill it before it does a great deal of harm. So you can leave right now, or you can stay and help us stop the infection," Alex said.

"But what about Mr. N. . .?"

"What about him? Mr. N is good at his job. Mr. N is not a nice man sometimes. Everyone needs a Mr. N, though, because if not, then the infection gets out of control. We don't want that—do we?" Alex said. He put down the silver milk pitcher.

"Now tell me about breast cancer. Everything you know. Is hers serious? I mean . . . what are her chances? I've no idea. You must have an idea. As you say, you're a doctor." Alex looked at him over the rim of his coffee cup, and Collin wondered if Law wasn't slightly drunk.

9

Are you strong enough?" Madani asked. "You don't have to do this."

"Yes. I'm strong enough," Dolores said. "I want to do it."

"Are you going to see the doctor again?" the old man asked in Arabic.

They were alone in the room. He'd followed Dolores up the stairs from the lobby after the doctor had dropped her off. Madani had gone out to his car and thanked the doctor for what he'd done for her.

"He's asked me to dinner," Dolores said.

The old man looked at her. "Maybe you shouldn't accept," he said. "You may leave soon, anyway. It won't be long now, I'm sure."

She put the plastic bag with a few things she'd bought at the hospital down on the bed. A blind covered the window. The old man switched on the weak electric light. She didn't like the room because she'd been so ill there. She'd been so frightened, lying in the penumbra alone.

She walked to the blind and raised it to see the street and the doctor's building across the way. He'd pointed it out to her from the car.

"I've had it cleaned," the old man said. "The bathroom. I told the girl to use Mr. Clean." He went in to check. "Yes. It's fine."

"He speaks a little Arabic," Dolores said, "the doctor."

64

"Yes, I know," Madani said, coming out from the bathroom.

"He's not a bad man," she said. "I like him."

"That's not the point; he's the enemy," the old man said in Arabic. *"Infidel.* But I like him, too. . . . Allah be praised, not all of them are the same."

He turned and left. She heard the door close.

She had wanted to ask him what was taking so long. She was anxious to get it over with now. Anxious to die, in fact, but she wouldn't let herself use the word.

She walked to the bed and looked at the little white plastic bag of things she'd bought at the hospital: toothpaste, mouthwash, a card from the shop in the lobby that said "Mexico City," with a picture of the *Zócalo* taken years before. She wanted to write her mother in London and tell her, in some way, where she'd died.

They could burst in on her at any moment and assassinate her. Many had been killed that way already. All along the way, since she'd left Baghdad, rumors had the Americans right behind them.

She thought that if she wrote her mother's address in her own handwriting and posted the card, her mother would know what became of her. She wasn't supposed to have any more contact with her family. She'd sworn not to. But lying in the hospital, she imagined what her mother would go through once she had disappeared. It was too cruel to leave her like that. She'd decided to post the card regardless of her promise. How could a postcard hurt?

She went to the little wooden desk and switched on the lamp. She found a cheap ballpoint pen in the drawer, and clicked it open. Only a few years ago, she'd been a young college girl with nothing to fear. She tried to imagine that girl now, but she'd changed so much since the invasion and her husband's injury that she couldn't even believe she'd been that girl. Yet she knew she had been. It was as if that girl had never left London, gone to Baghdad, married, had a child.

She put the card down and looked at the back in the bad light. *View of Mexico City's main square, 1960* it said in English. It seemed too short an explanation. She wanted to add something. *Underneath there is a ruined empire,* she wrote in her own hand, sure her mother would recognize it.

She'd found a book at the hospital on the history of the city and had read it while she convalesced. She couldn't stop reading books; the moment she did, the enormity of her loss would push her towards a physical panic. She'd never loved anyone the way she'd loved her baby son. How she'd looked forward to giving birth! She'd wanted to blossom like that.

She looked blankly at the back of the postcard. *This is what I'm left with. A room in a strange city.* She would not be a mother now ever again, but she would carry something to term. She had a new womb, where she'd carry a different kind of child; a monster, yes, but her child, nonetheless.

She could see her husband lying on the street, his clothes on fire—the way his feet moved in a slow awful way, his face destroyed and blackened by the blast . . . the baby ripped from his arms. No, she had kept reading books—any kind. She felt a sense of panic, as she always did when she thought of what had happened. She ran from the desk to the bathroom and was sick in the sparkling clean toilet.

Later, when she'd cleaned her face with cool water from the tap and come back to the desk again, she felt exhausted. She wanted to sleep. She wished it was all done and she could sleep forever. Sometimes she dreamt that she was asleep in her bedroom in London, her mother and father in the next room listening to the BBC news.

How can they sell such a stupid card, she thought. *What stupidity!* She crossed the description out in one neat strong line. Then she wrote down her mother's address in London and stood the card up next to the mirror.

At first she'd thought she might be losing her mind, but not anymore. She accepted her fits of anger now. She didn't care about the state of her mind or her body, or even her recent illness. She was made of hate now. Not the kind you see on the TV, the clenched-fist hate the TV people love to show. Hers was a different kind, small and pragmatic, and feminine. It was more like a shroud that covered her soul, a kind of burka that restricted her view of the world. She lived for vengeance, everything seen through vengeance's narrow slit, now.

She went to bed and slept, the sound of the traffic on the street below oddly comforting. She dreamt that the door was kicked in by American soldiers—dressed the way they were in Baghdad—and she tried to cover her face before they began to shoot. She felt the bullets enter her body. Instead of killing her, each one made her stronger. She looked into the bullet holes and saw pictures of herself, of her husband, and of the child she would never see again.

• • •

"He's dead, then?" Alex asked.

"Mailed back to Allah," Butch said.

"Did he talk, at least?"

"No," Butch said. "Tough guy, I'll give the prick that. I gave him to the Mexicans to see what they could get out of him."

They did what they always had done in a crisis. Alex had rented a hotel room in the *Zona Rosa* at the Hotel Presidente, under the name of James Ploughright. The cable traffic from Langley and elsewhere had reached the level of a blizzard; warnings were popping up everywhere in the world. Terrorists were deliberately creating an avalanche of misinformation to confuse them, or at least that's what it seemed like.

Everyone was saying that there was a real threat. Someone in Baghdad had confessed. Someone in Italy was reporting unusual meetings at the mosque in Naples. This was the kind of cable chatter Alex had learned to walk away from, because it could actually stop him from seeing the obvious.

What was obvious from the early reports was that someone linked to *al Qaeda* had bought a ticket in Saudi Arabia for Mexico City. A one-way ticket. That had been a mistake. That was where he'd started. They weren't perfect; he'd always believed that. They weren't supermen.

He'd gotten the routine cable about the one-way ticket a day after the call from Homeland Security. He'd flagged it himself, not passed it off to some underling. He still cared. After all of it, after all he'd been through with the agency, he still cared. It was about 9/11. It wasn't about his past or them, or even the people in power who, he knew, were running the country like a private fiefdom. It was about saving lives.

He'd immediately checked with the French airline that had issued the ticket in Riyadh. That person—a woman—hadn't shown up for the flight. Why not? Why had they bought a one-way ticket in the first place and not used it? And why a woman's name? It was a mistake, he was sure of that; someone had made a mistake and bought a one-way ticket to Mexico City and then not used it. It was a gift.

It was very late. Alex looked at his watch; Helen would still be en route to Washington, and he couldn't call her. He'd gotten her on a military flight. She would be in the States in a few hours. Her sister was going to meet her at the airport.

"Do you want something to eat?" Alex asked his friend. Butch was the only one he wanted with him, the only one whose advice he wanted. He felt they were close to the cell . . . did they have a bomb? One they planned to use—where? He had no idea. It was a gut feeling, but it was strong. The threat was real this time; he was sure of that. The enemy was doing *something.* They'd made a mistake, and if he could just tease out something from that mistake, he might have a chance of learning what they were up to.

"Why did you send the kid out—the doctor?" Alex asked.

"Because I don't like him," Butch said. "He's gutless. He's not one of us. Why do they hire little girls like that?"

"Is he? Why?"

"He's a pussy," Butch said.

Alex took a drink of red wine. He wasn't drunk, but he was high. There was a difference. He wouldn't allow himself to cross the line. The news about his wife had sent him running for the quiet place a drink gave him. He needed that quiet place.

"Helen might have breast cancer," Alex said. He was a little surprised he'd said it like that, dropping a bomb like that.

Butch had had his feet up on the coffee table. He'd taken his tie off, and files were piled on the table around their dinner trays. They'd been in the room most of the evening trying to wade thought the cables of the last two weeks.

Butch took his feet down and sat up. "How do you know? I saw her the other day; she looked wonderful." He looked shocked. Alex knew that part of Butch—as with so many of his friends— was in love with his wife. He was used to that. You had to be used to that when you married an exceptionally beautiful woman. It came with the territory.

"She found a lump. I've sent her to Washington to see an onco-logist, a good one. He's rich, anyway. I guess that means he's good," Alex said. "He's a friend of my brother's."

"It's great she found it," Butch said. "Early, I mean."

"The kid examined her, too," Alex said. "This morning. He was very nice. You shouldn't have thrown him out, old boy—not like that. I wanted him there. You went too far. I know he's just a kid, but I don't want one of these bastards to die before we get what we want. Don't send him away again. If he'd stayed with the guy, he'd probably be alive."

Butch nodded. If it were anyone else, Butch would have smiled

69

and promised and done it his way, but they were friends. He would do anything for Alex. It had always been that way. Alex was one of the few persons he'd ever really loved.

"Okay. You're the boss. If he'd just stop wearing that moral diaper. . . . I had to wake Osama up myself; he wouldn't help. You should have seen the kid look at me like I was—I don't know—a real *asshole. I'm* not the asshole who likes to kill innocent people."

Alex put his hand up. "Spare me the details, *amigo.* Personally, I don't care if you drop these guys out the third-story window after we're finished with them. Send them all air freight to Allah, whatever. I just want to know what they're up to—but we can't talk to dead people, Butch."

"It's here," Butch said. "I got that out of him, or at least him not talking like he was holding on to something really, really, hard every time we asked him if he knew where the bomb was. You could see it in his eyes. He knew something, all right."

"We don't know for sure it's a bomb," Alex said.

"No. But we know they like bombs," Butch said.

• • •

"We're alone," Butch said. He pulled the hood off the prisoner.

Setiawan Datuk was shackled to the bed. He was lying under a window with a view of the garden. The garden had decorative lighting, lit now so the safe house would blend in with all the other houses of the wealthy it was surrounded by.

"He thought I was going to drag you into the shower and get you all wet." Butch looked at the door. "See, I understand his kind. Spineless motherfucker, right? We're soldiers. We understand each other," Butch said to him. "You smoke?"

Setiawan Datuk looked at him. He was twenty-seven years old; he'd signed up to fight the Americans. They'd taught him how to make bombs, and he had a talent for it. His father had been a mechanic. He'd wanted to be an engineer, but it wasn't to be.

He'd listened to Jimi Hendrix in the market in Manila, and thought about America. He had liked the music. He'd bought the tape and brought it home. He'd read somewhere on the internet that Jimi Hendrix was "good with the ladies," and he too wanted to be good with the ladies. This was about all he really knew about America.

Now he believed they hated all Muslims. The young man was sweating. For some reason, he'd started to hear that music again, as if he were in the market on a sunny Saturday morning in March. The music came out of a cheap speaker in front of the store: "Hey Joe."

Where you gonna run to now where you gonna run to now/ Hey Joe, I said/ Where you gonna run to now where you gonna go/ I'm goin' way down south/ Way down to Mexico way . . . Ain't no hangman going to put a rope around me. . . .

"Hey Joe," the young man said finally. He looked up, and thought he saw the man from the record store.

He had a little bit of schoolboy English. He was out of his head, but he knew what the soldiers wanted. He had the place tucked under his heart, and they weren't going to get it. He wasn't afraid to die, not in the least. He was sure he'd go to heaven.

"Hey, yourself," Butch said. "You understand that I have a mission, right?" He looked at the kid. He wasn't a bad-looking kid; he needed a shave and a haircut, but not bad-looking. Butch dragged a chair over to the edge of the bed.

"I see you are going to need that the leg looked after. It needs attention, all right."

"Hey Joe," the kid said stupidly. He was delirious. He could feel the fresh air come into the room as Butch slid the window open.

"Is that better?" Butch asked.

71

"Hey Joe," the kid said. He wasn't in Mexico; he was back in his room, listening.

They took him to a place the Mexican intelligence service had. They did everything they could to him, everything they'd ever done to anyone, but he didn't talk. Butch was there the whole time, hoping he'd split open and talk, but he never did. Butch called Kwana from the hallway outside where Setiawan Datuk died and told her he was working late.

• • •

"I think it's here, in the city," Butch said.

"Yes. I think it's in the city. Only because we've rolled up one group, and I think they'll wait and see. The ticket from Riyadh was for two weeks ago, but they didn't use it. So we have a time frame. Setiawan Datuk left his ship two weeks ago and came here—or to Cuernavaca, anyway. Close enough. Maybe he brought a bomb to the city."

"We have a time frame," Alex said. The unused plane ticket could have been intentionally done to drag the blanket. They'd both had a teacher at Langley that used the term. It wasn't used anymore, but "dragging the blanket" used to mean creating enough confusion and disinformation to make it all the more difficult to learn what was real from what was fiction.

"They've probably dragged that blanket all over the world. That's why the cable traffic is so hot. The more they drag, the better their chances," Butch said.

"Well, I found a mistake. At least, I think it's a mistake. I don't know why. It's because of the woman's name. They normally don't use women, you know that. We *know* that. If you look at them, it's all men. That's where they're different from, say, the Palestinians, or Hamas. These *al Qaeda* pricks hate women. They'd never use them—we *think*," Alex said.

"If they hate them so much, why do they marry so many?"

"Very funny. You know what I mean," Alex said.

"Okay. Someone in Riyadh makes a mistake and actually— without thinking—tells us it's a woman who's coming at us."

"Pretty smart, right? They know their profile better than we do . . . that's what I think happened. A slip. He was angry about it. The little shit couldn't get it out of his head—angry—so he actually uses a woman's name on the ticket."

"And maybe he's just being clever," Butch said. "Another way to confuse us."

"If you're a woman, you can't leave Saudi Arabia without a note from your fucking husband. Why would he go there?" Alex said. "There could have been a question he couldn't answer. Remember, the Saudi police were certainly listening in when he bought the ticket. Or he had to believe they might be."

"I'm tired, Alex; we've been in here for six fucking hours. It's late. We've been at this for two days, in fact. You just found out Helen might be sick. You look exhausted, and I know I am."

Alex ignored him. "It's a bomb. That's their thing, isn't it? You're probably right. And they're going to use it—but where?" Alex asked.

Butch looked at his friend. Twenty-five years had taught him that Alex Law was not good at a lot of things. Staying sober, for one; he was too small to help in a bar fight. He'd been too good-looking to be taken seriously when they'd been in Africa, but he'd been a success when most had succumbed to the heat and the diseases.

The only thing Alex could do, and do well, was to *consider* the enemy and go from there. He had a knack for that, and for ignoring the intelligence bureaucracy and flying solo when it really mattered. The spy business, when it was all said and done, was about people. Alex understood people very, very well. The only one he probably didn't understand was himself, Butch thought as he picked up his coat from the back of a chair.

"I'll see you in the morning." Butch had a girlfriend at the embassy whom he was keeping a secret. He liked having secrets, especially from Alex. It was fun. He wanted to go see her before it really got too late. She was much younger than he was. It was the first real affair he'd had since his wife died; he didn't understand what she saw in him, but he didn't really care, either.

"Listen, I've gotten something from a friend."

"Really? What?"

Alex fished in his picket and threw out a foil of amphetamines.

"We can't sleep."

"What?"

"I said we can't afford to sleep. Not for a few days."

"That's crazy, Alex."

"Is it?"

Butch picked up the speed and put it in his pocket. "You're fucking crazy, you know that? I really didn't know that about you. You act so sane all the fucking time, too. You fool people. You fool me half the fucking time," Butch said. "Go to sleep. Jesus!"

"What if they get through?" Alex said. He said it not as the head of station or as an intelligence officer, but as Butch's friend. He had that dread now. It was a real dread that he wouldn't be good enough, that he was getting old and that he was past it. That he couldn't match them, and that a lot of people would die because of it.

"Then they get through . . . ; we're not perfect, Alex. We're just two old guys in suits."

"What's her name?" Alex said.

"What?"

"The girl, the one you're going to see. She's black, 37. Born in New Orleans. I think she's using you. Her brother has applied to the service. Maybe she thinks you can help," Alex said, watching him walk towards the door.

"Kwana. And I thought it was my good looks," Butch said, and left. He had no idea how Alex knew, but he wasn't surprised.

"I don't think we should assume it's a bomb," Alex said. But Butch, already gone, hadn't heard him.

10

When Dolores woke up, it was late, after eight in the evening. The room was cold and damp. It had no heater, and it was raining outside. She could hear the rain and the thunder rumbling over the city. Exhausted, she'd slept without dreaming, or at least it seemed that way.

She sat up. She looked for her shoes on the floor, then snapped on the lamp by the bed. *Maybe it will be soon,* she thought. She wanted it to be soon.

She heard a knock on the door. "Come in," she said. She thought it would be the old man, whom she was beginning to dislike. There wasn't any one reason; she was just beginning to resent him. All his talk about Allah, perhaps. She didn't really care about Allah. Allah belonged to children and old men, and people like Bin Laden who thought they were God. Allah hadn't cared about her wanting to be a mother. He hadn't cared about her husband. If there was a God, he seemed to love only Americans.

"It's me, Collin. Are you decent?"

"Yes. . . . Come in, doctor."

The door opened. She was glad to see him but didn't want to admit it to herself.

"I was downstairs having dinner. I thought I'd look in on you. They gave me this." He was carrying a tray with her dinner. She got up immediately and took it from him, embarrassed that they'd made the doctor carry the tray up the three flights of stairs.

"They shouldn't have asked you," she said.

"I offered, really. I need the exercise," he said. "How's the patient?"

"Better, thank you. I took a long nap. I'm still tired."

"Good," he said, "about the nap."

She stood by the desk where she'd put down the tray. She didn't know what else to say.

"You're going to eat, aren't you?" the doctor said.

"Yes. . . ."

"I'll keep you company, if you like?"

"You must be busy," she said.

"No, not right now. It's nine o'clock. I should go to the hospital later; I've got a patient. An American college student—alcohol poisoning. Stupid, really. . . I'm sorry; I'm intruding," he said.

"No. *Please* stay."

"Are you sure?" he asked. "I don't want to be a nuisance."

"Yes. I hate eating alone," she said, which was true. She ate most of her meals alone now, and she'd hadn't gotten used to it.

"I do, too, but I do it all the time. I skip meals sometimes because I can't stand another meal like that. You know, pretending to read while other people talk. I'd rather not. If you know what I mean," he said. "Breakfast is okay. You can be alone at breakfast."

"Yes, breakfast is easier," she said.

"You don't want to talk to *anyone*, then." He laughed.

"No. You're right," she said, and smiled. *I'm glad he's here.* She realized he was lonely. It had never crossed her mind that a man could be lonely like that, a young man. She thought men always had something more important to do. He took off his raincoat, the same one he'd been wearing the day he first examined her, and tossed it on the foot of the bed.

"It's chicken . . . ; it's not good, and it's not bad," Collin said. "Your dinner."

77

She smiled. It was the second time he'd seen her smile back-to-back.

"I've had it," she said, and then they both smiled.

"Nothing worse than a Mexican chicken," Collin said. "I don't know what they feed them, but whatever it is—old tires, or shoes—must be hard to cook."

"They can't all be like that," she said.

"The ones you buy in the city are. And an awful yellow color too, like those rubber ones you see in toy shops."

This time she didn't smile. He was trying too hard, he thought. That was it. *You shouldn't try that hard.*

He'd come because he was intrigued with her. He wasn't even sure why—her beauty, obviously. She had that kind of great beauty like Catherine Deneuve, the kind that compelled you to want to be with her, just to stare at her. But there was something else, too.

He let her sit down at the little table and uncover the dish of food. The silence wasn't awkward.

She was hungry for the first time in days. She ate the rice and chicken. He could tell she was better from the way she ate. He hoped she would make conversation, but she didn't. She just ate as if she were alone. He saw the postcard on the desk and reached for it.

"A friend in London?"

"Yes," she said, looking up. She stopped eating for a moment and watched him. He turned the card back around and looked at the picture.

"An old picture. Before the excavations and all."

"Yes . . . 1960," she said.

"Someone's scratched it out—the description."

"It was in the drawer like that," she lied.

He looked at her.

"Odd, what some people do."

"Yes," she said. "I don't know why."

"When I was a resident, a friend of mine used to write love letters on old lab results, between the lines. He became a psychiatrist."

She looked at him. Their eyes met.

"You look very young. Too young to be a doctor," she said.

"Am I? I feel quite old sometimes," he said. "Lately, especially."

"Did you . . . skip grades?"

"Well, I'm afraid I did. I finished high school in three years. My father was very very proud of that. He bought me a car. That's what he does if he thinks you've done something *really* good; he buys you something ridiculously expensive. He's a doctor, too."

"What kind of car?" she asked.

"A Ford Mustang . . . what are you doing here alone in Mexico, Dolores?"

The question took her by surprise, in part because she had difficulty reacting to the name Dolores. It wasn't her real name, and at times it seemed silly to answer to it. It was as if he were suddenly talking to someone else in the room.

"I'm sorry. It's just that . . . I thought about it, and I've decided you're much too beautiful to be traveling alone. Especially here. It's not really safe," he said.

"What color was it? The car," she asked.

"The car? My car?"

"Yes."

"Yellow."

"Did you enjoy it?"

"Yes." He laughed then. "I lost my virginity in it."

"Is that what you do in America? Have sex in yellow cars?" she asked. She was talking to him like an anthropologist. It all seemed so strange to her. What kind of people were these Americans, anyway? Were they like other people, or were they different?

She knew they weren't like the British. The British were simply preoccupied with themselves, like the French. But the Americans were more childlike, and so sure of their moral superiority. The French knew they weren't superior morally—just culturally, they thought. That belief in the moral high-ground was Anglo-Saxon.

"Yes. But not *just* yellow ones. What about you? Were you born in the States?"

"No. No, I was born in . . . London."

"Is that a secret?" he asked. She smiled. "The London part. Are you an international woman of mystery, like in the movies?"

"No," she said.

"You seem like a woman of mystery. I always wanted to meet one."

"I'm very ordinary. Really," she said. She pushed the empty plate away.

"Could I paint you? Your portrait?" he asked.

She wanted him to leave then—one part, a small part of her, that was lonely and frightened, wanted him to stay. But most of her wanted him to leave.

"Fully clothed, madam. Very dignified, just in case you thought I was some kind of lech."

"Doctor. . . ."

"Please don't call me doctor. Collin . . . please," he said.

She relented then in her heart. If she was going to die, she wanted to be like this with someone before it happened. At night talking, as if the world outside didn't exist. Silly things. What could be more silly than having someone paint your portrait? It had been that way with her husband, too; they'd laughed a lot about silly people or silly things they'd seen on the television. They'd once seen a man on *Al Jazeera* with a toupee that blew off while he was being interviewed. He'd carried on as if nothing had happened.

"Okay," she said.

"We would have to go to my apartment, there, across the street," Collin said. "My things are there. You see, I'm thinking of becoming a painter. A real painter."

"Will you be famous?" she asked. "Like Gauguin? I love Gauguin."

Each of them had a love for Gauguin, and they started to talk about his life. She knew his paintings very well.

"Are you a painter?" he asked, a little stunned.

"No. Architect," she said. It was the first time she'd confessed to being anything for two months. They called her *the wife, Alzawja,* in Saudi Arabia, where she'd been taken after she left Baghdad. She hadn't had the chance to speak very much at all. In fact, she'd worn a veil for the first time in her life there. She was locked in a room in a wealthy man's house while she waited.

"Big buildings and all that?" he asked.

"No. Houses for families," she said. "That's all I wanted to build."

They heard the sirens then, the police cars turning down from the *Zócalo.* They heard the cars stop in front of the hotel, their red lights bouncing off the buildings below, the red light painting the room's walls.

He went to the window and looked down on the scene below. He'd never seen so many police cars. They were still coming down the street.

"Are they coming here?" she asked. He turned and looked at her.

"Yes," he said. "I think so." She was pale. She came to the window and took his hand.

"I'm frightened," she said. It was the first time she'd touched anyone like that since her son had been killed.

"I'm sure we're all right. Probably some criminal staying here at the hotel. Exciting stuff," Collin said. He felt her squeezing his hand very hard. He realized she was frightened, and he was surprised.

They heard boots on the wooden stairs—faint at first, then louder, then in the hallway outside. Then the door was kicked in. Two plainclothes Mexican policemen ran into the room, one with a machine pistol pointed at them.

"We're Americans!" the doctor said in Spanish. He was indignant.

"Pasaportes," the man said. "Downstairs! Passports! Take your passports with you."

81

11

You could see the whole garden from the grand living room where they were standing. Well placed resort-style lighting lit the garden, making for a stagy *mise-en-scène* of light and dark patches, with brief moments of tropical green, where palms had been under-lit. The garden was capped by a large swimming pool at the center—it, too, lit up.

The house was in the Pedrigal and done in the International style that had been popular in the 60's with Latin American architects. Collin had been picked up at his apartment and driven there by an American who hadn't spoken a word to him during the entire hour it had taken to cross the city.

He had gotten a call in the middle of the night from the embassy to go to "see a patient," another friend of Butch's.

"Have you heard anything?" Collin asked Alex as he walked into the living room.

The room was huge with 20-foot ceilings. The space seemed to be swallowing them up whole. The foyer was brightly lit, but the living room was in a penumbra. Alex had been sitting with a highball glass on a big overstuffed couch. He was drunk. It was obvious from the expression on his face, slightly sardonic.

Collin wasn't surprised. The shock of his wife's illness, he guessed. He'd seen that kind of behavior before. The man was angry that a disease was attacking his wife. It was all too common a reaction, Collin thought. *He's angry at God.*

He'd lied to the police at the hotel and told them Dolores was his wife. They were asking for passports in the shabby lobby, and it was instinctual. He'd wanted to protect her. He'd been afraid the police would arrest her. He'd heard enough stories about attractive women at the hands of the Mexican police to know he had to do *something*.

He told the police he was an American doctor who worked for the embassy and that she was his wife, and the police let them both go immediately. They'd walked out of the lobby and across the street to his apartment. She'd never said a word to them.

When he'd sat her down in his tiny living room, in the chair where he read at night, she'd burst into tears. He'd given her a Valium and put her to bed in his room. He'd been asleep in his reading chair when the phone had rung.

"Not a thing," Alex said. "She's with her sister. I want to thank you for being so kind to my wife the other day. I do appreciate it. Drink? It's going to be a long evening. . . . I'm having a gin and tonic. Would you care for one? There's a housekeeper; she can make it for you."

"No, thank you," Collin said.

"Oh, I think you should," Alex said cryptically. "It's going to be a long night." The way he said it—the way he pronounced the word *long*—gave away just how angry he was, the doctor thought.

"No, thank you. Coffee, maybe," Collin said.

"Do you love your country?" Alex asked.

"Yes, of course," Collin said. "Is that why I'm here?"

"When you're being shot at, it never crosses your mind," Alex said. He tinkled the ice in his glass. "Patriotism never crosses your mind. Silly things do. Fear, of course, the great equalizer. The enemy is afraid, too. Have you ever been shot at, doctor? Probably not."

"No, sir."

"Butch and I have been. When we were your age. He's seen me piss myself, in fact." Law was drunk; it was obvious now, and Collin didn't know what to say. "I don't think Butch has ever really been afraid. Physically afraid, I mean. He's quite extraordinary in that way. Of course, it's difficult being someone's superior then. I mean, when they've seen fear in you like that. And you've pissed yourself. Not attractive in a leader," Alex said.

"Sir, is there a reason you had me come here?"

"I need your help. Will you help me?" Alex said.

"If I can," Collin said.

"Good. Sit down. We're waiting for Butch."

Law stood up and went to a window. He looked down on the pool. "It's strange; I remember when this house was new. I was on the Cuban desk at the embassy. We used to come here and throw parties." He turned around. "Of course that was illegal. Secretaries in the pool. Young men in the altogether, their dicks out. I cheated on my wife on several occasions here in this house," Alex said. "I'm very worried about my wife, in fact." Alex moved the ice in his glass again. "I don't like doctors; they speak in tongues, if you know what I mean. I had one on the phone from the States. He seemed to think there was a serious problem."

"I agree," Collin said. "I mean, about speaking in tongues."

"Malignant is the word he used." An agonized expression crossed Law's face. It was pathetic. The disease was something he couldn't control. He was a man who was used to controlling everything, Collin imagined. And now he'd met his match. There was no back channel for cancer. No air-strike. No assassination team, no one he could turn to to get secret information on the disease threatening his wife.

"There are treatments, sir. I wouldn't. . . ."

"We think *al Qaeda* has brought a bomb to Mexico. We think. Don't really know, of course. If it's true, only God knows where it is. Anyone's guess. Maybe they are going to move it to some

U.S. city. Los Angeles? It's close," Alex said. "Of course, if they manage to do that, tens of thousands of innocent people are going to die. Probably more.

"I want you to help me try and stop that—just in case it *is* true, I mean. . . . Do you think you can do that?" Alex said. "Of course, they may just want to use it here, in the city. Perhaps the embassy."

"Of course." Collin was stunned.

"Are you sure you don't want that drink now?" Alex said.

"All right," Collin said.

Alex rang a small bell on the coffee table and a man came out. The doctor ordered a glass of wine.

Collin's sister lived in Los Angeles. She was pregnant. He looked at the man. He was a Mexican.

"He'll have a proper drink. Gin and tonic. Make that two, please,"Alex said.

"Wine will be fine," Collin said, turning to the man.

"Do we have an understanding, then?" Alex asked. He was looking at the doctor. "If we don't stop them, I don't think they will be stopped. No one in Washington is taking me very seriously. They're busy with Iraq and don't really care what happens here. They'd be relieved if they blew up something *here*, probably. Wouldn't be *their* problem, would it. . . ? I'm viewed as an alarmist," Alex said.

"All right, I'll help," Collin said.

"Did you hear that, Butch? Our young friend said he'll help."

Butch was just then coming into the room. He was wearing a fresh, well-pressed suit, but looked haggard.

"I heard it. What if he understands it differently than we do, boss?" The doctor wondered why Nickels didn't like him. It seemed obvious that he didn't.

"Don't mind Butch. He's in love. He's got a girlfriend and she's much younger than he is. How old is she, Butch? *Exactly?*"

"Too young for me," Nickels said. "She wants new positions.

I don't do new positions." Butch loosened his tie. Collin wasn't used to their locker-room bonhomie. They came from a different generation, he supposed, where that kind of talk was common.

"All this screwing has put him in a foul mood. He's jealous of you, doctor . . . he wants to be twenty-nine again," Alex said. "Of course that isn't going to happen."

"I'd settle for thirty-five," Butch said, sitting down. "Have you heard from Helen?"

"Yes, she's got the all clear." Alex shot Collin a look. He didn't understand why Law would lie about something like that, especially to such a close friend. "She's right as rain apparently. She wants to stay and shop."

"What did I tell you," Butch said. "Jesus. What's wrong with you people?" Butch looked at Collin. "Fucking doctors. Worthless fucks."

"So, gentlemen. . . ." Alex said, looking at them in that controlled-yet-teetering way again. "The man upstairs. I want you two to get him to roll on everyone in his cell. We have forty-eight hours, and then we lose control of him. They'll render him to Gitmo, or wherever they decide to take this . . . person. The guest upstairs . . . he may be able to help with our problem."

"Who is he?" Collin asked.

"A Syrian, we think, arrested this evening. The man we arrested in Cuernavaca had called him three days ago. The one upstairs had Setiawan Datuk's hotel listed on his cell phone. Sloppy, really.

"I think the person upstairs knows exactly what is going on, or at least knows someone who does know. I believe that he is in the cell which is probably being controlled out of the mosque here in the city. I believe that this is the cell we're after, the one at the center of things. I know two other cells are operating in Mexico, *at least*. I don't believe they have our package, but they're acting as if they do have it. Very intelligent thing to do. They know that if we spread ourselves too thin, we won't catch anyone. Or

86

they'll pretend to make a mistake so that we can then spend our time talking to people who don't have a bloody clue where the package is."

"Are there guidelines of some kind? What we're allowed to do? How far we can go?" Collin asked.

"You see what I mean, boss?" Butch said.

"Maybe you don't quite understand what's at stake," Alex said.

It wasn't an act, Collin thought to himself suddenly. They were both crazy, he decided. One was vicious, and the other a drunk. But they were both crazy. He was sure of that now. It hit him, the reality of it.

"Do you know what waterboarding is?" Alex asked him.

"Yes," Collin said.

"Good. Butch is very good at it. I want you to go up and explain to the prisoner what it is."

"Explain *what?*" Collin said.

"I want you to explain what it is. Exactly."

"Waterboarding?" Collin said. "You're crazy."

"Yes. Tell him you're a doctor. Tell him that it would be better if he simply tells us what we want to know," Alex said.

"What is it you want to know?" Collin said, horrified.

Alex looked at the doctor, then at Butch. "I want to know what is going on," Law said.

"You're sure he even *knows?*" Collin asked.

"Yes. Don't be cheeky, son. I'm not in the mood."

"It's illegal. *Torture,*" Collin said.

"Well, waterboarding isn't," Alex said. "Haven't you been reading the papers? Read the papers. It's in the *New York Times.* It's fine."

"We're in the batter's box with waterboarding," Butch said.

Collin thought of his sister for a moment, and then looked at the staircase. He'd seen waterboarding in his training at the agency. They put recruits through the same program as pilots and other military personnel who might be captured by the enemy. Each recruit was waterboarded as part of the "prison camp" experience. He'd had no idea that his side was using it in the war against *al Qaeda*.

"I'm a doctor," Collin said. "You can't ask me to do that."

"Well, we're not asking *you* to do it, for fuck's sake," Alex said. "I'm asking you to go tell him to talk to us. You have a nice manner with people. I think he might listen to you."

"You have interrogation experts for that," Collin said, looking at Butch. "I don't understand. Why me?"

"You said you would help. I'm asking you to go upstairs and explain to someone that if they don't cooperate with us, there will be consequences," Alex said. He picked up his second drink.

"Jesus Christ," Collin stood up. It felt as if a jolt of electricity had run though him, straight to his face.

He was frightened. He was frightened for his family in the States because of all this bomb talk; he was frightened at his own anger at whoever was upstairs. He knew, even for his family's sake, that torture was wrong—but he understood its use now, in a way he couldn't have before. It was that *understanding* that was frightening him.

"Isn't there some other way?" Collin said.

"And what would that be?" Butch asked. "Exactly what would that be, kid? Take him to lunch and tell him over iced tea we think his friend Osama is an asshole and maybe he should reconsider killing a couple of hundred-thousand innocent people?"

There was a long silence. The ice shifted in Law's drink.

Collin reached for his glass of wine and had a long pull. He hadn't made the rules, he thought. As any good doctor would do, he was practicing a kind of moral triage. One man *might* have to be left behind in the cause of saving tens of thousands of innocent lives. He could live with that. He tasted the wine, swallowed it, and then stood up. *She's your sister for Christ's sake.* He felt a coward suddenly for not having wanted to do anything he could to save her or the rest of them.

"I may want to call my sister. She lives in Los Angeles," Collin said.

"Of course," Alex said. "Tell her she should go on vacation. I could arrange something. *Immediately*. I mean, Los Angeles is a logical target, isn't it? It's only an hour or so from the border."

"I'd like that," Collin said.

"Do you understand what we want?" Alex said.

"Yes," Collin said. "I understand."

"He's upstairs. Two men are with him now," Alex said.

"I'll want to see him alone," Collin said.

"Send them out of the room, then . . . if you like," Alex said.

He closed the door behind him. The prisoner was lying on a bed in the center of the room. He was shackled and they'd put a hood over his head.

The curtain was closed. The doctor went to the curtain and opened it. The man, when he'd heard the noise of the curtain, lifted his head, then lowered it.

"I'm a doctor," Collin said. "I want to help you." It was then he noticed the sandals.

He went to the bed and pulled off the hood. Madani looked up at him. They were both in shock, both horrified. He immediately replaced the hood, afraid the old man would use his name. And *certainly*, Collin thought, they were on some video camera. He did it without thinking about it. He could hear Madani breathing now, slowly through the black hood.

"Quiet," he whispered in Arabic. He didn't know what to do. He said it again. "I'm going to take the hood off again. I want you to say nothing. Do you understand me?" he said it quietly in Spanish.

"*Sí*," the old man said.

Collin lifted the hood off. This time the old man was crying.

There were tears in his eyes. He had a black right eye, and it was swelling up badly.

"I'll get you some water," Collin said, looking down at him. He went to the bathroom, found a glass, filled it, and walked back out into the room.

It seemed surreal. For a moment he thought of telling Law that he knew this man, but he stopped himself. They were going to torture him. If Madani did know something, Collin believed he would certainly tell him—someone he knew. It was a risk not telling them he knew the old man. *Perhaps they knew that already?*

He went back to the bed and helped Madani with the glass. He couldn't hold the glass himself because of the shackles, nor could he sit up properly. Collin helped him drink, the water spilling over his split lips.

"My wife?" the old man said in Arabic, between sips. The water spilled more when he tried to speak.

"I don't know," Collin said. *"Ingles,"* he said.

"My eye is damaged," Madani said.

"It will be all right," Collin told him.

"I can't see well."

"It's swollen. That's all. Let me see." He opened the lid and looked at the eye. It was terribly bloodshot, but he guessed it would be all right. "Do you know something?" Collin said. He put the glass on the table next to the bed.

"I don't understand," Madani said. "Why am I here? Who are these men?"

"They think you know something. Something about a bomb," Collin said.

"A bomb?"

"Yes. A bomb," Collin said.

"No. I don't understand. Can you help me, doctor?"

"I don't know," Collin said. "I don't know."

"How did you know I'd been arrested?" Madani said.

"I saw them put you in the car," he lied.

"Did you see if they took my wife?"

"No. I don't know," Collin said.

"I'm frightened. I've done nothing. They said they were going to kill me."

"You have to tell me if you know anything about this bomb," Collin said.

"How can I know about a bomb? I'm an old man," he said.

"Are you with them . . . with *al Qaeda*, Madani? Tell me the truth."

"No, of course not. It's ridiculous," he said.

"Why do they think so?" Collin said.

"Because I'm an Arab, perhaps. They hate us all now. May God help them."

"They are very . . . angry. You have to tell them something. Make up something. Anything," Collin said.

"Why? I don't *know* anything, doctor. I told you. How can I tell them anything, if I don't know what this is about?"

"They will . . . they will. . . ." Collin felt suddenly ill. He went into the bathroom and vomited. When he was finished, he ran the tap and washed his face with cool water. *What could he do?* If the old man was telling the truth, he was doomed. If he was lying . . . and he knew? Then he was a monster.

Collin sat on the edge of the tub and tried to think of anything suspicious he'd ever seen at the hotel: anything, or any person, who might, in the least bit, have something to do with a bomb; but he could think of no one. The old Arab shopkeepers who ate at the hotel had come to Mexico in the 1960s or '70s. They had all learned Spanish and had their children here. He never heard any of them talk politics. The worse he'd heard was them curse Israel, but that had been a kind of mindless boiler-plate hatred. He'd never heard them say one thing against America. Could they possibly be terrorists? It seemed absurd.

"I've been told to tell you that if you don't say where the

bomb is, they are prepared to use methods that will get you to tell them," Collin said. He'd come back into the room; he was desperate now. He thought that perhaps if he scared the old man into telling them something, he could get him, if not released, at least safe from torture.

"Are you working for them?" Madani asked. He seemed hurt by the idea that Collin would be the one to tell him this.

"No. I'm a doctor. I want to help you. You have to tell them *something,*" Collin said.

"Will you see if my wife is all right, doctor? Please."

"For God's sake, Madani. Are you *listening* to me!?"

"Are you going to do it?" the old man asked.

"Do what?"

"Hurt me."

"No, of course not." They looked at each other. "I'm your friend. *Sadeek.*" Collin used the Arabic word.

"Tell them I'm an old man who runs a hotel," Madani said. "Please."

"My sister and her family live in America, Madani."

He watched the old man's eyes. The good one, the one that hadn't been hurt, seemed to register something. "Why would anyone want to kill innocent women and children, Madani? Why in God's name would they want to do that? Can you blame them for being angry. . . You *do* know something, don't you?'

"No."

Collin was angry with the old man now. "I'm going to tell them that I think you do! *Right now.*"

The old man stopped talking then. Collin could see that the fear had now been replaced by something else—anger, or resignation, perhaps. He'd brought his doctor's bag, and checked the old man's blood pressure. It was high. He unwrapped the cuff. Madani watched him with his good eye.

"When I was a boy, there was a family dog. It went mad. My father and uncle didn't kill it because they thought that it would somehow be cured. The veterinarian, an Englishman, said it should be destroyed, but they loved the dog. It was the family dog, you see. They tied it to an olive tree we had. My father told me to care for the dog, but it never got better, and one day my father shot it. It broke his heart but he had to do it. Do you understand?" Madani said. "It was a mad dog."

"He has high blood pressure. It's 165 over 100. If you waterboard him, he might not survive it. He could have a stroke. He's probably on medication for it. I would have it lowered before you put him under that kind of stress," Collin said.

"My aunt Tilly has high blood pressure, but she still drives a big rig," Butch said. "And she's *old*."

Collin looked at Alex. He was quite drunk now, but oddly sensible underneath it.

"How soon can you get it down?"

"Two days," Collin said. "No less than two days. If that."

"Don't have it. We have to take the chance. I take it he didn't tell you anything?"

"No. He claims he doesn't know what you're talking about."

"Do you believe him?" Law asked.

"I think so. I'm not sure."

"You think so. Why?"

"He's an old man. He said he's been here in Mexico for over 20 years. What could he have to do with *al Qaeda*, for God's sake?"

"Tell him I'm going to start on his wife if he doesn't tell us where the bloody thing is," Butch said. "He's lying. We have pictures of him going into a mosque downtown run by a real fire eater. Wants all the western devils to go back to hell where they come from. I've just heard some of the tapes."

"Is she here?" Collin asked. He was frightened that she would be led in and give him away. "I know this man. He owns the hotel across the street from my apartment. I eat at his restaurant," Collin said.

Alex smiled. "I told you, Butch. It wouldn't take him but an hour to tell us. We already know that. Or at least, we thought it possible. The watchers have had him under surveillance. They said that a young American doctor ate at the hotel."

"My apartment is across the street. I often eat dinner there."

"Butch said you wouldn't tell us. I bet him a hundred dollars you would," Alex said.

"Sorry, kid. I just thought you might want to keep us in the dark. I might have, if I knew the guy."

Nickels seemed different suddenly, not so angry at him.

"I thought about it," Collin said.

"I'm sure you did," Alex said. "I was hoping he'd tell you. That he'd feel safe with you."

"You have his wife?" Collin asked.

"Yes. Not here," Alex said.

"Tell him I'm going to beat her up. It will take me about an hour to get over there to where she is," Butch said. "He has an hour to tell us where the bomb is."

"You aren't serious. . . . We're *Americans*, for God's sake," Collin said.

"Just tell him that . . . of course we wouldn't dream of hurting his wife," Alex said. "But then, we aren't holding her. The Mexicans are. And only God knows what *they* might do to her."

12

"A re you drunk, Alex?" Helen said. She'd had difficulty closing the door of the limousine because it was armored and weighed so much. Alex had had to reach across and help her with it. The Coldwater guard had helped her in but had stupidly forgotten to help close the door.

"No. Intoxicated," Alex said. "There's a difference."

"Is there, dear?" she said.

She'd gotten into the limousine, and they'd sat there for a moment because Alex hadn't said anything to the driver. A chase car waited behind them, a black Suburban filled with Coldwater contractors. Alex didn't like Coldwater, but turned to make sure they were there. It was filled with dregs, men who'd lied about their experience. Half of them said they were former Navy Seals; the other half said they were Delta Force. Most of them had been neither but *had* been in jail. A lot of them were Russians with colossal accents and psychopathic instincts.

"The house, please," Alex said finally.

"Yes, sir," the driver said.

His wife looked out the window.

"How was the flight?" Alex asked.

"Crowded. I saw an old chum from college."

"Really."

"She's divorced, and I think she's a lesbian," Helen said.

"Well. Things happen," Alex said.

"I think you can be too old to be a lesbian. I mean, as a starting-off lesbian, shouldn't you get that done before you're forty?" Helen said.

"I suppose it's never too late to learn," Alex said.

Helen smiled. "Do you think there's a class?" she said.

"There's a class for everything nowadays," Alex said.

"Not like when we were kids. No classes then."

"No." He thought she looked tired. "I was a little surprised when I called, and your sister said you were on a flight back to Mexico City. I don't quite understand," Alex said. "You just got there, didn't you? It's only been three days, anyway," he said. "I think."

"It's cold. And the weather—hurricanes. I didn't think it was a good place to be for someone in my condition," she said.

"How did it go with the witch doctors? One of them called me."

"Yes . . . you promised me you wouldn't drink again. That was our deal. We had a deal, remember, dear? I took you back. You'd stopped drinking. Only you've started again," she said.

"What did the witch doctors find out? He seemed very keen on keeping you there," Alex said, ignoring her.

"What's wrong?" she said. She took his hand, and he let her.

"Problems at work. The widgets came out blue; I wanted red. The home office is angry and very obdurate," Alex said.

"That's no reason to drink," she said.

He looked out the window. They were on a freeway; it was late, without too much traffic. So much of the city had a sinister drab quality, almost worse at night.

"Are they still behind us?" Alex asked the driver. "The chase car?"

"No, they've fallen back," the driver said.

"Wonderful. You see what I have to put up with? Inferior employees. It would drive anyone to take a drink," Alex said.

"I want to see your doctor. The one who came to the house, the young man," Helen said. "I didn't like that doctor in Washington. He never once looked me in the eye. I didn't like being alone without you, either."

"Reeves? Really, dear, he's much too young for you. Granted, he's handsome, but can't you wait until I'm away on business or something?" Alex said.

"Alex . . . I want to see him. I like him."

He turned away from the window. He was frightened for the second time in his life, in a way that no one could help him not be. He couldn't call for reinforcements, the way he had in Africa. It had taken him 25 years to realize how much he needed her, and now he saw that maybe he wasn't going to be able to make it up to her the way he'd planned. Everything he'd done wrong came back to remind him that he might be too late.

"You haven't told me what the doctor said," Alex said.

"And you haven't told me why you're drinking again," she said.

"For Christ's sake, Helen. This isn't a game. You should be in the States. Not here."

They went up onto an elevated freeway. It had a view of anonymous neighborhoods with satellite dishes and ugly hard-faced concrete buildings, some with old-fashioned neon signs advertising *Carta Blanca* beer in a blinking black and red script.

"If I forgive you being drunk, can you do me a favor? Just don't ask me a lot of questions right now. Can you do that? *Please,* Alex. I just want to be here with you and ride in the car and talk about silly things. Can we do that?"

She was wearing jeans and a car coat, and looked almost young. She was so beautiful. Her black hair was as silky as the day he'd met her. He'd gotten butterflies in his stomach because she was so pretty and he was so out of his league. All his friends had been jealous when they met her. All her boyfriends before him had been big strapping football types. He wasn't an athlete—unless, as he told her, you counted poker. She'd fallen in love with him that first night because he seemed kind, unlike the others.

"The ambassador has invited us to a party," Alex said, acquiescing. "I think she's going to do a Texas Barbeque. Should we wear cowboy hats and boots?"

"I think we should," Helen said. "And I'll get you some Hermes chaps from a place on Rodeo Drive."

"Shall we go, then?" Alex said. "For fun?"

"Oh, let's go. The bitch is wonderful when she's in all her glory," Helen said. They laughed like they always could, even when things had been dishonest between them because he had a problem with women and alcohol.

"Would you mind terribly if we stopped somewhere on the way home?" he said. "It won't take long."

"No."

"There's someone I've got to see."

"Is it about a widget?"

"Yes. He knows how to fix my problem, I hope. . . . Robert, can you go by Mr. Hussein's house? You know where it is," Alex said.

They were standing in a foyer that also held an original letter written by Napoleon. Hussein was a collector of things Napoleonic. "Mr. Hussein, you know my wife, Helen," Alex said.

"*Señora*. My pleasure. It's been too long!" Hussein said. Hussein was Alex's age and generation. He was intelligent and charming and Alex knew had an eye for the ladies, because in the old days, they'd been bad together. He was born in Egypt and had come to Mexico as a very young man, where he'd prospered as a "venture capitalist" in the capital's financial world—at least that was what he paid the press to always say when they gave his bio. What they couldn't say was he'd been an enterprising money launderer. Reporters that did suggest anything sinister quite soon found themselves without employment.

"Thank you for seeing me again, very decent of you," Alex said.

"I've met your wife before. At. . . ."

"The Westins'," Helen said. "I remember your charming daughter."

"Yes. Conco. She's at Yale. Everyone is away right now, and I'm all alone. I miss them terribly. . . . Can I offer you something to drink?"

"I'd love a glass of wine," Helen said. "I've been on a plane for hours."

"Of course. And you, Alex?"

"He'll have a ginger ale. . . . Good god—is that Napoleon?" Helen asked.

"Ginger ale it is. And yes," Hussein said.

He stepped away into the living room, told one of the security men they'd have drinks there, and came back into the foyer.

"Shall we go and sit down?" He took them to a smaller sitting room with a Velásquez on the wall. It was a landscape of the valley of Mexico painted in the 1870s. The room had red wallpaper and Restoration furniture. Large French doors led off to a dramatically-lit patio, with a view of the city below.

"Were you in the States?" Hussein asked Helen.

"Yes. Visiting my sister. She's moving houses and always gets excited about showing me the next one." Helen gave him a quick smile with her lie.

The drinks came via a dark-skinned maid who was used to being anonymous.

"I haven't seen the garden," Alex said. "I'd love to see it, if you don't mind." He got up and looked at Helen, then at Hussein.

"Yes, well, I have my drink. Run along, boys," she told them.

They went out onto the patio. Helen could see them through the French door. Hussein lit a cigarette. He was very elegant, the way he did it. She wondered what this man had that her husband wanted so badly.

Alex watched him light his cigarette. Hussein held the tiny gold lighter for a moment, then put it into his pocket as he exhaled smoke. Everyone liked Hussein, even the people who feared him. He had style and grace, and that counted for a lot with Latins.

"Alex, I've been with you people for such a long time. Why all this, now? For god's sakes, you know me." It was true; they'd used Hussein to keep track of certain men in the Mexican government over the years. He was close to the President now. In return, the CIA had turned its back on arms dealings of Hussein's that were less than legal—or, as Hussein called them, extra-legal. Like everyone else, Alex liked Hussein and always had.

"Someone called Madani mentioned you."

"If he did, I don't know him," Hussein said.

"He convinced me that you know something about a bomb that *al Qaeda* has brought to Mexico."

"Don't be absurd, Alex. *Al Qaeda*. Really! That's quite absurd. It's the first I've heard of it." Hussein inhaled and looked at him, making eye contact.

"Mr. Madani didn't think so. He was very convincing," Alex said.

"Let me talk to him."

"I'm afraid you can't."

"Why?"

"He's dead."

"Dead?"

"He had a medical problem." Hussein smiled. It was a rather painful smile, and Alex thought that finally he was getting through to him. "It was unfortunate, but these things happen," Alex said.

"I'm sure they do."

"He suggested that you had been instrumental in arranging for a bomb to be hidden in the city—in fact, that you know who has it. Is that true?"

"No, it is not true. Alex, I've known you for how long? Twenty years—no, longer."

"Yes. A long time."

"Well then, *surely* you must know that I've no interest in Mr. bin Laden, or his ideas. Nor have I tried to help them in any way. I hate them."

"Oh, I doubt you have. But you *might*. Your father was an important figure in the Muslim Brotherhood. Your brother is the Imam here at the mosque. And I have a very big problem that needs solving. Look at it from my point of view. I can't go to the mosque and ask them where the bomb is, and who has it—but I think you can," Alex said.

Alex moved closer to the end of the patio, putting his hands on the balustrade.

"I'm not my father, Alex. Don't you see that this is their way of bringing me down? These people don't like me because they know I've cooperated with you in the past." Hussein came up behind him. "It's just a ruse. To confuse you."

Alex could smell the cigarette smoke, a French brand.

"Then prove to me that we are still friends. And find out where this bloody thing is and who has it."

"How?"

"Go ask your brother Abd. And we don't have much time."

"Is that what this is about? Why didn't you just come and ask me for my help."

"Because the stakes are too high, old boy. That's why. Bring me the package and you are free to do whatever it is you're doing these days. And we'll continue being friends. But I need results. Tell your brother we'll pay him, if that's what it takes."

"You're quite mean, Alex. Has anyone told you that?"

"Am I? I suppose so. I've been in a rotten mood lately. Are you going to at least tell me what I need to know?"

Alex turned from the balustrade. He knew Hussein was innocent, and that his brother probably wasn't.

• • •

Alex thought the old man was lying. He'd finally gone up and spoken to him before they took him away to be questioned. He had the room cleared. He'd sent the doctor away and brought a chair to where they had the old man chained to the bed.

"My name is Tom," Alex said. The old man had looked at him in a way Alex remembered from Vietnam—the way that prisoners looked when they were confronted finally with The Great Satan, the boogieman they'd heard about all their lives. The man who wore no uniform, but gave orders everyone listened to, and obeyed.

"You have very little time under my control. Others will come and take you away, and you won't come back again . . .do you understand?" He'd watched the old man nod yes.

"If you help me find this thing I'm looking for, I can help you. Do you understand? But we don't have much time."

"Let them come," the old man said. He was staring at Alex.

Alex had sat back in the chair, and heard it creak. He reached down and touched his tie, letting his fingers travel down the length of it.

"Do you think your God will love you for killing innocent people? People who don't deserve to die, other Muslims? They'll die, too. Is that what you really want?"

"I want what God wants," the old man said.

"Do you think God wants your wife to be killed?"

The old man looked at him, then. He was dirty and needed to shave. His gray beard was coarse, and his left eye was completely swollen shut despite the ice the doctor had put on it.

"Do you? Not so easy now playing God, is it?" Alex said.

"She has nothing to do with it," the old man said. The tone of his voice had changed. It was quieter, the realization of what he'd done to his family finally coming home to him.

"Oh, but she does. Just like those people you want to kill. She has everything to do with it. You see, we can all play God. I can play it, too. And I will . . . I promise you. I'll call somewhere and I'll play God unless you help me. Do you understand? I have no problem with that," Alex said.

He watched the old man rest his head back down on the pillow. He wasn't completely sure whether the man was telling the truth, or whether he himself could allow the woman to be mistreated for the sake of saving innocent lives. He thought he could. He took his phone out, as if testing his resolve.

"What's your wife's name?"

"Asmira."

"Tell me, does Asmira deserve to die because of what you've done? Does she, goddamn it?"

". . . No."

"Where is it, then?"

"I don't know," the old man said.

"Who does?"

"I don't know."

"But you know *something*," Alex said.

"I know nothing about a bomb. I own a hotel called the Gobi. That's all I know," he said. He was crying.

Alex opened his phone and started to punch in a number.

"People at the mosque near *Insurgentes*. Go there," the old man said.

"Why?"

"Someone there might know something."

"Who?" Alex closed his phone.

"The Imam. Hussein." The old man closed his eyes and started to pray for forgiveness.

Alex put down the phone, relieved. He was sweating, his face wet to the touch.

13

She shouldn't have come back," Collin said. "Your wife should be in the States with real doctors and real hospitals. Not here in Mexico City."

"Can I come in?" Alex said. Collin nodded and let him pass.

It was very early, before nine in the morning, when Collin heard a knock at the door. He was on his way out to the hospital. He opened the door and was surprised to see Law, sober, standing in his doorway alone. No guards, no one with him, in a sweater and looking less glamorous than when he was with his retinue of security men.

"Yes, well, I know all that," Alex said. He'd driven himself alone to the doctor's apartment. Alex had expected him to be angry because the old man had died the night before.

"Can I sit down?" Alex said. "It's been a long night."

Collin led him into a kind of anteroom where he saw some of the local people for free, and then past that into the living room. Alex had caught the doctor on the way out; he was holding his medical bag.

The doctor cleaned off a chair piled with art books so Alex could sit down.

Collin was frightened that Dolores might be involved somehow in the plot, but he couldn't or didn't want to believe it. He didn't know what to do. He'd sat wide awake in bed for hours, putting it all together. If she'd had a passport, it would all be different—but she didn't.

He'd asked her point blank where it was. If it was stolen, why hadn't she allowed him to apply for a replacement at the embassy? He decided she was an innocent—an illegal immigrant, most likely, nothing more. Probably an illegal Arab trying to get into the States. But that, he'd told himself, certainly didn't make her a terrorist.

He judged her on the quality of her spirit. He was attracted to her, not just physically but emotionally, as if she needed something from him but was unable to tell him what. She was no mass killer; he was certain of that. He felt as if he were treating a very young child who had come into the office crying, and he had to guess the nature of its malady.

"I'm sorry, but your wife is not my patient. Under the circumstances, I don't think it's a good idea that I see her again. Besides, she needs a specialist," Collin said.

Alex didn't sit. Collin looked for a place for his stack of books, and finally found one.

"What circumstances?" Alex said.

"You're my *boss*. You call me in the middle of the night and have me go see people who end up dead. You say that if I don't help you, I'm helping terrorists do something horrific. I think I'm busy, don't you?"

Alex rubbed his hands together. He saw the postcard of the *Zócalo* that Dolores had left for the doctor to post for her. He picked it up off the coffee table.

"Were you good friends? You and the old man?" Alex asked.

"Yes. Friends. We played chess. I let him win on occasion—and now he's dead, and you say it's fine because he was a terrorist. I'm not convinced. In fact, I very much doubt it." He watched Law look at the postcard.

"My parents have a place near this address in London," Alex said, glancing at the card. "Well, my father now. My mother died. Two years ago."

105

"How interesting," Collin said. "I'm sure it's very nice. Now I'd like to go out, as I have real patients whom I've had to neglect—unless someone else is chained to a bed somewhere, waiting to be helped into the next world."

"He confessed, your friend," Alex said. "Before he died. He said that an *al Qaeda* cell is active in the city, and they are in possession of a bomb."

"And you learned this on the basis of torture? I'm sure I would confess, too."

"Interrogation," Alex said.

"I don't believe it. I would tell you I was Bin Laden's best friend if you beat me long enough."

Alex looked at him. "Why are you living like this?" he asked. He looked into the tiny, dark bedroom and saw the watercolors taped to the wall.

"I like it," Collin said. "It suits me."

"Does it have to be quite so grim? . . . I suppose so."

"It's always been a doctor's office. Remember? I'm a doctor."

"So it suits you?" Alex said.

"Is that a crime? Anyway, it was part of keeping me gray. No one to notice me, just an eccentric young doctor's choice of digs. Very suitable, I thought. Lots of *drunks* in the neighborhood." He eyed Alex.

"My wife likes you," Alex said, ignoring the remark. He looked at the postcard again, then set it down. He saw Collin's work book; the doctor had been practicing his Arabic. "I didn't know you wrote Arabic. Very impressive."

"I'm studying it," Collin said. "It's in my file if you want to check. Will I be arrested? You should know I also have French and some German. Is that a crime, too? Will I be arrested and chained to a bed because I speak a little German? Perhaps you'll want to arrest my parents too—waterboard my mother? Her father was Dutch. Very dangerous, the Dutch."

"This isn't going well," Alex said. "You're very angry."

"No, it isn't. I told you, I can't see your wife . . . as a patient. I'm sorry."

"But she *wants* to see you. You made an impression on her. She says you're kind."

"I'm sorry. It's impossible," Collin said.

"All right, what do I have to do to get you to see my wife?"

"What do you mean?" Collin said.

"Come on. There must be something. New car? A trip home after all this is finished? Whatever it is, I'll do it. I'm very rich. I don't care what it costs. Do you want out of this assignment? I can arrange that, too. The Embassy in Paris?"

"You're joking?" Collin said.

"No. I'm not joking," Alex said.

It took a minute for Collin to realize that his boss was blackmailing him. The outrage turned quickly into something else. He did want out, he thought; not just from the assignment at the embassy, but out of the service altogether. He could not help them do again what they'd done last night. He was in danger of losing something about himself that he couldn't afford to lose.

Then he thought of what was at stake and realized he couldn't leave the assignment, not right now. No matter how awful it might be, he had to try to help. It was oddly because he *was* a doctor that he couldn't just turn and quit. *First, do no harm,* he thought.

"I have a friend. I think she's an illegal of some kind. I want her to have an American passport," the doctor said.

"Jesus, is that all?" Alex said.

"That's all. But I want her to be able to go to the States on a plane. Throw in some kind of background story for her and a Social Security number while you're at it. Her name is Dolores Rios."

"Fine. She'll have it by tomorrow. I'll need a photograph. How old is she?"

"Just like that?" Collin said.

"Just like that," Alex said.

"She's about my age. Thirty or so. Make her twenty-seven."

"Now will you come see my wife?"

"Yes. This afternoon, send a car here at three," Collin said.

"Thank you," Alex said, and stood up. "How much Arabic?"

"Enough to get into trouble," Collin said.

"I wouldn't have let you leave—if that's what you were thinking. I need you right now. I was lying about that part."

"And if I refuse to help again?"

"You won't. I understand you."

"Do you?"

"You're like me. You just don't want to admit it," Law said.

"Like *you!* Hardly," Collin said.

"Everyone thinks you're soft. Butch, everyone at the station says so—but you're not. You're very hard, in fact. You just don't show it. That's why I know you'll help find the package. You don't give a damn that Butch hates you or any of the rest of it. In fact, I doubt you give a damn about much. That's what they liked about you in the first place. You're arrogant. Aren't you?"

"Maybe," Collin said.

"You'll stay because you always want to do the right thing. It's a curse. I have it, too. It doesn't seem like it, I know. But I do. Not about the small things, God knows, but about the big things. You care."

"And you think doing the right thing was letting that old man be taken away by those thugs," Collin said.

"I couldn't have just let him go. Could I? You were so sure he was innocent. And it turned out he wasn't."

The doctor had no reply to that. It was true, he'd thought the old man was an innocent who had somehow gotten involved with terrorists without realizing what it was really about.

"Three o'clock," Collin said.

"Would you like me to mail that card?" Alex offered. "I could send it out in the pouch. Get there quicker. You know what the Mexican mail is like."

"Sure," Collin said. He picked up the postcard and handed it to Law. "You're right; the mail service is shit," Collin said.

"Glad to do it," Alex said.

The doctor walked him to the door and watched him leave. Law got into a car with embassy plates that he'd parked illegally at the corner. The doctor watched it disappear into the traffic on the boulevard and was relieved he was gone.

• • •

"Allahu akbar," someone said to Hussein in the parking lot.

"Salaam Aleikum," Hussein answered.

The mosque was near the archeological museum. It had been built in the Sixties. It had a golden dome reminiscent of Qubbat As-Sakhrah, the Dome of the Rock, as it was known in the West. It had been built with money from Saudi Arabia and from a few rich Muslim families in Mexico who'd come to settle after the Six-Day War. The mosque became a Wahhabi stronghold in the Eighties. Hussein's brother had been part of the transformation, having come back from a long stay in Pakistan, a changed man whom he barely recognized.

Hussein took off his shoes. It was a Wednesday morning, and few people were at the mosque at that time of the morning. The mosque's offices were on the second floor, but he'd wanted to pray for a moment.

He stepped onto the floor and walked under the brightly painted classical arches, similar to what he remembered as a child in Cairo. Hundreds of empty rugs lay in lines across the floor. For a moment he stood and looked at the morning light that streamed through the door. It illuminated the dome, and he felt he was certainly in a blessed place. In God's place.

It had been a long time since he'd gotten on his knees and

prayed. He was a man without God, without even the need for a God. He always thought of himself as a man of this world. Money had been his god. Money had given him everything he'd ever wanted. He'd been good at making it, good at keeping it. It had given him the power over other men that he found satisfying; he remembered what it was like to be powerless, something he dreaded even now. God had a brother, he thought, as he entered and bowed his head. He was called Mammon, and each had his place.

Hussein had married an American girl, an airline hostess, part of his escape plan from everything he'd known and had been taught by his father. She knew nothing of his God, and he wanted it that way. His children didn't think of themselves as Arabs, even though they had their father's dark skin and black hair.

It wasn't until the morning the twin towers fell that he'd thought seriously about his father's God, about how—if he existed—he could let that happen to innocent people. What kind of God was he? His wife had lost a brother in the towers. She wasn't the same after she got the news. She wasn't the same toward Hussein either, because he was an Arab. He tried to tell her that he was innocent and she tried to listen, but something had been poisoned between them. She'd left him and gone home to New York, and never came back to him. Even his children had treated him differently afterwards. They saw him as part of that strange world they'd heard about on CNN.

He knelt down now on a prayer rug. He'd been a very young boy when his father first brought him to the mosque in Cairo. He remembered the trip in the car, the riotous street, and the call to prayer. It had been the week that England and France had invaded the Suez Canal.

"I want to see Abd," Hussein said in Arabic.

The young man in the white *keffiyeh* looked at him from behind a computer screen. He was black and his black skin looked very dramatic in the traditional dress. He was from Nigeria.

"He's with someone," the man said.

"Please tell him his brother Hussein is here to see him," he said, in such a way that he couldn't be put off. The man picked up the phone and called into the inner office.

"He asks you to please wait a few moments," the man said.

Hussein nodded and went to the couch. Above him, on the wall, was a framed quote from the Koran: "God loves the clean."

"You can go in now," the man said, finally.

Another man, in western dress, came out of his brother's office as Hussein was entering. He was carrying a briefcase and didn't bother to look up at Hussein as he passed.

14

Dolores looked out the window to the street three floors below. It was a Saturday, and the traffic was light. She saw an older man leave the doctor's apartment. In a moment, she watched Collin leave.

She held the curtain's cord, letting her fingers touch its plastic knob as she watched Collin. She wanted to call out to him, to say yes to whatever he had in mind for her—an affair? Her husband seemed to be calling to her also. She saw him as he had been at the hospital in Baghdad, his doctor's coat bloodied, a queer combination of exhaustion and anger stamped on his unshaven face. The corridors chock-full with the wounded and their families.

She stood in the window long after she'd seen Collin leave his apartment. Her room phone rang. She'd made a call; Madani had given her a number to use if something happened to him. He hadn't come back to the hotel, and she'd decided to use the number.

She'd borrowed the doctor's cell phone and called from his apartment. She'd pretended to talk to a friend of her sister, saying that she was passing through town and wanted to meet her.

They'd sent the young man who was standing in her room now.

"You'll have to leave the hotel," he told her.

"Are we going to leave the city?" she asked. She turned away from the window. She was looking forward to getting on with it, whatever it was.

"No. Not yet. Nothing is ready yet," he said. "But you must leave here; they've decided it."

He seemed a sweet boy, she thought. Not at all what she'd expected, now that the police were so close.

"No. If I'm not leaving the city, I want to stay here," she said.

The boy looked at her, puzzled by her refusal. He turned away from her slightly, as if he'd been pushed physically.

"Madani is dead," the boy said in Arabic. The young man was a Palestinian. His great grandfather had been an Irish policeman, and the whole family had looked European since. He thought telling her about Madani would somehow get her to obey.

"Are you sure?" she asked. She turned from the window.

"Yes. He's dead. His wife has been taken out of the country, we think."

Dolores looked at the young man, who looked like any young man. He wore baggy blue jeans, a white t-shirt, a gold chain around his neck, and new expensive Nike shoes.

"They killed him?" she asked.

"Yes."

"He didn't tell them, then? About. . .?"

"Perhaps he did, and they are just watching you," the young man said. "We don't know."

"No, he wouldn't tell them." She was certain of that. "No. He didn't tell them. And his wife?"

"We don't know. She's gone. They arrested her, too. That's all we know," he said. Dolores nodded. "Only God knows where she is by now."

"I'll stay here," she said again.

"What do I . . . what do I tell them?" he said.

"Tell them I want to stay here." The young man looked at her. "Until they're ready for me to leave. Tell them I've been ill. I'd rather not move again."

The young man nodded but didn't like it. "Whosoever disobeys Allah and his messenger, he has gone astray," the young man said, quoting the Koran. He turned and left. He didn't bother to close her door.

She walked across the room and closed it herself.

Where is my child . . . ask your God that, she said to herself. *Where is my son now?* She suddenly wanted to sin against God, to challenge him for his cruelty to her. She wanted to go to hell or worse, to get back at *everyone.* That's what I want, she thought. To get back at them all.

She went out and had lunch by herself, and walked the streets. The doctor came by while she was gone and left a note reminding her that they were to have dinner together.

• • •

"He's not here?" Helen said.

Collin looked at her. She seemed too beautiful to be sick. A line from somewhere popped into his mind: *Beauty too rich for use.* She was the Praetorian's wife and looked the part because she stood so straight and tall.

"Are you afraid of him? Everyone is, of course. Except me," she said.

"Naturally," Collin said. "Shouldn't I be?"

She smiled. She took his hand for a moment. They were standing in the foyer, and it was cold. The huge living room, so busy with workmen the first time he'd seen it, was empty. It was a Friday; no workman in Mexico worth his wages worked on a Friday.

"We've the place to ourselves. Thank you for seeing me again," she said.

The woman had an affability and charm that he couldn't resist, no matter how he felt about her husband. He'd been angry, but suddenly he softened. He couldn't blame the poor woman for

114

her choice in men. It was a relief to let his anger go. After all, he told himself, he'd warned them; it was they who hadn't listened to him about the old man. It wasn't his fault he'd died.

"Shall we go to the bedroom? It seems odd for . . . well, for you to examine me here," she said.

"Of course."

"Would you like something to drink?" she asked.

"Perhaps later," he said.

He followed her up the terrazzo staircase. She told him that some kind of robber baron from the Diaz period built the place, and Diaz had stolen it from him. It dawned on him that Law was truly very wealthy; it was so obvious now, looking around.

She took off her blue sweater and laid it on the bed. It was a huge antique canopy bed, but the canopy part was missing.

"I'll just warm my hands." He stepped to the bathroom and ran hot water on his fingers. When he came out, she was sitting on the bed in just her bra. She looked worried.

He examined her, all the time wondering why she'd come back here. He felt the lump. It was perhaps bigger, but he wasn't sure.

"Well?" she asked when she was dressed again.

"Maybe it's grown a little," he said. "You shouldn't be here. You should leave immediately, Mrs. Law. Go home."

"Helen. You can call me Helen," she said.

"Helen. All right. You should go home, Helen."

"I'm afraid," she said. She started crying. He sat down on the bed next to her. The room seemed cold, and too big for a simple bedroom.

"But you can't stay here," he said. "We can't help you here—here in Mexico."

"I want Alex to come back with me, but he says he can't. I don't understand. I can't do this alone."

He was shocked. The hatred he felt for Law left him, replaced

115

by a kind of respect. Law must want to be with her, but he knew how serious it might be if he failed at what he was doing, so had decided not to go. For the first time, the whole fight to find the cell of terrorists seemed real to him. And he was frightened, truly frightened, because there was no morally safe place anywhere in it.

"Can you speak to him, doctor? Tell him that he should go back with me."

"Of course," he said. "But if he doesn't, you have to promise me you'll leave and see someone."

"I did see someone. He was *awful*. He didn't care. They just want to cut off my breast," she said. "I can't have that. How can I be a woman if I don't have my breast?"

It seemed such a simple question. He knew the answer, the answers he'd learned in school, the answers he'd read in the literature, but he couldn't answer her. Lately there was something wrong with him. His doctor's muscle seemed to have atrophied completely since he'd seen Madani lying shackled to that bed.

"You see? You agree . . . I can see it in your eyes," she said. "And Alex? What am I supposed to tell him, that he's going to get half a wife?" He held her hand again. "I can't be half a wife to him. A *monster*."

"I promise to talk to him. I'll go see him today," he said. "I promise."

"You will? Thank you. You see . . . I said you were kind. And I think he likes you and will listen to *you*. We had a son. If he'd lived, I think he would have been like you," she said. "He would have been kind."

"Do you have other children?"

"We have a daughter, but I don't want to tell her." He nodded. "She's just been married. It should be a happy time. Don't you think? . . .Coffee, then?"

"Yes. That sounds good," he said. "You have to go back, with or without your husband. If you don't. . . ."

"I'll die." She said it with finality, and smiled. But he thought she was angry at the cancer. It wasn't unusual; he'd seen this kind of anger before, the quiet kind, a profound resentment.

"You just don't have the luxury of time with this," he said. "And no, you aren't going to die. No reason even to think that."

"What's so important that Alex can't leave?" she asked.

"You'll have to ask him," he said.

"I can't. He wouldn't tell me, anyway," she said.

After they had coffee, she took him for a tour of the house. He enjoyed it; it took his mind off what was happening. He asked if he could come back sometime and paint the courtyard. She told him he could come anytime.

• • •

Hussein's younger brother, Abd, was dressed in white. He wore glasses. He was forty-five, but looked much younger.

"Salaam Aleikum," Abd said, standing to greet him.

"Aleikum Salaam," Hussein answered.

"Why didn't you phone and tell me you were coming?" Abd said. "I'm sorry you had to wait." Abd smiled, which surprised Hussein. His younger brother had become very serious, not at all the clown he'd been as a child.

Abd's grand office had a computer and a large desk but was oddly empty, except for a few quotes from the Koran on the walls, a bookcase, and a large aerial photograph of Mecca during the *haj*.

His younger brother hugged him in the prescribed manner of Arab men, but not as a brother, Hussein thought. When he'd been a child Abd had been devoted to his older brother, perhaps because their mother had died when they were both so young. It was different now. Their father, knowing Mubarak would arrest him, had sent Hussein and his brother to live with an aunt in

117

Mexico City. He had brought them to Mexico himself and then gone home. They'd never seen their father again.

They'd fought with their aunt, who was afraid that she would get into trouble for harboring her brother's children, even in Mexico. For a few years, they'd been poor. It had been difficult for his younger brother to be an outsider in a strange land. The Mexicans didn't like Arabs any more than they liked Chinese or other foreigners. The racism they encountered had changed them both, made them both harder.

Desperate to get away from their aunt, Hussein discovered things he could do: small illegal things at first, cigarette smuggling, then laundering money. It was small amounts at first; then, when he was seen as efficient and honest, very large amounts in the Gulf States, where few questions were asked.

Hussein had gotten very, very rich, and married the American girl who'd been studying Spanish in Cuernavaca. He'd told her he was a merchant banker, which he was, in a way. He'd branched out into other legitimate businesses over the years: textiles, a cement factory, arms. Now he had a business empire.

Somehow during all this, his little brother, whom he'd sent to England to study, had become a Wahhabi fanatic instead of a good Englishman. It was as if the brother he'd loved had gone and never returned. Hussein blamed himself and blamed those strange years they'd spent in a no-man's land of small apartments with their crazy, spiteful aunt. He had the odd feeling that they were both lost on a sea of small misunderstandings.

"We need to speak," Hussein said.

"Sit down," Abd said. "Please."

"Not here." Hussein gave his brother a look. "Perhaps we can go outside."

"I can't right now, Hussein. I'm very busy. I have meetings. Can't it wait? I'll come by the house tonight. I promise."

"No, it can't wait, Abd. Please."

His brother gave him a look, then nodded.

"We can go down into the courtyard."

"Yes," Hussein said. "That would be fine."

"The Americans think I'm part of a scheme to bring a bomb here."

"That's ridiculous," Abd said.

"Of course it is."

"You have to convince them. You have connections. You don't even come to the mosque."

"I've tried," Hussein said. "I think they are going to arrest me. They'll arrest Claudia and the children, too. I'm very frightened, Abd. You know what they're like when they're angry."

They were walking along the reflecting pool, which the Saudi royal family had built as a gift to the mosque. It was an exact copy of the pool at the Alhambra in Spain. King Abdullah had come himself in the 80's to the dedication.

"What can I do?" Abd said.

"Is it true? Is there a bomb in the city? Do you know anything about it?" Hussein stopped. The sky was gray; a few raindrops hit the ground around them. "If it is true, you have to tell me. You'll help me stop it. It's wrong," Hussein said. "Our father would curse us." He meant it.

"Our father is a great martyr," Abd said.

"Is he?"

"Of course he is. He died for the cause."

"I would have preferred to have had a father than a martyr. Is it true, Abd?"

"Is what true?"

"Is *al Qaeda* passing some kind of bomb through Mexico? Is it here, already in the city? Do you know where it is?"

"God willing," Abd said.

"Do you know where it is, then?"

"No. I know nothing about it."

"But you've heard something?"

"Go home, Hussein. Pray to God that he gives us strength and that we vanquish the Infidel. *Inshallah.*"

"I don't know you anymore," Hussein said. "What about my wife and children? You know what they'll do to them."

His brother turned and left without answering him.

Hussein had loved his brother once, but he didn't know him anymore. The boy he'd loved had died a long time ago.

15

Mexico City's sprawling central market—a tin-roofed warren of alleys—was a casbah of sorts, where she liked to go to try to forget what had happened to her. And to forget that soon she would be facing a martyr's death.

She had special ways now of hiding from the world. Closing the door to a bathroom and sitting alone at the hotel, concentrating on the drip of the faucet, she would open slightly. Or pretending to sleep on the bus from Veracruz. She'd found a zone—a land of memories. Half-asleep, she stayed for hours in that land, the bus's diesel engine noise mixing with the noise of someone's radio as the bus drove towards the end of a story that seemed to belong to someone else.

The language on the bus, Spanish, too dense and strange for her ever to parse. She'd taken a long journey through her childhood in this dreamlike state. She'd watched herself as a young girl talking to boys, walking on the High Street with her friends in their school uniforms. She'd been clean in a dirty city, all the while on a lonely road from Veracruz, plunging on towards the destiny that had been hers since she was a girl.

Could the doctor who delivered her have guessed? That first scream, had it said something? Had it been special? Probably not. No Greek chorus by her mother's bed.

But there was the central market, where she could just be another young woman with olive skin walking with other young women quietly. Sometimes the rain beat on the market's tin roofs, soothing, the air smelling of radishes and fresh meat.

She'd gone the first time with Madani's wife. It had reminded her of Baghdad, when she'd first come with her husband as a new bride. Something about the hubbub, being part of the normal life of the city, made her feel safe. She bought little things. A small round mirror for her handbag, a package of dates.

She'd wanted to buy something to cook. It had been months since she'd cooked. She'd been cooking a special dinner the day her son had been killed; it had been her birthday. The meal had been waiting for them at home, never to be eaten.

She had a fantasy of cooking something for the doctor. Impulsively she started to buy the ingredients, thinking that it might be the last meal she would ever cook. He had a small kitchen, and she was sure the doctor would let her do something so normal, something that would help her forget everything.

She wandered down the line of poultry-mongers in their bloody aprons.

"Would the *señorita* like something today?" a young man asked. It was the way her husband had looked, his white coat blood-splattered from his work at the hospital, after the war started. He'd smelled of carnage when he came home. She wanted to turn away. The young man's boss smiled at her, his apron even bloodier. But the older man's smile gave her strength. *I want to buy something. That's all I want to do, to cook something for the doctor, to say thank you.*

"Something for the family?" the older man said, looking at her. She'd forgotten that she was beautiful until she came out in public. The men were doting on her, immediately smitten. What would her life have been like if she hadn't been beautiful, she wondered. Had it been a blessing or a curse? Her sister was plain; nothing went as easily for her sister as it had for her. Nothing.

"Yes," she said finally. "A chicken. Please," she said in English.

"You've come to the right place, *Señorita*. We have only the best

. . . . the *Señorita* is not from Mexico?" the older one asked as he was digging through the chickens. He spoke English.

She tried to look away. The wooden cutting boards, with short brutal-looking knives, caught her eye. She tried to look away, but saw the head of a pig, its face nightmarish without its body.

She ran away. The man called after her, not understanding what was wrong.

She ran along the crowded alley, until she couldn't hear the man calling anymore. She was shaking. People were staring at her, their brown faces darkened by curiosity.

• • •

Her husband had changed. They were walking home together, the three of them, her husband holding their son. The streets were full of shoppers.

She'd gone out to find a bottle of white wine for their dinner. They were going to celebrate her birthday; she would be twenty-five. It was a luxury now, as the shops had less and less since the Americans had invaded. The streets of their neighborhood were more and more dangerous, especially for women. Her husband, calling her on her cell phone, had told her to come by the hospital. He would walk home with her, angry that she'd gone out with their child for something so frivolous.

She wanted to tell him that they couldn't stop living. It was her birthday; she had cooked something special for them, and she wanted to serve wine. She was a Christian and it wasn't wrong. She was thinking, as they walked home, that it was ridiculous to feel guilty for wanting to buy a bottle of wine. But everything was strange now. They had to think and live like victims, not like human beings. Everything had changed.

She wondered why they were staying on. They had money; they could leave and go live with her parents in London. Her husband had qualified as a surgeon in England and could work there. She was going to ask him if they might not go now. Things in Baghdad were getting worse and worse even *before* the war started. What hope was there for Iraq now?

Her husband and son had stayed out in the street, talking to one of his nurses, who'd happened by while Dolores checked in one of the shops. To her joy, she found bottles of wine from Italy and was bringing one up to the counter by the door. She felt happy.

Then the street outside in front of her changed—the light very bright for a moment—then gray, from the dust of the explosion. A bottle of cooking oil glinted as she passed. She heard the noise and later remembered the sound of the glass hitting the canned goods around her.

It was the shelf so tightly packed that had saved her, or she would have been killed. Later, the people in the neighborhood found pieces of the rocket. It was American made, in Tucson, Arizona. At her son's funeral, she wondered if the young women from Tucson, Arizona, were like her. She saw herself going there, carrying her dead mutilated child and asking them if it was *this* particular child that they had intended to kill with their rocket.

They were forced to bury him, covered only in a shroud, in the back of the Al Yarmouck hospital grounds, along with hundreds of other children killed during the American bombing of the city—all of them guilty of nothing more than being born.

• • •

She turned around suddenly, determined to buy the chicken. She wiped her tears and walked back through the market. People had already forgotten that she'd made a scene. Embarrassed, she caught the younger man's attention at the poultry-monger's stall.

"I'm sorry," she said, looking down. The young man looked at her nonplussed for a moment, then decided to smile because she was so beautiful. She had that effect on men. She smiled back.

"I'd like a chicken," she said again. "Please."

"Of course, *Señorita*. Large or small?"

"Small. Yes, small," she said.

"Grape leaves. Where might I find them?" she asked in English. The young man didn't understand her, but he found someone who spoke English better than he did, and they told her where to go. There was a shop not too far away, a few streets from the market, they told her, near the mosque.

She counted out three dollars from the money they had given her to live on until it was time to leave the hotel. She went on and found fresh grape leaves in a shop near the market.

She saw the mosque then as she was coming out, saw its minaret against the sky. She couldn't help herself. She started to walk toward the mosque. She was not religious, but it was Friday, and it was something she wanted to see. For the sake of her son's memory.

On the way, she crossed a small plaza packed with professional letter-writers, plying old-fashioned manual typewriters for the city's analphabetic—mostly Indians who came to them to write letters to loved ones, mostly in the United States.

"Letter, *Señora?*" an old man asked her as she passed. He was dressed in a white shirt and black tie, his hair still coal black. She stopped.

"English?" she asked.

"Yes, I have some English," the man said, sitting up straighter. He looked at her carefully as if to say he was capable.

She looked at him, then sat down. She put the package with the food she'd bought on her lap.

"How much?" she asked.

"Six pesos a page, *Señora*," the man said.

"Dear husband," she said. The man looked at her.

"Address, *Señora?* Do you have the address?"

"Address?" she asked.

"Yes, *Señora.* For the letter."

"Baghdad," she said. She gave him the address of her apartment. She thought of the curtain blowing out the French door, the view of the Tigris River the first time she'd seen it. She had him type the address. Then he looked at her, his fingers poised over his machine, ready.

> *Dear Mohammad,*
>
> *I've fallen in love with another man. You should not be angry with me, as I still love you. Will you understand? He is a doctor too. I think if you could meet him, you would allow it. He's kind and he has blond hair, and he looks at me the way you used to look at me before the war.*

The old man's eyes lifted for a moment, but she didn't notice. She shifted her package, then went on dictating. She had done everything she could not to feel anything since her son's death; now, suddenly, this unexpected attraction. She started to weep, and the old man stopped typing out of respect.

"No, it's all right," she said, and went on.

> *I miss touching you so much, can you understand? He is a doctor, too. But he never wears the white coat. I wish he would; I loved your white coat so much. I loved to see you coming down the boulevard in it. I could see you sometimes from the window. Did you know that? I looked out for you in the afternoons.*
>
> *It's worse in the afternoon now, when you don't come. Can you understand me? The afternoons are the worst, sullen, awful. He's kind, and he has blond hair and is called Collin. He knows nothing about me.*
>
> *I miss touching your hair, the way I used to do it from the back. When I see him, he reminds me of you. Have I done wrong? He's an*

American, so that makes it even harder.

Can you understand what happened to us that day? I couldn't. I hate the people who told me to go on with life. In this, we agreed. I don't believe in anything now. I wish to God I did.

His name is Collin Reeves.

She stopped. The old man was looking at her. He hadn't said a word.

"Is that all, *Señora?*"

"No."

He looked down again. He was a kind man and didn't want to ask any questions. He'd written thousands of letters, but never one quite like this.

"No," she said. But this too. . . .

Will we see our son in heaven? I wish I could believe that, but I don't. That's what is so horrible.

The old man rolled the page out of his machine.

"Twelve pesos, *Señora* . . . I'm sorry for your loss," the old man said. He folded the letter carefully. He gave her the envelope for free. Usually he charged for the envelopes, but she seemed so sad and so beautiful, he didn't have the heart. He typed the address she gave him onto the envelope quickly.

"Return address?" he asked.

"Mexico City, Hotel Gobi," she said.

"Do you know the street address?"

"No," she said. "But it doesn't matter. I'm leaving soon." She took the letter with her. "I'll be gone."

She crossed the street. Men were walking towards the mosque for Friday prayers. Cars were double-parked in front; some, she noticed, were chauffeur-driven. The rain had picked up, and people were walking with their heads down. Umbrellas appeared.

127

She walked through the gate into the mosque's courtyard. A few men stole glances at her, thinking that she would take the women's entrance to the tiny gallery, as women were barred from the mosque's main floor.

She slid off her shoes. She didn't have anything to cover her head with, but she wanted to see what her son had died for. They had intended to bring him up a Muslim. Her husband had never been religious until after the bombardments started and people started looting from the hospital. He'd turned to God then to save the city.

She thought that if she went into the mosque, she might hear God tell her that what she was going to do was all right. She'd never been in a mosque in her life. Her parents were Christian Arabs. They had left Baghdad to study in England and had never gone back. They both liked the West.

A small man stepped in front of her as she walked through the door to the mosque. He was wearing traditional garb and was bearded. She saw hundreds of men lying facing the niche that marked the direction to Mecca.

She smiled at him, thinking he was going to show her where she could go to find a place to pray. He slapped her in the face. The bag she was carrying fell out of her hands. He pushed her roughly towards the door.

"Get out!" he said in Arabic. "You are a woman and are unclean."

She held her burning face. She looked at the food spilled on the floor. Other men close to them turned to see what was happening. She thought they would come to her assistance, thinking that the man who had slapped her was mad.

She stooped to pick up the chicken in its clear plastic bag. She could see the blood-stained parts.

He hit her on the shoulder as she squatted down. She fell. The pain in her arm was terrible. She screamed.

The Imam who had been praying stopped. He watched from

across the room as the man picked her up and hit her again. Other men, who'd been praying nearby, came running over and began to beat her, too.

She never let go of the chicken. It leaked onto the floor, grotesquely. While they beat her, she held onto it as a way of defying them.

Finally, one of the religious police dragged her out to the street by her hair, and left her there.

When she stood up, it was raining. No one in the street had come to help her. Cars drove by, their tires making a sound in the rain-washed street. A few shopkeepers watched her try to stand up. They thought she was a drunk, or that it was a lover's quarrel. They were afraid to get involved.

She felt for her purse, which still hung over her shoulder. She was bleeding from her nose and saw the blood dripping onto her wrist, then onto her shoe. Her dress had been torn so that she had to hold it up in front. Her bag of food, which she'd held onto while they were beating her, was gone.

She walked unsteadily back toward the front of the mosque. She saw the bag of chicken in the garden where they'd thrown it. She stood a moment, unsteady; then she turned and started to walk toward the hotel, her hands holding her dress up in the front.

Because of the rain, people didn't notice as much. The blood from her nose ran down her chin and onto her scuffed hands and knees. In the plaza, the scribes had hauled their desks under the arcade and were all gone now. The small plaza was attacked by the rain as she crossed it. It was the first time that she'd felt totally alone. Even the moment she'd seen her son's body on the street, she hadn't felt so alone.

16

"Hello," he said. Collin glanced at his watch. "What time is it there?" he asked his sister. He'd been trying for an hour to get a cell connection to the States.

He'd taken a nap at the American Hospital and had a frightening dream about Los Angeles, about his sister, about all the pregnant women living in that city and their babies waiting to be born. It was as if he were living inside a daydream that at moments turned to a nightmare.

In his waking dream, he was in a hospital. He was dressed in his clinician's coat, but the buttons were missing and he was swearing because he couldn't button his coat. He stopped to ask a nurse what kind of hospital this was, if he couldn't even button his coat.

The hallways were lined with seated young smiling mothers-to-be. It was midday and very bright, and then the hallway turned dark suddenly. All at once the women started to give birth, their babies protruding from their bloody legs. He was helpless and alone, the nurse having disappeared.

"Three-fifteen," his sister said. "Where are you? Did you come home?"

"Mexico City." He was sitting in his apartment now.

"Oh . . . I thought maybe you'd gone home. How are you?"

She sounded disappointed. He heard a television playing in the background.

"Good," he said.

They hadn't spoken since he'd been home for Thanksgiving. His sister had emailed him, asking why he wouldn't come home to the States to practice. She told him, in a nice sisterly way, that he was throwing his life away. She wasn't writing because their father had asked her to, but because she was truly concerned for him. She didn't understand why he didn't want to have a *real* life. She equated a real life with a life in the United States and everything that implied, as if the rest of the world weren't *really* living. Despite her education—she'd been to Stanford and studied art history—his sister was mindlessly chauvinistic. It surprised him; he'd always thought she was bigger than that. But she wasn't, and he had to face it. It was as if she hadn't been educated at all.

"How's the mother-to-be?" he asked, trying to change the subject.

"This call is going to cost you a fortune," she said. His sister had always been very practical.

"Is it? I'll have to charge more next time I take out a kidney or something extra. That's what I do if I'm getting low; I do something extra," he joked.

"I'm okay. We're due next week. It's getting hard to walk, so I was watching Oprah. I'm an expert on a variety of subjects now. Especially everything Tom Cruisean," she said.

"I liked him in *Collateral*," he said. He stood up and walked to the window with a view of the boulevard. It was raining.

"Didn't see it. Collin, why are you calling me in the middle of the day? It's not like you."

"I wanted to hear your voice," he said.

"Did you get my email?"

"Yes."

"Why didn't you answer me?"

"I thought I'd call instead."

"Thanksgiving was *awful*. It can't go on like this, Collin. Dad has been acting *crazy*. Really crazy. He's built this huge practice and he did it for you. Mom is talking about flying down to see you. She isn't even going to tell Dad because he'll want to come, too. She thinks you're in love with someone down there, and that's what this is all about. I've had to talk her out of it *twice* already."

"Me? It's too late; I've married. And she left me already. We had three kids and they're all brown as berries. I'm bringing them up for Christmas," he said.

"See, you think it's a big joke, but it's *not*, Collin. They're hurt. I mean, what are you *doing* there? No one understands why you don't just come home and have a normal life. You can't save the world. You're just working part-time, treating American tourists with the runs. We could all understand it when you were in Africa. I understood that, but now? I don't understand. I really don't. Are you trying to ruin your life, Collin?"

"No," he said.

"Bob said that a nurse practitioner could do what you're doing." His sister had married a doctor—a plastic surgeon. He was just out of school and eager to build a profitable practice in the "City of Angles," doing facelifts. His brother-in-law's father had been a factory worker in Detroit; he saw medicine as a free pass into the middle class, and he wanted it *all*. They'd moved to L.A. because he'd read in *Doctors Are Entrepreneurs* that L.A. had more cosmetic surgeries performed per day than any other city in the world, except for Moscow and Saõ Paulo. If he could have been allowed to trade stocks and operate at the same time, he would have.

"How is he—Bob?" he asked. He didn't like his sister's husband. Something about him was profoundly unctuous. It seemed unnatural for such a young man to be so preternaturally materialistic.

"He's opened up a new office. I never see him, but that's okay.

We're doing okay, and most young doctors aren't these days. We've bought a beautiful place. I want you to see it," his sister said. "I'm sorry for asking you all those questions. I'm not quite right, either. I feel and look like a balloon, and I wish Bob were here more than he is. I hope he doesn't miss everything . . . you know, the way Dad did."

"Why don't you have the baby in the Bay Area, so Dad can look in?" It was the reason for his call. He wanted to convince his sister to leave L.A.—without telling her what he was afraid of, of course.

"Go home?"

"Yeah. Why not? There's that Bernstein guy, that OB-GYN in Dad's building. He's good. And they've been good friends for years. You could stay in Mill Valley, show off the baby to your high school chums. You wouldn't have to cook when you got back with the baby. I'll come up and see the little mite. It can be old home week. I'll take you to the movies the way we used to—remember, at the Sequoia? I'll buy you popcorn."

"And what about my husband? Do I just roll him up in a carpet and take him with me?"

"Not a bad idea," Collin said.

"Very funny. That's a sweet idea, but I can't. I've got a good doctor here."

"What if I asked you to?"

There was a long pause then.

"Collin, are you all right? *Really*. I mean it. Do you think you might have a psychological problem? It's okay, you know. If you did. I'd still love you. You could tell me. Are you gay or something? Is that it? Is there something you can't tell us?"

"No. I was gay last week. Would you do it as a favor for me? Have the baby in the Bay Area. I worry."

She burst out laughing.

"Oh, my god. You *are* crazy. God, I knew it. I told Bob you were crazy. He said you had to be crazy to go to one of the best medical schools in the country, graduate at the top of your class, and then be a diarrhea doctor."

"Is that what he calls me? That's funny." Collin had gone to the window. It was glazed with rain. He smiled. For a moment he felt better; Bob probably didn't like him either, and he didn't have to feel guilty anymore.

"Yes. But you can't blame him. He's jealous. Your father was a doctor, and you have a practice you can walk right into and take over any time you want. He has to build one, or go work for an HMO and see fifty patients a day. Anyway, he's jealous of *everyone*. Believe me," she said. "I love him, but he is."

Then she had to go, because her husband was calling on her cell. She barely said goodbye. He heard the doorbell with its awful buzzing sound as he folded up his phone.

Dolores stood in front of the doctor's door for a moment as people passed her on the street. She was drenched from the rain and looked like the countless street people who plied the area around the *Zócalo*, begging. She'd stopped bleeding from her nose, but her dress was stained and torn.

She thought for a moment that she should call them and have them pick her up, and stop this drift towards the doctor. The beating had nothing to do with her revenge, but she couldn't do it. It wasn't that she was angry with them; she just couldn't be with those types of people anymore. They were so empty, so full of death and hatred.

She stepped up to the door and rang the buzzer.

She didn't want to do it anymore. She didn't want to be a martyr. The beating had broken her anger somehow. She'd been somnambulistic for months, oddly mindless. Now she felt awake for the first time since she'd walked out on the horrible scene on the street that day. She was awake and terrified. The blows had brought her back to life and out of the dream.

The door opened and Collin looked at her, horrified.

"I'm sorry," she said. "I didn't know where else to go."

"Jesus."

He brought her inside and closed the door. She started to cry. At first it was slow, and the doctor watched as the water dripped off her. Then she put her arms around him and began to sob. He just let her cry, not understanding. He finally asked her what had happened, but she wouldn't answer him.

• • •

"God is good," he said. "He's brought us the package from heaven."

It was a tailor shop. The office was dark and very long and narrow. Women in the front of the store ran the pressing machines. Every few moments they would hear the hiss of the machines as they put something in and brought the top down on it.

There were three men in the messy tailor's office. Boxes and boxes of fabric lined the walls. The package sat on the floor, surrounded by boxes of fabric so it looked like just any parcel in the shop.

The men had planned for this for two years. Now that it was here, they were excited.

"What is it? I mean, what is it exactly? Inside?" the tailor asked.

"I don't know," Hafiz said. He didn't know. All he knew was that it was some kind of bomb, and it was powerful. He didn't even understand the word "dirty" the way the scientists understood it, but he'd heard the term, and he wondered if it wasn't that kind of bomb.

The fact that it was a ruse to help confuse the Americans had been kept from them. The cell they belonged to in fact did not belong to *al Qaeda,* but to the Muslim Brotherhood's network.

The Brotherhood's leaders in Egypt were very experienced, and knew that sometimes they had to lie even to their own.

"But you must send it on. Let the boy take it for now," Hafiz said. "I've probably been followed."

"But I thought. . . ?" the tailor said. He was excited, but he was very scared, too. He had a big family and a profitable business. He was taking a big risk, more for his family than for himself.

"Not here. It can't stay here. Not after Madani's arrest," the tailor said.

The tailor and the young man knew about Madani. He'd been their cell's fourth member. No cell had more than four men in it, and Madani had been the fourth and all-important "contact" man.

"I think they will arrest me," Hafiz said. "They must know."

"God be with us," the tailor said.

"Yes. May God be with us," Hafiz said. He looked at his watch. He'd only been inside the shop for a few minutes. "Now I must go."

The young Palestinian boy watched the two leave the office together. Then he waited. He heard the hiss of the press, then bent down, picked up the box and carried it out the back door into the alley. He strapped it to his motorcycle and pulled out into the traffic.

17

He'd cleaned her up. There were no broken bones, but she was bruised and would have a black eye. Otherwise, her injuries were superficial and not serious.

Sometimes he thought in the vernacular of medicine. Staring at her, lying on his bed now, it was easier to do that than in more human terms. A civilian would have thought in terms of a beating and violence done to her. He wanted the freedom to be angry at whoever had beaten her, but he couldn't. He was afraid his feelings for her would push everything else out of the way. So he'd forced himself to react solely as a doctor, and it helped calm him down.

He'd given her a Valium and put her to bed. He'd gone out twice while she'd slept; once to the Gobi to get her some clean clothes, and once to the Radisson hotel to treat a young American couple on their honeymoon, who had both gotten dysentery. They'd never been really sick before and were terrified they might be dying.

"You've been asleep," he said when she opened her eyes. He'd taken her dress off and couldn't help but notice her body. He looked away from her for a moment, a little ashamed that he'd looked at her that way when he was her doctor.

"I'm sorry," she said. "I didn't know where else to go. I didn't want to go back to the hotel. Not like that."

"No. I'm glad you came here," Collin said.

"I'm afraid your dress is . . . I had to throw it out. I put you to bed. You'd fallen asleep and I didn't want you to get cold. I had to go see a patient."

"Thank you." She slid up onto the pillow. He saw her soiled bra, and she covered herself.

"I have a robe you can wear," he said. He went to his closet.

"No. I . . . I don't want to get up just yet," she said.

He stopped in front of his closet.

"I got your things from the hotel. I didn't check you out. I don't know who's running the place. I don't know what's happened to Madani," he lied. "I can't imagine why he would be arrested. But then it's Mexico, isn't it?"

"Yes," she said. "It's Mexico."

He came and sat on the edge of the bed.

"How are you feeling?"

"Better, I think. I cried an awful lot, didn't I?"

"Yes. Complete waterworks." He smiled. He thought she was going to say she was sorry again, but she didn't.

"Was it a robbery?" he asked.

"My purse? Did I have it?"

"Yes. You had it with you. It's here, in the kitchen." He went and got it. It was still soaked and wretched-looking, but he took it in to her anyway. "What happened?"

"I went to the market . . . it happened on the way back," she said.

"Bastards," he said, and meant it. He wished he'd been with her. He'd had a protective feeling toward her the moment they'd met, as if she were waiting specifically for *him* to come and save her. It was very odd, but he had it every time he saw her.

"Do you mind if I smoke?" he asked. "I don't very much— smoke—but sometimes late at night I like to when I'm alone. I sketch and I smoke. I enjoy that. It's the little things in life."

He went to the dresser, got his cigarettes, and lit one. He was wearing dark slacks and a clean white shirt. He looked quite handsome, she thought, his blond hair freshly cut. He'd had it cut since she'd seen him last, and it made him look even younger.

"You're a doctor . . . but you smoke," she said, watching him.

"I know. Stupid, isn't it? I can't tell you how easy it is. I used to have friends in medical school who would smoke a pack a day despite everything we were learning about cancer. There's a disconnect, you see, between you and all that. It's as if . . . as if we were protected by everything we'd learnt. It's hard to describe, but there's a distance. I only allow myself one a day, though," he said.

"Then you'll be all right," she said.

"I think so. But I have brandy, too. Would you like one?"

"Yes."

"I've pulled you into my web of sin," he said.

She smiled a little. He went and got the brandy and two glasses from the kitchen. He poured out the drinks and put them on the nightstand. He noticed how beautiful she looked despite what had happened to her eye, like a doll that had been damaged slightly where everything else was perfect.

She reached for the drink. He saw the cup of her breast and tried to look away. She surprised him; she let go of the sheet altogether and held the glass, not caring that he saw her like that. Their eyes met.

"What do you think of the world?" she asked.

"Well . . . I think it's very big, and obviously . . . full of brutes," he said.

"When I was a little girl, I liked everyone," she said. She took a drink, and then put it down on her lap. "When we were out walking on the High Street, my mother and I, I would invite everyone home for tea."

"Do you want to talk about what happened?"

"No," she said. "No, not at all. . . . Where was that painted?" she asked.

He turned and looked at a second painting he'd done of the pool at the *pensión Javier.* Marita was sitting with her back to him, the orange of her bathing suit very bright. It was the first painting he'd done with a passable figure in it.

"Baja California. A little town, San Javier."

"You painted it?"

"Yes."

"Is she your girlfriend?"

"No," he said.

"But I sense something," she said. She took another sip of her drink. "An intimacy."

"Well . . . artistic license. Student's enthusiasm," he said.

"You're lying," she said, in an odd tone of voice. Not angry or reproachful, but very much to the point. Like a scholar looking at some ancient text, seeing something no one else saw.

"We were good friends," he said finally. "I think she's gone back to Germany now. I'm not sure."

"I thought so," Dolores said.

He turned and looked at the painting. It was larger than he'd usually done. He'd borrowed the paper from Alfredo, he remembered, because he'd brought no large paper with him.

"I like it," Dolores said. "Is she beautiful . . .the girl?"

"Marita? Yes, very," he said.

She nodded, accepting that information like someone buying something and hearing the price from the owner.

"Did you make love there?"

He didn't know what to say. She'd been so guarded up to this point. Perhaps it was the valium, he thought. He started to slip back into his doctor mode, fashioning an analysis.

"Did you?" She didn't let him go. Perhaps she'd seen it on his face, the change in expression, moving away from her. She closed the distance quickly.

"Yes, we did."

"There . . . in the pool?"

"*No.*"

"Do you love her?"

"No. Too different. She's a bohemian. I'm a doctor."

"But you slept with her."

"Yes."

"Is that what you do?"

"Dolores . . . I'm not sure I understand."

"I . . . I just thought she might be your girlfriend and perhaps she would come here and be angry with me for being here, in your bed. I'm not a child. You must have a girlfriend."

"No. I guarantee she isn't going to come here and get angry. And she wasn't my girlfriend. Not really. We were friends, and that's all. It was very brief. A brief affair."

"Will you tell me about the place . . . there? The one in the painting."

"The hotel?"

"Yes."

He took a drink. "Well, let's see. It's in the desert. Very rough, very little town, hardscrabble place. It's hard to believe there are still places like that."

"Where is it?"

"Near the States," he said.

"Is it beautiful?"

"Yes. If you like the desert."

"Do you think *I'm* pretty?" She was looking at him. Her bad eye had swelled up now, and was a little monstrous.

"Yes. Very." He didn't think about his answer.

"Do you want to make love to me? . . .Can I have some more brandy?" She held the glass out to him.

The word *manic* came to him. Just the one word. But it came from the doctor side of his brain, and it registered. He knew he had to back away.

"No. We have to get you something to eat. And to do that,

we have to go out. But I'm very flattered." He tried to play the question off.

"You didn't answer me," she said. She was looking at the painting again, her hands on her lap.

"I think you're upset," he said. "You've had a rough day."

"Are you going to be my lover, or my doctor?" she said. "You can't be both. I don't think that would be right. And I'm not like the German girl in that painting. I'll be different. I'm not like her. Easy, like that painting."

He didn't want to, but when she got up from the bed he kissed her. She kissed him back, and they held each other as travelers do when they meet again unexpectedly. It was as if they'd known each other for a long time.

The phone woke them. He thought he would let it ring and not answer, but he knew he couldn't. He looked at his clock radio. It was four in the morning. She moved against him, her nakedness warm and stirring, even now. She reached for him as he answered.

"This is the embassy. Someone needs to see you. We'll send a car."

He turned over and kissed her. It was different this time; it was as if they were still making love and had only stopped for a moment, and now they were resuming.

"I've got to go," he said.

She kissed him and didn't let him finish. She reached for him there; her touch was perfect, and she knew the power it would have on him. Then they were making love again, very softly at first; she rolled on top of him and started quickly. He could see her black hair and her breasts and the way she rocked. He saw she was crying perhaps, and it was very strange. It was as if there were two women making love to him at once: a frantic girl, and someone else. One of them, he was sure, he would never really know.

142

• • •

They met in the lobby of the Four Seasons.

"I've got your brother," Alex said. He said it as if it were a package or a car.

"Can I see him?" Hussein asked.

"No," Alex said. "Absolutely not."

"Let me see him and talk some sense into him. I can get him to talk, Alex."

"I've got him. That's what's important."

"It's my brother, for God's sake, Alex."

"I'll send him to people you don't want him sent to if you don't find what I want—and very soon. I know you know people . . . very hard people," Alex said. "They don't believe me in Washington, so I've no help at all. I've got to find this with what I have, and that isn't much. Do you understand me? I don't care about your brother at all.

"Now go to those people and tell them that I want that package. If they get it for me, they'll have a powerful friend at the embassy, and they can call in any favor they want within reason," Alex said.

"Can I see him first?"

"No. First find this kid. Get me this kid and you can see him. I'll give you 48 hours." Alex handed him a photograph of the young man on his motorcycle, taken near the tailor's shop.

"I could ask my brother who he is."

"I've already *asked* him," Alex said, and he turned around and left.

Hussein had never seen Law act like this before. Law was sober and it frightened him, because he wasn't at all the man Hussein knew. He was someone else entirely: someone he had never met before, someone he couldn't really reason with.

• • •

The town car slid to the curb and the doctor got in. He'd brought his doctor's bag, and he put it down at his feet. A man with a hood over his head sat in the back. Butch Nickels was sitting next to him.

"If it isn't the good physician," Nickels said.

The doctor looked at him, then at the hooded man, who was handcuffed, his hands behind his back.

"Where to, sir?" the driver asked.

"Towards Popocatepetl. The road to *Popo*. You know it?" Nickels asked the driver.

"Yes, sir, I know it," the driver said.

"Go there. We used to go there in the old days. Before you were born," Nickels said. "When were you born, kid?" he asked Collin.

"I'm not a kid," Collin said. "This man is bleeding."

"Is he? I wouldn't be surprised."

"Yes." He could see the blood staining the man's shirt, below the hood.

"Well, he should be," Butch said. "He's had a rough time of it. But he should have expected that."

Collin heard the man mumble something in Arabic.

"I need help. Are you a doctor?" the prisoner asked in Arabic.

"Yes," Collin said. He glanced at Nickels.

"Go ahead and parley. Fine with me," Butch said to him.

"Please help me. I am hurt, badly hurt. Where are they taking me?" the hooded man said. His voice was weak.

"You didn't answer my question," Nickels said.

"Nineteen-seventy." Collin reached over and pulled up the hood so he could see the prisoner's face. "*Jesus!*" Collin said.

"Why did you join up?"

"None of your business," Collin said.

The prisoner's nose was broken and it was bleeding badly. The tailor, in his fifties, was looking at Collin as if he might finally have found someone who could help him.

"Ooh, touchy?" Nickels said.

"You know what? I don't like you," Collin said, lifting his medical bag onto the seat next to him.

"So what? I don't like you, either," Nickels said. "So we got that out of the way. Don't you feel better?"

"Where are we going?"

"On a treasure hunt," Butch said.

"What does that mean?" Collin said.

"You're the medical-school-top-of-your-class motherfucker. You figure it out. I got to college on a football scholarship and never went to class."

"I'm going to treat him while we drive?"

"Go ahead. That's why you're here, isn't it?"

"I'll have to take off his hood."

"Go ahead."

The doctor reached over and pulled off the hood.

"Jesus Christ," Collin said again. He had to breathe through his nose in order not to lose it. The man's face was horribly battered.

"I've seen worse," Butch said, glancing at him. "Much worse."

Collin put cotton in the man's nostrils to stop the bleeding.

"Do you speak English?" Collin asked him, cleaning up his face, looking into the prisoner's eyes. The man was terrified. The other two hadn't been, but this man was frightened. He shook his head no. "Spanish, then?"

"*Un poco,*" the tailor said.

"*Muy poquito,*" Nickels said. "Enough to be an asshole, though."

"My wife and children. They don't know where I am," the man said in Arabic to Collin. "Can you let them know I'm alive?"

"He wants to contact his family," Collin said. He got a butterfly bandage and used it to close a laceration on the man's cheek.

"Tell him my nephew lives in Los Angeles. He's got two kids. Tell him that," Butch said.

Collin looked at Nickels. He couldn't think of the word for nephew in Arabic, but he remembered the word for sister.

"I have a sister in Los Angeles," Collin said in Arabic. He watched the man's face.

"I told him my sister lives in L.A.," Collin said.

"Is that really true?" Nickels asked.

"Yes."

"Yeah. Good."

"What's that supposed to mean?" Collin said.

"I want to know something. Why is it people like you look down your fucking nose at people like me? That's what I want to know. I really do . . . because I'm getting really sick of it. Do you think I do this for kicks? Huh? What the fuck do you think I'm doing this *for?* Do you think I made this motherfucking world? Do you think I'm the fucking problem? I'm the only solution you got, kid. You and all you fucking rich people. I'm your solution. Like it or not. 'Cause these guys are for real, baby. Look at him. He wants to send your sister to kingdom come. And you're all watery-eyed about it. I don't get it. I really don't," Nickels said.

Collin just looked at him. He didn't know what to say.

"Did you ever hear the expression dog eat dog?" Butch said.

"I'm a doctor. Not a dog," Collin said. "Can you understand that? I was taught to help people. Why can't you understand that? That's what they teach you in medical school." He got a small light out and looked into the prisoner's eyes.

"Yeah, I can understand that," Nickels said. "Go ahead and patch him up. But if he doesn't tell me what I want to know, you're going to need more than a fucking cotton ball."

146

18

W ell?" Helen said. "Have you decided? . . .The doctor wants
me to go back to the States, as soon as possible."

"Can't I meet you in a week or two?" Alex said.

He looked up at the ceiling. The ceiling, fifteen feet up, was
freshly plastered and perfectly smooth. Helen was sitting at an
art deco mirror they'd bought, brushing her hair.

"No. I won't go without you. I don't understand what could be
more important than this, Alex."

She looked in the mirror at him. He was lying in bed. It was
late. He hadn't had anything to drink at all for two days. She
hadn't said anything about it. She'd probably never known him
sober, until recently. He was quieter, not voluble the way he was
when he was drinking. There were long spells of silence now.
Not angry silence, but silence of a different kind, as if he were
taking his sobriety in.

"A week is all I ask," he said. "Ten days. I promise to come."

"Did you ever really love me?" she said.

"Yes. I've always loved you," he said. "You have to believe
that."

"Even when you were with other women."

"Yes. Even then."

She stopped brushing her hair and put the brush down
carefully.

"I'm begging you to go, now," Alex said.

"I won't go without you," she said. "I won't. I don't care what happens to me . . . I won't go. Not unless you come with me." She snapped off the light and slipped into bed next to him.

"I'm afraid," he said. "I'm afraid . . . if you don't go. . . ."

She put her arms around him. It was pitch dark in the room. She loved being alone with him like that.

"Do you remember once we went to London to see your father, when we were first dating?"

"Yes," he said.

"I was so impressed with your father and mother. I thought, if I can be like her, I'll be all right. I miss her."

"So do I," Alex said.

"We went out every night, remember? We saw *The Mousetrap.*"

"Ate at a place called the Oratorio."

"Yes," she said. "And you took me to the Savoy for lunch with your father, and all those people kept coming by to say hello. Your father seemed to own the city."

"He'd been there during the war."

She kissed his neck. "Let's go see him."

"Okay."

"He's lonely, I think." she said.

"I think so," Alex said.

"We'll go see him," she said. She touched his lips. "I love you. Is it because of work? Is that it? Why you can't leave? Is it something you can tell me? Something to do with that man Hussein we visited?"

"Yes, with him," Alex said. "I'll quit after this if you'll just go back tomorrow." He was cupping her breast, the one with the lump. "*Please.*"

They made love then. She pretended she was only 22 and they were in London, and there was nothing in front of them but good things. Her mind played tricks on her lately, making the past seem more real than the present.

148

• • •

There was a good smell even in the stairway. It was the smell of his mother's cooking. The young man, Omar, walked up the stairs towards his parents' apartment. They'd come to Mexico from Gaza, after Hamas had killed his uncle for being an informer. No one ever found out if it had been true or not. Enough is enough, Omar's father had told his mother that night, and they'd borrowed money and flown from Jordan to Mexico because they had a cousin there.

All the children except their oldest boy, Omar, had been born in Mexico. His father had opened up a small market. Now he had four of them, and considered Mexico home. He didn't miss Palestine. He told his son that Palestine was dead, a land full of killing and suffering. Why in the world would any sane man want anything to do with it? Nothing was worth that kind of suffering, he told his son. Omar thought differently. He had a romantic notion about the place he barely remembered.

The young man carried the package up the stairs with him. A man he knew well, from one of the other apartments, walked down the stairs past him and smiled. Omar smiled back, making sure the man didn't bump the package.

"May God be with you," the man said.

"And with you, too," Omar said.

His mother was cooking. He greeted her and she smiled at him. She was on her cell phone, and he went back to his small bedroom in the flat and put the package on his bed. Then he took it off and tried to put it under the bed, but it wouldn't fit. He put it on the chair and stood for a moment, trying to decide what to do with it. His mother opened the door to his bedroom, still talking on her cell phone.

"Your father wants to know where you were all morning," she said to him in Arabic.

149

"I was. . . ." He was staring at the package. "I was having the bike looked at. I'm thinking of selling it," he said.

"Praise be to God. I hope you sell it soon, before you're killed," his mother said. They'd had a friend of the family killed the summer before on his motorcycle on the road to Puebla, and his parents had been trying to get him to sell his since. It was a lie; he had no intention of selling it. But he knew it would make his mother happy.

"What's that?" his mother said. She was looking at the package.

"I bought a new computer from Pablo," Omar said.

"You have two computers already," she said.

"It's a Mac," he said.

"What's that?" she said. He shook his head and smiled at his mother as she was closing the door. "Lunch will be ready soon. Your father is coming home. He wants to talk to you about store #3." They'd numbered the stores. Three was in a very tough neighborhood and was being robbed almost continuously.

When his mother left, he suddenly had a strong desire to open the box and see what was inside. It didn't weigh much, which puzzled him. The box was computer-sized. For some reason, he thought that he should see what was inside.

The cardboard box was bound with string. It looked quite ordinary. He went to the kitchen and came back with scissors and cut the string. He heard his little sister come in from school. She was with a friend. He was about to peel back the top of the box, but stopped.

His sister opened the door. She was 16 and very cute, and he worried about her. He knew what the boys in the neighborhood were like. She was wearing her Catholic school uniform.

"What are you doing?" she said in Spanish. She didn't really speak Arabic, although she understood it.

"Out," he said.

"Your porn stash? Why don't you get a girlfriend?" she said.

"Go," he pointed.

"Lunch is ready," she said, and started to close the door. "You look weird."

He tied the string again, put the box back on his chair, and went and had lunch. He couldn't really eat. His father was talking to them about store #3 and what to do about security. All the time their father was talking, his sister was looking at him.

"Okay, what's in that box?" she said.

"What do you mean?" He'd come back to his bedroom after lunch and was staring at the box, trying to decide what to do with it. He'd told his father he would meet him at store #3, and he'd promised not to be late. But he had no idea what he was going to do with the package. He decided at lunch to take it with him to store #3 and leave it there. He thought it would be safer.

"You look weird. There's something weird in that box," she said. "I want to know what it is."

"Don't act crazy, Sofia." His parents had given the rest of the children non-Arabic names, all taken from film stars.

"I'm not. But I want to see what's in that box. It's drugs, isn't it?"

"No."

"You've been acting strange. And I don't believe all this religion crap you've been telling mom and dad. Trips to the mosque and all that bullshit. You've fallen in with that crowd from Montecitos," she said. "Are you on crack?" They'd grown up in a rough and tumble neighborhood. A lot of the boys and girls he'd studied with had gone to work for the myriad neighborhood gangs.

"No."

"Then let me *see* . . . Mom said it's a computer."

"It is," he said.

"Then let me see it," she said. She obviously didn't believe him.

"*No*. Now I have to go. I promised Dad I'd. . . ."

151

"Why can't I see it? If it's *just* a computer."

His mind froze. He didn't have a quick lie to put her off with.

"Okay . . . it *is* porn," he said. "I don't want you to see it, okay?"

"I *thought* so. Good *Muslim* boy . . . yeah. Nasty boy is more like it," she said. "You're just like Miguel. God. Yuck! Is it gross?" She smiled, interested. "What's it called, *Booty Call #6?*"

She was already having sex with her boyfriend, but she didn't want to let on, as she knew it would destroy her mother and father. She got her birth control from a women's group that worked in the neighborhood. The young women there were kind and told her that if she was going to have sex, she should protect herself.

"Yes."

"Can I see it? I won't tell mom. I want to see what it looks like. Gross!" She thought that this was a perfect way to prove to her brother that she was still a virgin. She was very worried what he would do if he found out otherwise. In Palestine, there'd been murders when fathers or brothers found out their daughters or sisters had compromised their virginity. The girls had been killed by their own families.

"No! Now can I have some privacy, Sofia?"

"Are you going to watch it now? Can I watch it with you? *Yuck!*" She shut the door, glad that he wasn't a drug addict.

• • •

"*Shukran*," the tailor said.

"You're welcome," Collin said, in Arabic.

The tailor was watching the road carefully, now. Collin had stopped the bleeding from the worst lacerations. The tailor didn't seem to notice while Collin had been working on his face. Once the tailor had turned and looked at Nickels, and then turned back towards the window.

"Where are we going? He needs rest. His jaw might be broken. I want to take an X-ray," Collin said.

"*X-ray?*" Nickels said.

"Yes. He might not be able to eat if it's broken. He'll have to have a liquid diet. Anyway, I want to take an X-ray to be sure," Collin said.

Butch rubbed his hand over his short hair but didn't answer.

"Are you going to tell me where we're going?"

"His house," Butch said.

"What?"

"This guy's house."

"Why?"

"I want to have a talk with his family," Butch said.

"Jesus Christ. Don't you ever let up?" Collin said.

Nickels looked at him a long time.

"I'm still having that sleeping problem. What do you think it is?" The doctor shook his head, closed up his medical bag, and put it back down on the floor of the car.

"Maybe if you stopped beating the crap out of people, you might sleep a little better," Collin said.

"No, that's got nothing to do with it. And I didn't do it. The Mexicans did it."

"You were standing there," Collin said. "In the room, no doubt."

"Yeah, I was. Come on; you're supposed to be a doctor."

"How old are you?"

"57."

"You're lying. How old?"

"Okay, I'm 59."

"Have you been having a lot of sex lately?"

"Yeah. Why?"

"How often do you get up at night to pee? More than twice?"

"Yeah."

"You might have a prostate infection. Or it's swollen because of your age."

"Prostate, huh?"

"Yes," Collin said.

The car slowed and turned off the toll road they were on. Collin looked out the window and saw one of the countless ramshackle unplanned suburbs that surrounded the city.

"I've got a young girlfriend," Butch said. "I'm trying to keep up. You know what I mean. She likes sex. Hell, *I* like sex."

"She may have given you an STD," Collin said.

"STD?"

"Sexually transmit. . . ."

"Yeah, I know what it means," Nickels said.

"Maybe you've bitten off more than you can chew," Collin said.

"I've been fucking longer than you've been alive, kid."

"Exactly."

"She's not that kind of girl." Collin shrugged his shoulders. "Can you treat it?"

"You need a doctor."

"*You're* a doctor," Nickels said. "I don't care if you don't like me. Can you treat it?"

"Depending on what's wrong . . . yes, *someone* can treat it."

"I want *you* to treat it. You inspire confidence. Look what you did for him."

"Why did you bring me?" Collin had never met anyone like Nickels.

"Because you speak Arabic. And we have no one at the embassy who does right now. Can you believe it? I'd have to fly someone in from Washington. The Company spends billions of dollars every year, and I can't get anyone who speaks Arabic to have on hand. It's a hell of a way to run a railroad," Butch said.

"I speak it *very, very* badly," Collin said. "I can't be of much use to you."

"Well, we're about to find out."

It was three in the morning, the street lit by weak lights from the top of thin steel utility poles that brought electricity up from the city. A fog that sometimes appeared in the mountains above Mexico City at night shrouded some of the buildings.

The tailor had known for over an hour that they were probably going to his house, but he hadn't been sure so had kept it off his face. He was sure, now. There was an American car and a police cruiser on the corner with two Coldwater types behind the wheel.

"Pull in behind them," Nickels said. He got out of their car and went and sat in the American car.

"Why are we here?" the tailor asked the doctor in Arabic. His damaged face was more swollen that it had been before.

"I don't know," Collin said. "Do you live here, nearby?"

"Yes."

"You have to tell them what they want to know," Collin said in Arabic. For a moment he had to think of the verb to tell, so it came out wrong the first time. But he repeated it.

"Why?"

"Because," Collin said. "If you don't, they'll probably arrest your family and send them out of the country." Collin turned and looked at the driver. He was looking at them through the rearview mirror.

Nickels came back and slid in next to the tailor. He took out a pistol and laid it on his knee. He looked at Collin.

"Okay. Tell him that if he doesn't tell us where the package is, we're going to go down the street and arrest his family. The kids, too. Go ahead and tell him."

"Children? You can't be serious."

"Try me," Butch said.

"Okay. No need for that," the tailor said in perfect English. He spoke English, but hadn't let on until then. The doctor was a little shocked.

"*Motherfucker!*" Butch said. "You see! You see! He speaks English."

The tailor looked at the doctor, then. It was a strange look, as if to say he was sorry for misleading him because he'd been kind to him.

"Sneaky motherfucker," Butch said.

The tailor told them that Madani had, in fact, been the key player in their cell. There were four people in the cell, he told them. One of them was the Imam at the mosque; he'd even given them his name. Collin had wanted to ask if the tailor knew of a girl at the Gobi, but was afraid to. Instead, he'd listened to Nickels question the tailor on the way back into the city. The man tried to prevaricate, saying that he didn't know anyone's address, but only met them at his tailor shop. Nickels finally lost his patience and told him that he was going to go back to the tailor's house and arrest *all* his family, including his young children, and make sure that he never saw them again. It seemed to work.

The tailor said the person who had the bomb was a young Palestinian man named Omar who still lived with his mother and father. He said Omar had taken the bomb with him the day they were arrested. He gave them the boy's address.

19

She let me in, *amigo*—your charming friend," Alfredo said. Collin put down his doctor bag in the hall.

The two were sitting in the small living room. Dolores was dressed, her right eye discolored and still half-shut from the beating.

"Your young friend is very interesting to talk to. *She* thinks you should be a painter, too," Alfredo said to him. Alfredo had not asked the girl about her eye at all, deciding that it would be impolite to bring it up.

"Should I introduce you two?" Collin asked.

He looked at Dolores. She was wearing jeans he hadn't seen her in before. The pants were more revealing, tighter; with her hair down, she looked very young. Before this, she'd dressed as if she'd been going out of her way to look plain.

"Out making sure Montezuma doesn't get his revenge?" Alfredo asked.

"Yes," Collin said, smiling.

He came into the room. Alfredo had brought a bottle of wine, and he and Dolores were having a drink. He'd been out painting, Alfredo said, and he'd decided to come by on the spur of the moment.

"Alfredo, this is my friend, Dolores Rios," Collin said.

"How do you get so lucky, *amigo?*" Alfredo asked him, nodding towards Dolores.

"Just lucky," Collin said. He poured himself a drink.

"Listen, I thought we could go back to San Javier again. Would you like to go? Dolores said she would love to. I've told her all about it."

"When?" Collin asked.

"Friday? We could leave early. Fly in again," Alfredo said. "Spend the weekend."

"Who's going?"

"Just us. I want to stay a week or so. And no one I know can afford it right now. Come on . . . I don't want to go all alone."

• • •

"I need your help, Don Chepe," Hussein said.

Don Chepe was a very important man, not only in the Mexican underworld but in the emerging trans-national mafia, a loose alliance of cartels that were politically connected and financially sophisticated—and, some argued, important to the stability of the world banking system.

Don Chepe had given Hussein his start in the money-laundering business years before. The man was a Class One offender, in the parlance of the DEA, but he also happened to be the new head of the *Mexican* DEA. He was an untouchable.

Don Chepe's father had been a brick layer. When he didn't work, the family starved. That was the Mexico City Don Chepe had grown up in, and the world he understood. He'd become a policeman because he saw, when he was still a child, that the police always worked, and their families never went hungry. And, the police could steal with impunity.

"Tell me, *amigo*. What is it?" Don Chepe said.

"It's a very serious problem. Perhaps we should talk outside," Hussein said.

"No. Here is good," Don Chepe said. "Don't worry."

Hussein told him the problem, and finished with what Alex Law had said about rendering his brother.

158

"I know Law," Don Chepe said. "He won't take our money. We've tried with him twice. He's very clever. He uses us when he needs us, but I've never met him. He avoids me at parties."

"Maybe that's why he's asking for help. He's convinced they are trying to get some kind of bomb into the States."

"Terrorism is bad for business," Don Chepe said. "Hell, I go to Los Angeles myself." Hussein shook his head. "These fanatics are smart. You see what they're doing in Iraq. But what can I do?"

"He wants you to help find the package," Hussein said.

"We can try," Don Chepe said. "The police are best for this, the Federal Police. I have two I use to find people in the city when I have to. I know them a long time. These two are very thorough. Like rats at the dump. Everything gets turned over. What's the package look like?"

"I don't know," Hussein said. "Nobody seems to know."

"Okay, we find it," Don Chepe said. "Stop worrying. But I need a thread. A name."

"I don't understand."

"A place to start to pull from," Don Chepe said. "Someone my men can talk to first."

"Okay. I'll get you someone," Hussein said.

Don Chepe walked him to the office door. His office was right down the hall from the President of the Republic. "Tell Law I said hello. Maybe one day we can have lunch," Don Chepe said, and smiled.

"I'll tell him," Hussein said. They embraced, and he left feeling uneasy.

He called Chepe later and gave him two names: the Hotel Gobi, and the name of a woman his brother's secretary had overheard Madani mention once on the phone. It had cost Hussein $100,000, paid to his brother's secretary, but he'd gotten a name. It was a start.

• • •

"Are you sure you want to go?" Collin asked.

"Yes," Dolores said.

"What about Chicago?" Collin asked. "Don't you have to get home?"

"I want to go to that place. The place in your painting. The desert place," she said.

Alfredo had gone home. Collin had said he would call if he could go back to San Javier. He was a little high from the wine they'd drunk, and he wanted to ask Dolores questions.

He was uneasy, because the tailor had said that Madani was their cell's leader, answering only to the Imam at the mosque. Butch Nickels had read all the names registered at the Gobi the night that Madani was arrested to see if the tailor recognized anyone. Collin kept expecting her name to be read, but it wasn't. *Did they know she'd been staying there? She must have been registered,* Collin thought, looking at her.

"What do you know about Madani?" Collin said. He'd been waiting for Alfredo to leave so he could ask her.

"He's an Egyptian, I think. That's all. I didn't like him, really."

"Why? He seemed to like you," Collin said.

She didn't answer him. She had a way of not answering, and instead looking away, that was annoying him. Despite it all, he wanted to take her to the desert. He wanted to be with her. He didn't want her to leave; he was afraid he wouldn't ever see her again, and he didn't like the thought of that.

"I think Alfredo likes you, too," he said, changing the subject. "I'm jealous."

"He's very nice," she said. "I liked him. He's different."

"He's a real painter," Collin said. "I saw him looking at you when you got up. Have men always acted that way around you?"

"Yes, I think so," she said.

"Unless you dress like an old woman," Collin said. She smiled. "Madani may be a terrorist."

"Why do you think that?" she said. Her face went blank.

"Because. I have a friend; a policeman. I called him about Madani. They think he's a terrorist—the police."

"I doubt that," she said. "All Arabs aren't terrorists." He thought she sounded a little angry. It was the first time he'd ever heard her sound angry.

His cell phone rang, but he didn't bother to answer.

"I didn't say all Arabs. I said Madani may be one," he said.

She looked at him a long time.

"What about his wife? Is she supposed to be a terrorist, too?" she asked.

"I don't know. Where's your passport?"

"It was stolen on the bus from Veracruz. I told you."

"Why don't you speak Spanish? Your name is Dolores Rios. You said you had family in Veracruz. I don't understand."

"Why don't you speak Dutch?" she said. "You said your grandfather was Dutch."

"I want to be your friend," he said in Arabic. He looked at her face carefully.

"I'm sorry . . . I don't understand what you said to me."

"I heard Madani's wife speak to you in Arabic one day."

"Did she?"

"Yes. Are you going to tell me the truth? I'm not stupid, Dolores."

"Truth?"

"You have no passport. You were staying at the hotel, but you weren't listed on their register."

"How do you know that?"

"I just do," he said.

"Are you a policeman?"

"What if I was?" he said.

"I thought you were a doctor," she said. "Maybe I was wrong

about you. . . . I never liked policemen." She got up. "Thank you for what you've done for me," she said.

She went to the bedroom and lifted her suitcase onto the bed. He picked up his cell phone. His sister was calling from Los Angeles. He held the phone for a moment.

He watched her bend forward, opening the suitcase. He rushed into the room and held her around the waist. He shoved her suitcase onto the floor. It made a big sound on the wooden floor as it fell. She let him hold her.

He didn't care who she was. He felt possessive for the first time in his life. He wanted to *have* her. He wanted to take her clothes off and make love to her, and he didn't give a damn who she was. Something about her beauty was very profound and was most powerful when she was naked. He'd never thought that before about a woman. It was strange, but true. It was perfect, and he wanted to steal that beauty for himself.

She turned and held his face and kissed him.

"I don't want to go," she said. It surprised him, the way she said it.

"Can I paint you like that?" he said, watching her later. She was lying on the bed, like Goya's Maja.

"Yes," she said.

They didn't talk anymore about who she was or where she'd come from. "Men are so predictable," she said finally, watching him work.

She'd never really let her husband see her naked, not like this. She had always wanted to, but he'd seemed afraid of her nakedness. It seemed to make him uncomfortable, as if enjoying it were loathsome. As if Allah thought being naked were somehow a sin.

"Will you take me to the desert?" she asked.

"Of course," he said, "if you want."

• • •

"You see, they got her name at the hotel. It was in the police report when they arrested Madani, but she wasn't registered. Her name never appears on the register.

"The old man made a mistake. If he'd registered her, I wouldn't have thought anything about her—just another tourist. But I think she's the one, the one who's supposed to take the package. They said it was a woman in Riyadh who was buying the ticket. You see? They don't ever use women. It was brilliant," Alex said. "Then the doctor gave me the postcard. I had it on my desk to mail when I read the report from the Gobi that night."

"It's a risk we shouldn't take," Butch said. He was looking at the postcard. "Let's just arrest her now."

"Why?" Alex said. "They'll just get someone else. She doesn't have it yet. This way we can find out what they intend to do with it."

"Because she just might be smarter than us. And she might know where the hell it is."

"I think she's just a girl," Alex said. "A girl who lost her son and wants to get back at the world. She's only 26. I'm getting a complete report this afternoon from London."

Alex picked up the postcard from the booth they were sitting in. "This is her mother's address. Her father's dead. He was a barrister. She grew up in London. She's not even a Muslim; she's a Christian Arab. She married a doctor and they moved to Baghdad a few years ago."

They were sitting in a bar on the third story of the *Banco Industrial* building. It was a pick-up bar for bankers and well-heeled types in the *Zona Rosa*. It wasn't party time yet, so the waiters milled around, looking out the windows down on the traffic.

163

"I say we should pick her up. This doctor is something *else,*" Butch said.

"Who would have thought it?" Alex said. "He must have treated her. She was ill, probably. The old man naturally would have gone across the street to someone he thought he could trust. Someone who wouldn't have given her a second thought."

"But she was pretty, and one thing led to another," Butch said.

"That's it. Now we have her."

Butch picked up the postcard again and looked at the back.

"But we don't have the package."

"No, we don't. But she's the messenger. She's the one that's intended to take it wherever it's going, I think."

"Probably," Butch said. "Have you told anyone?"

"Of course not. They'd have her arrested and rendered before you could say Coldwater Associates . . . I'm telling *you,* Butch." Butch looked away for a moment.

"I'm thinking of asking Kwana to marry me," Butch said.

"She's a little young for you, old boy, isn't she?"

"No shit, Alex. Tell me something I don't know. I miss being married. I like it. It's nice having someone to come home to. I'm tired of living alone, you know? I could have a kid. I'd like that. A boy. I could teach him things. When I retire. What am I going to do? When I'm not doing *this?*" he said.

"I thought you could take care of *me,*" Alex said. "Push people out of the way in the old folks'. Get me an extra dessert."

"Very funny," Butch said.

"So, I want to dangle this girl out there. Let her go. That way we see who she gives the package *to,* on the other side. That way we roll *them* up, too. There's got to be an *al Qaeda* cell in Los Angeles, or wherever. Why not take them out, too?" Alex said. "It's a risk, but we could roll them all up. Why not?"

"Well, because we might blow up the fucking city and let a lot of people die. How's that for a reason, Alex?"

164

"We'll turn her," he said. "She obviously likes the doctor."

"What do you mean?" Butch said.

"We flip her. That way, there's no risk. We can turn her first."

"With the doctor?"

"Yes. With the doctor," Alex said.

"I've been giving him a hard time. You know why? Because he's young, and I'm jealous. That's why," Butch said.

"No kidding. I would never have guessed . . . well, what do you think?" Alex was looking at a glass of wine. But he hadn't touched it.

"Okay. Let's turn her," Butch said.

"In the meantime, go turn this kid Omar's house over and see if he's got our package," Alex said.

"But. . . ."

"We want them to think we're looking for it, right?"

"And if I find it?" Butch said.

"We give her a phony to take. If we're really dealing with a cell system, the other cell probably won't know what the damn thing looks like. That's my guess," Alex said.

20

I'm older than you," Butch said. "I'm fifty-five years old. That's exactly how old I am. I wanted to tell you."

He finished cinching up his pants. He'd gained weight in Mexico, and he could feel it. He'd been a linebacker at Notre Dame; he had that linebacker's bulk and strength. He had a long scar on his back that went from his scapula to under his left arm, a gift of the North Vietnamese. When he told her how he got the scar, she'd listened carefully, but he could tell that it all seemed like ancient history to her.

"I know that," Kwana said. They had started to live together at his apartment. She watched him put on the harness he used to carry his weapon.

She knew, as did most employees of the embassy, who were probably the spooks and DEA agents. He was a spook, an old spook, another woman had told her. Her friend remembered him from the embassy in El Salvador. He'd been married once, the woman told her, but his wife had been murdered in Mexico.

"I'm thirty-two," Kwana said.

"I know how old you are," Butch said. Since his time in Vietnam, Butch had always used a backup revolver; and he picked it off the bureau and slipped it into an ankle holster.

"I want to get married," Butch said.

"I'm black," she said. Then she got out of bed. "You don't want to marry me. I'm black."

"No shit; I hadn't noticed," Butch said.

"No . . . I'm black. All right? That's okay here in Mexico, but not back home. No one will like it. My family won't like it. Your family won't like it. We'll be out and people will say things. I've heard them. *Ugly* things," she said.

"Yeah. Well then, let's not go back home," Butch said.

He opened the revolver. He always used a revolver in the ankle holster, because he never wanted to worry about a jam. He looked at the primers. Just stared at them for a moment.

She was very black, and he loved her ass. It wasn't right, maybe, at his age, but he loved her ass. He liked to do it like that, so he could see it. He liked the curve of her spine as it traveled up to her shoulders, and he liked to see her walk around his apartment while she was getting dressed. He wanted to have a kid with her, but that was too much information for one morning. He closed the revolver.

"What do you do with those guns? I thought you were an AID official. I don't even know who you are," she said. "Not really."

"I am an AID official," Butch said. Then he slid the revolver into his ankle holster. It was a little harder than it used to be to bend down. *Because you're really 60! Dumb ass.*

She went out to the kitchen, sat down, and poured a cup of coffee.

He wondered what that meant about his viability in a gunfight. When he was young, he'd been very strong. It had counted for a lot in his ability to survive. There's a physicality to a gunfight. Now he wasn't as strong, and it was starting to worry him. They wanted him to retire; it was only because Alex had insisted he be kept on that he hadn't been bounced back to the States, to some empty condominium in Virginia and a future full of nothing. No family left. Nothing. All he'd known was this life. Embassies, war, gunslinging for rich people. He wasn't a fool; he'd seen too much to believe in the bullshit they fed the public. He'd never even said that to Alex, not what he *really* thought. He was a hired gun and always had been, and that was fine with him.

He rolled his cuff down over his ankle. She'd gone into the bathroom. He stood up and looked at himself in the mirror. He wanted to lose some weight. He was dyeing his hair now and it helped make him look younger. But he needed to lose some weight, too.

"Shit," he said out loud. He dreaded that more than anything: his future when this was over, the loneliness he saw in front of him if he didn't replace it with her and a child, a family he could support and guard against all that out there that he'd seen close up. It was a mean world.

"All my people are dead. Except for my brother, and he won't care. If that's what you're worried about." He went to the bathroom door and spoke through it. "I love you. Can you hear me?"

He could hear the shower running. She hadn't said yes. She hadn't said anything but that she was black. He just stood there and listened to the water running. Finally he heard the door click, and she pulled it open. She was wearing a towel, her hips very narrow. *Pretty. Damn pretty,* he thought, looking at her.

"I can't marry you, Butch. I'm not going to lie to you."

"Why?" he said.

She looked at him a long time. She was a kind girl, and she didn't want to hurt him. She wasn't sure why it had gotten this far, but it had and now she had to tell him the truth.

"I don't know. I just can't marry you."

"Okay," he said. He saw the future in front of him. That condominium and the emptiness of it, with its cold kitchen and its coupons stuck to the refrigerator and the random noises that come through the walls in those places. He wanted to stop her as she walked by him, but he didn't.

He liked the girl. He didn't love her, either; he had only ever really loved his wife, but he liked her an awful lot, and he would have made a good father. That wasn't going to happen. Not now. It was too late.

"Okay," he said again. "I understand. I got to go."

"Maybe we should . . . you know. Slow down on this." She was getting dressed now. He loved it when she got dressed in front of him. He shook his head.

"Yeah. Okay," he said, and left.

He called her later on her cell, but she wouldn't take the call. He left a stupid message—he'd take care of her, he had a pretty good bank account—and then he hung up. He'd filed for her to be his next of kin the week before. It had made him feel good.

No one wants to feel like there's no one who will show up to the funeral. Just an empty room and you in the box. That's what he thought in the elevator, going to pick up the tailor.

They had a jail in the basement of a building near the embassy that technically belonged to Mexican intelligence. When the elevator door closed, Butch saw his own funeral. It was just a room in some church basement, with his box and no one there.

He'd stopped the elevator mid-floor, took out his back-up gun and put it to his head. He pulled the hammer back and waited. He heard the elevator's alarm bell going off, but it seemed far away. All he saw in his mind's eye was the box and the empty room and the folding chairs.

He tried, but he couldn't pull the trigger. Finally he put the gun down and let the elevator go on down to the street level. When he brought the tailor out of his cell, he thought he might be angry, maybe hit him—but he didn't have that kind of hate in him anymore, the way he had when he was younger.

When he was younger, he had a lot of hate in him. It hadn't been easy, being the son of a steelworker who wanted his boys to be better than he was. Ironically, his father had been a communist, hounded by the FBI all through the '60's. There had been lots of people at his father's funeral. He'd been lucky.

169

• • •

She was wearing her Catholic school uniform: white socks, a pleated dress, and a green sweater with a white shirt. Her father paid for the Catholic school because it was one of the best in the city. He was determined that his daughter would be someone and that she would socialize with a better class of people. He was disappointed in his son, who'd shown no interest in education once he'd started up at the mosque.

"I looked in the box. I opened it," Sofia's boyfriend said in Spanish. "There's no pornos in there." Her mother didn't understand Spanish, and he knew it. Sofia's mother smiled, and he smiled back at her.

"You went into my brother's room?" Sofia said.

"Yeah. So?"

Her mother came back into the kitchen.

Sofia had invited her boyfriend for lunch. They were waiting for her father and her brother to come home. They always ate lunch together on Wednesday afternoons; it was something she'd looked forward to since she was a little girl.

It was the first time she'd asked her boyfriend to come along. He was a handsome boy. All the girls wanted him, and she felt she was lucky that he'd wanted her. The fact that she was very beautiful in her own right seemed to make no impression on her. She still thought of herself as the ugly girl who'd been a good foot taller than the boys in her primary school.

"There's no box. No movies. It's just a box with some clothes in it," he said under his breath.

Sofia looked at her boyfriend. Her mother told her to go down the street and get some fresh bread, because she'd forgotten to pick it up. The two of them got up, but Sofia told her boyfriend to stay. She wanted him to get to know her mother a little. He didn't want to stay, but she left before he could stop her.

"Carlos is here," she told her brother. He looked at her. "Please be nice."

Her brother and father were coming up the stairs as she was leaving for the store. She stopped to kiss her father on the cheek. She'd been missing him since he'd opened a new store; he was always gone by the time she woke up now. She told them she would be back in a moment, that she was going to the *panadería*.

"Do I have to?" her brother said as she passed him. She made a face, as she had when they were children, then went down the stairs, her hand running along the concrete balustrade.

She stopped suddenly, for no reason, and looked up the stairwell. It was the stairwell she'd grown up on. She heard her father's voice and the Arabic word for daughter. He had stopped to speak to one of the neighbors. She wondered who. The building was full of Arab families. In her childhood it had been like a village, with the adults looking after everyone else's children. Doors kept unlocked. She'd always felt safe. She hurried out the door of the building. It was a beautiful clear spring day, and she felt happy because her boyfriend had come to lunch.

The Coldwater team was made up of Russians. Butch didn't like the Russians; they were mindless, and he didn't trust them to fight if they really had to. But he'd had no choice. In the old days they would have had their own teams, but now everything was being privatized. He had to use rent-a-thugs, as Alex and he called them.

He showed the men, eight of them, the photo of the Palestinian kid they'd gotten from the surveillance people. He made sure they all saw it.

"I want him. This kid, you understand? That's what we're here for."

A big Russian with blond hair looked at him. He was the team leader. They were making $2,500 a day, Butch had heard. The sergeant looked at the photograph and then at Butch.

"Dead or alive?" the Russian asked.

"*Alive*, asshole." The Russian gave him a dirty look. "Jesus."

"Dead is easier," the Russian said, and smiled. He barked some orders to the others in Russian.

"I'm going, too," Butch said.

"You no go," the Russian said. "Maybe too old."

"Fuck you," Butch said. "And I'm going first. You think you can manage not to shoot me?"

"Maybe," the Russian said. "We should put man on roof first. Call helicopter."

"I did. They didn't show up. I didn't have time to bribe twenty motherfuckers. Welcome to Mexico. Your fuckers know how to clear a room?"

"Yeah. They know," the blond said. "You can put a man on the roof when we get up there."

"Teach you that at Sears . . . how to clear a room? It's the fourth floor apartment. Number eight. We'll put everyone in the kitchen once it's secure, okay?"

The blond went and told the others. None of them spoke English except the blond. It seemed odd to hear Russian on the streets of Mexico. Butch leaned against the car for a moment and looked at his flak jacket in the front seat. He didn't feel like putting it on.

The blond turned and looked at him. Butch drew his pistol and walked to the head of the line of mercenaries. He could tell they couldn't care less about what they were doing. They were all very young and yet looked tired, as if they were bored at the prospect of a gunfight. He noticed as they all walked towards the building that the sky was very blue.

He wasn't right in the head. Maybe he hadn't been for a long time, he decided. It was the first time he admitted it to himself— admitted that he was suicidal and angry. Only God knew what that would lead to up in that building.

People on the street—people coming home for lunch, as was the custom—started to notice them. Some stopped and stared; others ran to get away.

Butch went first into the building. What people on the street saw was an older man in a suit, with a gun. The other men had U.S. Army flak jackets on, the kind they'd seen soldiers wearing on TV. The older man didn't.

The stairwell was darker than he would have liked. Because of his experience, he had not done what the Russians were doing, which was viewing everything from the tip of their gun sights. He dropped the front sight enough to see clearly, relying on instinct shooting, but at one moment lowered his weapon, knowing it was the one thing he wasn't supposed to do. As he did, he heard the sound of boots climbing the stairs behind him. It was a sound he'd heard many times before. *If they kill me, good,* he thought. *Fuck it.*

• • •

"My name is Tom," Alex said. "May I come in? I'm a friend of the doctor's."

Dolores nodded her head. She'd been packing. They were leaving that evening for Baja.

Alex had called the doctor and asked him to go see his wife, to convince her she had to go to the States for treatment. Alex had watched Collin drive away from where he sat, waiting in his car. The doctor had asked him if he'd gotten his friend the passport. Alex told him he had, that it was all fixed. She could leave whenever she wanted.

Alex followed her into the living room. He was wearing a raincoat, his blond hair plastered down from the rain.

"We haven't met," Alex said.

She was a pretty girl, younger looking than he'd expected. The

173

little bit he'd been able to get from London was that she'd been born in Baghdad and gone with her parents to London when she'd been only five. She'd married an Iraqi doctor the year she finished her degree.

She looked at him a moment.

"He's gone out," she said. "Are you a painter?"

"No," Alex said. "Not my line of work. May I sit down?" She nodded nervously, and he smiled. "I'm in public relations," Alex said.

He turned and looked into the bedroom. He could see her suitcase on the bed. "Going away?"

"No," she said. She instinctively told a lie. Something about the man frightened her. "Unpacking, actually."

"Well. Terrible day to travel," Alex said.

"Yes," she said.

"Have you known the doctor for long?"

"No," she said. "I don't know when he'll be back," she said, hoping he might leave.

"Oh, that's fine. I can wait . . . I thought we might talk, in fact. You see, I'm really here to see you."

"Me?"

"Yes," Alex said.

"Why?"

"Well, I have a client who is very interested in you. Your name isn't Dolores, is it? You grew up in London, and you were married to someone called Mohammad. Your son was killed in a bombing eight months ago in Baghdad. Your husband was terribly injured."

She wanted to get up and run, but she knew that someone would be waiting for her on the other side of the door.

"We've spoken to your mother. She's very concerned. Apparently, she hasn't heard from you in months. She was very glad that my company knew where you were. The Brompton road, right?" Alex said.

174

She couldn't stand it, then. She bolted, and he let her. She threw open the front door; two men were standing there in the rain. They looked at her. One of them had a machine pistol. He raised it.

Alex took her hand. He signaled the man with the gun, and he lowered it. Then Alex led her back inside to the living room.

"I just want to be left alone," she said.

"I'm afraid it's too late for that, my dear."

"I haven't done anything," she said.

"Well, I don't know. Is that true? What about working for Mr. bin Laden?"

"That's absurd," she said.

"Is it?"

"Yes. Of course it is. I'm a British citizen."

"Of course you are. May I see your passport?"

"It's been stolen. In Veracruz."

"Why are you traveling under an alias?"

"It was convenient. People are suspicious of Arab names these days."

"Are they? I suppose so. I'm afraid you'll have to come with me."

"Who are you?" she said. "You haven't shown me anything."

"I told you . . . I'm Tom," Alex said. Then he stood up and walked towards the door. "Please don't make this unpleasant."

• • •

Law had *ordered* him to go and read the riot act to his wife.

"He wants you to go to the States. He's right," Collin said.

He reached for her breast; she winced a little. He looked at her. He always felt a kind of panic when he thought a patient was ignoring him and his science. When that happened, he felt as if he was being forced to deal with both a medical and a psychiatric problem. It always made him nervous and a little frightened,

175

because he knew only too well that the medical problem probably wouldn't wait for the other to be resolved.

"Yes. Alex says he's going to ship me back home in one of the agency's planes. Whether I like it or not . . . oh, I know what Alex does, dear. My father was in the game, too. I've known for years. I pretend not to. You must be in the game too, or you wouldn't be coming here at odd hours just because my husband asks you to.

"You won't like it. It changes people. It changed Alex. When we went to Saigon, it changed him. I don't know what he did there, but it changed him," she said.

The workmen were making noise in the room below. He thought that for the first time, she looked truly scared, verging on terrified.

He looked at her a moment. "I'm leaving it, in fact," Collin said.

"Good. May I get dressed now?"

"Of course. You have to leave, Helen. It's very serious, this lump."

"Is it?"

"*Yes.*"

"Have you ever been in love, doctor?"

"I don't know. Maybe." He thought of Dolores. He knew he wanted her with him. He wanted to leave Mexico and the agency and take her with him. Was that love?

"Well, you see, I don't want to be without my husband. Especially now. You'll understand someday."

"Helen, for God's sakes! Don't be ridiculous. You could die if you don't get this treated." He'd raised his voice, and he was immediately sorry he had.

"This is silly." He spoke in a normal tone of voice. "You *have* to go." He realized suddenly that Law wasn't going because he couldn't. It was terrible. He saw Law in a whole new light. He was willing to sacrifice his marriage to find these terrorists and their bomb, and he couldn't tell his wife there was a reason—a *very* good reason—for wanting to send her on alone.

"You see, no one understands. I'm used to that," she said.

"He can't go with you."

"Excuse me?"

"He can't go with you," Collin said.

"Why?"

"Because someone has brought a bomb into the country, and he's worried it might be intended for the States. He is trying to stop them," he said.

She looked at him a long time.

"I didn't know. I thought. I thought he was ashamed of me. Of . . . that he didn't love me."

"No. Now you know. If you tell anyone I've told you, I don't know what will happen to me. I'm sure it will be very serious," he said.

"I knew the day I met you that there was something special about you. You were so kind. You're kind. You're kind to tell me the truth."

"I wish I hadn't," he said.

She smiled.

"I won't say. I promise. I'll call him and tell him I'm going. I'll go tonight."

"I want you to see my father," he said.

"Your father?"

"Yes. He's very good at what he does. I'll call him and make the arrangements. He's a surgeon. But he's got a friend, an oncologist, who's one of the best in the country. Do you know anyone in San Francisco?"

She looked at him a moment and burst out laughing. It was as if she were a different woman.

"I'm sorry, did I say something funny?"

"No. I'm sorry it's just that—Alex. His father, his family is there. That's where we—our home is. Our daughter."

177

"Good. Then I'll call my father," Collin said.

"Thank you," she said.

"He's very . . . he has no bedside manner, my father. Believe me, you may not thank me after you meet him," Collin said.

She gave him a big hug then, very tight, and told him he was a good doctor.

21

He'd had a bad feeling going up the stairs. Butch kicked at the front door, but it didn't budge. A woman began to scream somewhere behind the door as he tried to kick it in.

The Russians had failed to bring the battering ram that he'd asked for. He'd put his shoulder to the door twice and couldn't get it to open. One of the Russians had joined in with him. They got in synch with their kicking; and the door jamb suddenly snapped and gave way, and they were inside.

He heard the shrieking of women's voices now, very loud. The Russian and he ended up bouncing off the hallway wall, colliding together. They grabbed at each other to keep from falling. For a moment he was disoriented. Then he saw the kid in the photograph. He was running down the hall away from them, and Butch followed him instinctively. He waited for a moment at the bedroom door.

The Russians were waiting for a cue. Butch nodded towards the kitchen angrily. He pulled the hammer back on his pistol and opened the door, all of it seemingly in unconnected movements.

The kid was looking at him, then fired. Butch saw the muzzle flash as he fired back. He hit the kid in the head. The shot's impact knocked the kid into the dresser. The women were still screaming. The kid's bullet had creased his neck. He felt a searing and knew what had happened. The kid had almost killed him. *Why hadn't he let him?*

He walked over and looked at the kid's body. The kid was holding a cheap handgun, a twenty-two. Butch picked it out of the kid's dead hand and flung it across the room.

One of the Russians was standing in the hall behind him, just watching. He seemed completely inexperienced.

"Clear the other rooms, you fucking idiot. *The other rooms!*" But the man was staring at the dead kid and didn't understand.

The Russians had probably lied. They'd probably never been soldiers at all. Butch pushed past the one in the hallway, and alone cleared a bathroom and two more bedrooms. When he came back out to the hallway, the Russian who had been standing in the hallway was going through the kid's dresser drawers. Butch raised his gun and pointed it at the small of his back.

"Get away from there." The man turned and looked at him. "I said, get away from there," Butch said. The man didn't move. Butch was going to shoot him, but the blond came up the hallway.

"Clear," the blond said.

"Tell this *motherfucker* to get out of here," Butch said.

The blond told the other Russian to leave the room. He brushed by Butch and gave him an evil look.

"Dey in kitchen," the blond said. "Moder, fader and dauder's friend. No one else."

Butch nodded. He could hear crying coming from the kitchen. He started to see things he hadn't noticed before: the color of the walls, the runner on the floor of the hallway. Inexplicably, a red balloon—partially deflated, hugging the ceiling, left over from some celebration.

"He dead?" the blond asked.

"Yeah," Butch said.

"You bleeding. Not serious," the Russian said. He pointed to his neck. "But you bleeding."

"No shit," Butch said.

180

"Okay," the Russian said.

Butch went down the hall. He looked down at the arm of his suit coat. It was wet with blood from his wound. He touched his neck and winced. He could feel the blood oozing from around his fingers. He was going to scare the people in the kitchen, but he couldn't do much about that. He took a hand towel from the bathroom and put it on his neck.

"We're looking for a bomb," he told the blond. "You start looking for that. Send two men down to the street." He spoke as he walked down the hallway and walked into the kitchen. *Why hadn't I just let him kill me?*

He saw they had the mother, father, and daughter and someone else on their knees on the kitchen floor. They'd handcuffed them with plastic cuffs. The daughter looked at him first. She was terrified.

"Where's my brother?" she asked in Spanish.

The father looked up at him and gave him a strange look. He already had guessed that the son was dead and was giving Butch a look that he hadn't seen in a while. The father was dangerous now.

The father tried to stand up before Butch had a chance to decide what he was going to do with him. One of the Russians, standing over the father, hit him with the butt of his rifle and he fell down hard, out cold. He hit his head on the edge of the kitchen table. The wife started to shriek again and tried to get to her husband, even though her hands were tied behind her.

He decided right there and then to get the Russians out of there before it got any worse.

He called Alex's cell number. "It's a goat fuck," Butch said on the phone. "I need help over here. People who speak the language, for starters. You think you can do that? And I'll need a repairman too, as I've dinged the merchandise."

"All right," Alex said. "Do you have the package?"

"I don't know yet. It may not be here. And that party we wanted to talk to is going to be unavailable now."

• • •

Collin put down his bag. An embassy driver had taken him back to his apartment. He expected to find Dolores, but she was gone. When he saw her things still there, he wasn't worried. She'd probably gone out for a walk, or to buy something for their trip. She'd seemed excited about the trip.

He went to the kitchen, got a soda from the refrigerator, and dialed his father's office number on his cell phone. It was a number he'd been dialing all his life, one of the first phone numbers he'd ever learned: LO 6-4413.

The receptionist put him on hold. His father was seeing a patient, she said, but she would let him know he was on the line. As he waited to speak to his father, he felt like a child again. He felt guilty without wanting to. The guilt overtook him, an involuntary guilt for making his parents suffer because of what he'd decided to do with his life. Crazy, he thought.

"Collin?"

"Dad."

"What is it? Are you okay?"

"I'm fine."

"I've patients. Can I call you back later?"

"Yes, I understand. I'm sending you someone, a friend of mine. She's got a lump on her breast. I want you to have Jerry Bernstein take a look, as soon as she gets into town. Can you do that for me? She's put things off and needs to see him right away."

"Jerry's in Europe," his father said.

"Well then, someone else. Someone you'd send mom to," Collin said.

"Marvin Lee, then. I'll call him myself. What's your friend's name?"

"Helen Law. She should be able to see him day after to-morrow."

"The name is familiar. Okay, I'll take care of it. Tell her to call here."

"Dad . . . thanks."

"You got it. You sure you're okay?"

"I'm fine."

His father rang off. Almost immediately, his phone rang. It was Law.

"Thanks for coming again, old boy. I won't forget it," Alex said. "Listen, Butch has had an accident. He fell off his bicycle. Could you see him—*now?* The car is still out in front of your place. I know it's a lot to ask. You just got in . . . I can call someone else, if you like."

"No. No, I'll go," Collin said. He left a note for Dolores telling her he had come back but that he'd had to go out again.

• • •

"I'm afraid I can't be patient about this," Alex said.

They were sitting at the dining room table of a safe house, the same house they'd used for Madani. "I'm going to order some lunch. Would you like some?"

"No," Dolores said. "Where are we? And who are you? I want to see someone from the British embassy."

Alex smiled.

"Well, they don't want to see you, I can assure you. They'd rather not. You're a problem to them, you see. English terrorist?"

"I haven't done anything," Dolores said.

She looked across the big living room of the house. It was well-furnished. It was obviously the house of some very rich person—but whose, she wondered.

"You keep telling me that," Alex said. "I don't believe you."

"Are you going to tell me who you are?" she said, angry now.

183

"I told you, I'm Tom," he said.

"Can I see someone from the British embassy?" she asked again.

"No. Would you like some lunch?"

"God damn you," she said.

"Is that a yes, or a no?" Alex asked, but she didn't answer him this time. He got up and rang a bell. A steward came from the kitchen; Alex ordered two lunches and sat down again.

It was overcast, and the garden was dull-looking from the dining room; the surface of the pool flat, a few white clouds reflected in it.

"You're some kind of policeman," she said.

"It really doesn't matter who I am, dear girl, but rather who *you* are," Alex said. "That's what I want to know . . . *Fatima*."

"I don't have to talk to you," she said. The fact that he had her real name frightened her.

"You do if you don't want to go to Abu Ghraib . . . or worse," he said.

"For what?" She was trying to put on a brave face, as if she were honestly indignant.

"As a terrorist. As a member of *al Qaeda.*" He looked at her and put his hands down on the table. "Now, I want to find this bomb of yours. I realize that you may or may not know where it is. But I know that you could help lead me to it. That's what I want. If you help me do that—find it—then things might go very differently for you. And not just you," Alex said cryptically.

"What do you mean?"

"Your friend . . . the doctor, for starters. He's involved."

"I barely know him. Don't be ridiculous," she said.

"But you see, I've no way of knowing that, do I? I know you used his phone to call a number in the U.S. A number in a one-bedroom apartment in Chicago that was abandoned when the police went to check on it. Something tells me the name of the person renting it is going to turn out to be a fiction. They seem to have left in a hurry. I wonder why?

"Did they hear about your friend Madani? I think so. Did you warn them? Or was it someone else? Perhaps the doctor is part of this. I don't know him that well. I know he speaks Arabic. Perhaps he sympathizes. I find that odd, don't you? A Christian. Or is he just in love with you?"

"I don't know anything about a bomb, for God's sake!" she said.

"Did you call that number in Chicago?"

She wanted to answer him, but she was afraid to. She looked down at the garden. Everything seemed so orderly, but she felt that no one lived here and it frightened her. It was too orderly: no sign of real life, a cold, unlived-in quality to the place.

"I met someone on the bus from Veracruz. He gave me his phone number. I may have gotten it wrong. I did call it once . . . that number," she said.

"Do you have it now? What was it?"

"I lost it. I don't remember."

"And the man's name?"

"Steve something. An American."

"Spielberg, maybe? Or was it Smith? Come on, Fatima! You're no terrorist; you're an architect. You father was a successful barrister in London, until he died of cancer. Your father died two years ago from lung cancer, but he didn't smoke. Your mother has two other daughters. One lives in New Jersey, in fact. Why are you doing this? Some personal revenge? Your son's death? Do you think he'd want you to kill innocent Americans on his behalf? I seriously doubt that. From what I understand, Dr. Mohammad was a good man. No sane human being would want this. Certainly not a doctor. . . . He is a doctor, isn't he? Your husband? We're looking for him now, in Baghdad."

"Stop it!"

She looked at him a moment. The anger that she felt that

day seeing her husband's blackened body seemed to have lifted, until now. It came back. She'd loved her husband in a way no one could understand. But she realized then—sitting with this man—that it wasn't like the way she loved Collin. It had never been like that. A small part of her was ashamed to admit that her child's death had liberated her. She'd been in love with the idea of going to Baghdad, of being a wife and mother, but she hadn't really loved Mohammad.

She felt the tears stream down her face. How could she feel that way about a man who'd been so good to her? It made her sick. Was it *that* guilt, and not her son's death, that had made her decide to be a martyr? Guilt that she'd never really been in love with her husband?

"I suppose you're in love with this Collin fellow. You're young; he's handsome. You were alone in a strange country. He took care of you, I suppose."

She slapped him. His cheek turned red. She expected he would hit her back. She hoped he would. But he didn't.

"Well, I see I've hit a nerve. Guilt, I suppose. It was bound to happen," was all he said. Then his cell phone rang and he took the call, answering in monosyllables. His face was red from where she'd struck him.

• • •

"Who are these people?" Collin asked. He'd caught a glimpse of four hooded figures sitting on the floor of a small, tidy living room. Their heads had turned towards the sound of him coming through the broken doorway. A group of Mexican uniformed police stood at the entrance to the apartment building. One of them had taken him up to the apartment.

"Terrorists," Butch said. The doctor had him sitting on the toilet lid. He'd taken off Butch's shirt and was looking for any other wounds.

186

"A few stitches is all it needs," Butch said.

"It will be more than that," Collin said. "You're lucky. It missed the carotid artery by a few centimeters."

"Am I?" Butch said. He looked across the hallway. He could see the bottom of the kid's shoes in the other room.

"What's that mean?" Collin said.

"Just a question," Butch said. "Thanks for coming." It was the first time he'd said anything nice to him, and Collin was taken aback.

"Well, I didn't want you to think I didn't care," he said finally. "Anyway, that's my job, isn't it? Helping the needy?"

"I suppose so. Can you help me interview these people? I've no one to help. They sent me some dumb-ass Russians, and I had to send them back. I've been here alone. The father won't talk to me. There's no one at the embassy at all who can help. They want to send some SEALS from San Diego. I don't need muscle; I need someone who can speak fucking Arabic. I've got some Mexican policemen in there with them right now, but I'm afraid their language skills aren't too good."

"You've lost some blood. You should probably rest," Collin said.

"Right. When I'm dead, I'll rest a lot. Can you talk to the woman? She speaks Arabic. No Spanish at all. She's the wife."

"Is that her son in there on the floor?"

"Yes . . . I guess so."

"What happened?"

"We had a difference of opinion," Butch said. "These people may know where the bomb is. I've looked. I couldn't find anything."

"Do you know what you're looking for?" Collin said. He got out his kit with the suturing equipment.

"Not exactly."

"Do you have a Geiger counter?"

"No, I don't have a Geiger counter. I don't have a translator. I don't have a terrorist, and I don't have much time. The FBI is supposed to be sending a team that can help tell us what we're looking for. Personally, I'd rather have the *Queer Eye* guys than the FBI. They'd be more effective. Sorry—are you gay?"

The doctor looked at the wound. He ran a Q-tip over it harder than he might have. Butch winced, but didn't say anything.

"I don't understand," Collin said. He laid out his equipment on a towel he'd put on the floor of the bathroom.

"No one believes us. That's why we aren't getting any real help," Butch said.

"Why not? Law is the head of station."

"The first rule in the war on terror is cover your ass." One of the Mexican policemen, in plain clothes, came in to ask if they could send out for something to eat.

Butch said they could, and to get him something, too. His Spanish was pretty good.

It took twenty-five stitches to close his neck wound. Collin told him he was quitting the agency as soon as this was over. Nickels looked at him but didn't say anything. Collin supposed he couldn't have cared less.

They heard a horrific scream. One of the Mexican policemen was leading the girl to the bathroom, and she'd seen her brother's body.

"God damn it!" Butch said. He stood up and pushed the doctor out of the way. "God damn it! Get her back into the kitchen. Jesus!"

22

"At least have some tea," Alex said.

The steward put their lunches on the table. She pushed hers away immediately.

"Bring the young lady some tea. Something English, if you have it. Not that damn Mexican herb tea," Alex said. Then he tucked into his lunch. He was hungry.

He thought about his wife for a moment. He remembered her being even more beautiful than the young Arab woman sitting next to him. It didn't seem possible that his wife could be sick. She'd always been so strong physically. Stronger than he was . . . he looked up at the girl. *How long ago was that—that Helen had looked like that?* He wished for a moment he could go back in time to that first day he'd met her and just look at her.

Helen had pretended to ignore him. It had been at a friend's apartment in New York. He'd seen her from the top of the stairs. She was there visiting his friend's sister. It was summer, and he couldn't have been more than twenty-two.

"Do you remember Hansel and Gretel?" Alex said finally. The steward brought a pot of tea and a cup and left them alone again.

"I want to see the British Consul," Dolores said.

"They left bread crumbs. Do you remember the story?" Alex asked.

189

"*Yes.*"

"Why did you write your mother? I have her address. That's what led me back to you, really. I have your mother now in custody —well, the Brits have her."

"What do you mean?" Dolores said.

"I'd drink that before it gets too dark." Alex poured her a cup of tea. "She's part of this, isn't she? You were in communication with her. You are a bona fide member of *al Qaeda*. We can't let your mother run about loose, can we? I'm afraid your sisters will be next. They're standing by. The whole family will be arrested. Your older sister—Lillian—her children will have to go, too," Alex said. He buttered a piece of bread.

"What do you want?" Dolores said. She was holding the tea cup and looking at the cup as if he weren't there.

"I want the bloody bomb. Where is it?" Alex said. He put his butter knife down. It made a little sound on the china plate.

"I don't know," she said finally. "I never saw it."

"But you were going to see it, weren't you?"

"Yes. I don't know. I don't know what it was they wanted me to do. I just know I was going to die . . . I want my sisters and mother left alone. I want to talk to them on the phone. And leave the doctor out of it, too. He has nothing to do with it. I've only just met him," she said in a monotone.

"I'm afraid it isn't so easy, dear. What if I told you they will be released when I get the bomb?"

"How can I get it? Don't you understand! I don't know where it is, or who has it. Or where I was to take it. I don't know *anything* about it."

"You can go back to the Gobi and wait, can't you? They still expect you to take it, don't they? I would imagine so. There's no reason to expect they won't go forward with their little plan."

"You've arrested Madani and his wife. Why would they go back to the Gobi? Certainly, they must suspect the police are watching the hotel," she said.

"Because. Why shouldn't they? *Someone* has to take it . . . north.
Don't they? I'm betting they want it to be a woman, a very pretty
young woman, who will get people to help her all along the way,"
Alex said. "That's what I would do, if I were them."

"Then will you let my family go? And the doctor? If I help you?"

"Yes," Alex said.

She took a sip of tea. Her hand was shaking slightly.

"Why?" Alex said. He pushed his plate away.

"What do you mean?" she said.

"Why would you do this? Mass murder. Do you really hate us
that much? You were brought up a Christian. It isn't religious
with you."

"Yes," she said. She took another sip of tea. "Yes, I hate you
that much."

"I don't believe you," Alex said. "It's something else, isn't it?
You blame us for your son's death, I suppose."

• • •

"I was worried about you," Collin said. He let her pass him
and he closed the door. "I'm glad you're all right."

He'd been sitting in the dark. He'd noticed her suitcase was
lying out on the bed when he'd come in.

"Your hair is wet."

"Is it?" she said. He nodded. She touched it.

They'd let her off a few blocks away. It was better, they'd said,
that she walk the rest of the way.

"Can I ask you where you've been?"

"I'd rather you didn't," she said. "I was with a friend. Someone
I met here."

"I was worried. I didn't have a way of getting ahold of you,"
Collin said. "Do they know Madani?"

"No," she said.

"I thought it might have something to do with him. I don't care if it does. But the police know. Suspicious, anyway. I was going to warn you. You see, I don't believe you are a terrorist. Whatever it is you are . . . you aren't that," Collin said. "Are you?"

"Of course not," she said.

"I've got you a new passport," he said.

"I don't understand."

"I know someone . . . at the embassy. They arranged it. It was a favor. You won't have to worry about not having one now."

"Thank you," she said. She walked into the bedroom.

"It's on the desk," he said, following her.

She took her coat off and laid it on the bed, then went to the desk and picked up the passport Law had left for her.

"There's a plane ticket to Chicago, too—if you want it," Collin said.

She turned and looked at him. "Do you want me to leave?" she asked.

"No. Of course not," he said. "But I didn't want you riding the damned bus if you *did* leave."

"Thank you," she said. She found the passport and opened it.

"I want you to go to Baja with Alfredo and me this weekend. I promise you you'll love it. It's beautiful . . . the town."

She put the passport back on the desk. "I think I'm moving back to the hotel," she said.

He watched her go to the closet and start to take out her things.

"I don't understand," Collin said.

"Thank you for all you've done. But I think it's best." She didn't turn around.

"You don't have to," Collin said. He walked up to her and put his arm around her waist. She looked at the wall across from her. He'd tacked up the drawing of her lying on the bed. "I don't want you to go," he said quietly. "I'd like you to stay. I don't want you to go to the Gobi, or to Chicago, or anywhere, for that matter. I'm in love with you."

"I'm married," she said suddenly. "I wanted to tell you . . . I'm sorry. I shouldn't have let it go this far."

He let go of her. It was as if he'd been hit in the stomach. He didn't speak. He didn't know what to say.

"Well, you can't love him . . . or this wouldn't have happened," he said finally.

"No. I *do* love him. I'm sorry. I made a mistake. I'm going back home. Going back to Chicago. In a day or two," she said. She continued to pack her things. Her suitcase was still open where she'd left it when they'd come for her.

"I don't believe you," he said. She turned around. She was folding up a white sweater.

"It was just a holiday romance. Can't you understand? I didn't mean it to go this far. I'm going home to my husband. And that has to be the end of it; do you understand? I don't want to see you again," she said. She laid the sweater in the suitcase.

"All right." He felt foolish. He looked for his coat. He was going to say something—that he didn't believe her—but it was all sounding too ridiculous. Perhaps she'd just used him, he thought. He picked up his coat. *She was a very beautiful woman. It must happen all the time. All the time.*

He put his coat on and walked out onto the street. He'd never really been in love before. He'd been sexually infatuated, of course, but never in love. He thought that in a day or two it would go away, the pain he felt in the pit of his stomach.

He went down the sidewalk, not really looking up until he got to the bar on the corner. Then he went in and ordered a mescal. It was an awful place, but he didn't notice any of the pathetic loathsome types sitting in the shadows or at the bar near him. Instead, he saw only her holding the sweater and laying it in the suitcase. He relived it, again and again. He felt an utter fool for getting involved.

When she walked into the Gobi, she was surprised to see

Madani's wife at the desk. The old woman greeted her in Arabic. They looked at each other for a moment, each one unsure of what to say.

"Would you like the same room?" Madani's wife asked, deciding to avoid everything.

"I'm sorry," Dolores said. "About your husband."

"We had a life; it doesn't matter. We have children," was all she said. She handed her the key. "Are you going to be here long?" she asked.

"A few days, perhaps. Do you want me to pay?" Dolores said.

"It's paid already," the wife said. "They've paid everything. Meals, everything." Dolores was going to ask who had paid, but didn't.

• • •

"Leave the girl," Butch said.

"But I thought. . . ."

"I said, leave the girl," Butch said. The Mexican from their intelligence service nodded. "You can take her parents," Butch said, "but leave the girl."

Nickels was sitting in the kitchen. Dirty plates from their fast food lay on the counter and on the table. The mother and father spoke to their daughter in Arabic. The daughter, frightened, answered her parents in Spanish. Butch went to the kitchen door and watched the parents and the boyfriend led away. He waited, drinking coffee until that was over and it was quiet in the living room.

It was almost six when he walked into the room. His neck hurt, but he didn't care. He'd gotten used to all kinds of pain in his life, and something about this pain was reassuring. This pain fit, and he was glad for it. *Why hadn't I just let the kid kill me?* He'd been asking himself that question all afternoon and didn't have an answer.

Training? Or was it something else—hope? He was 60 years old. Why hadn't he just let the kid kill him? He was heading for that empty apartment in Virginia, and frighteningly empty days with no one to talk to. Long walks where he would remember his days of derring-do. Park benches? A dog, perhaps.

No, he didn't think so. It would never get to that point. He would never see the inside of that horrible place.

The daughter was sitting on the couch with the hood over her head. She heard him coming and he saw her draw herself up, terrified and probably exhausted. He reached over and pulled the hood off of her head.

"Mi nombre es Tom," he said. He asked her name in Spanish.

"Sofia," she said. She looked around the living room. Then she asked him where her parents had been taken.

"Jail," he said.

"Why?" she said. "Why?"

He looked at her, then. She was just a kid. She wore the ubiquitous uniform of Catholic school girls in the city: pleated skirt and white shirt, her hair in pigtails. She was maybe 16, he guessed. He'd always wanted a daughter. It was never going to happen, now.

"Where is it?" he asked.

"Where is what?"

"The bomb," he said. "Please tell me. I can help you if you tell me where it is. Everything will be all right if you tell me that. Or just show me where it is."

"You killed my brother," she said.

"He tried to shoot me . . . it wasn't my fault." He was surprised he answered her that way, defensively. He sat down next to her. He could see the smashed door jamb in the hallway from where he sat.

"Who are you? What do you want?" she said.

"I'm Tom," he said. "How old are you?"

195

"Sixteen."

"That's a good age." She just stared at him, terrified. "Sixteen. You have to tell me where it is."

"I don't know what you're talking about," she said.

"Your brother. Did he bring something home? Turn around." He dug into his pocket and got a short-bladed policeman's knife. He touched her shoulder. "I'm going to take off the handcuffs. *Las esposas,*" he said.

She shifted on the couch and he cut off the plastic cuffs. Her wrists were red where they'd cut into her flesh.

"Do you want something to drink? You can't run, do you understand that? I would have to shoot you. I don't want to do that. Do you understand me? I want you to answer me," Butch said. He knew he couldn't shoot her. It was the first time he'd had that thought in almost forty years. Always before, something had been in front of all that. Duty, whatever—a horrible misguided loyalty, perhaps. He'd been able to do things that he knew now, since the moment he saw her sitting there with a hood over her head, he couldn't do anymore.

He sliced easily through the plastic handcuffs, the blade razor sharp. He'd sharpened it himself with a small whetstone he'd carried since Viet Nam. He enjoyed that, sitting at a kitchen table wherever he happened to be in the world and sharpening it in a circular motion, listening to the rasping sound the blade made. He'd done it all his adult life.

He felt suddenly different about everything. He was sure he'd never see that apartment in Virginia, and he was happy.

"Get out," Butch said. "Go on. Get out," he said in Spanish. She stood up, confused.

"What about my father and mother?"

"Get out," he said. "Go on before I change my mind. Don't come back here, whatever you do. Do you understand me?" He said that in English. She looked at him a moment, then left.

23

Collin knocked on the hotel door.

He'd known from the moment he'd left the bar that he was probably doing the wrong thing. She would be angry with him for following her, but he didn't care. He had to see her again. He couldn't end it the way she had. He didn't even have a phone number for her in the States. He was sure, too, that the husband—if he existed at all—was someone she didn't love. He was sure of that.

He tapped on the door a second time, frightened by what she might think of him for coming here. A Latin man opened the door, surprising him.

Dolores was standing across the room. She looked at him, obviously frightened. It was written on her face. He noticed her suitcase on the bed, unopened.

"I'm terribly sorry. I'm here. . .." Collin said.

The man slammed the door closed. Collin had caught a glimpse of another, much younger man, standing near the bathroom before the door was shut in his face.

For a few seconds he stood at the door, his heart racing. *They could be police. They had to be watching the hotel. Nothing to fear if they were the police.* And if they weren't? He couldn't just leave.

He raised his hand and knocked again. In a moment, the door opened. The older man looked at him angrily. He wore a cheap black leather jacket, and his hair was greasy and combed straight back. His face was pockmarked. He looked like a criminal.

"I'm sorry; I'm from the embassy. Doctor. I'm looking for a Ms. Dolores Rios. Is that her?" he said officiously.

"Policía," the man at the door said. He began to shut the door in Collin's face again. Collin stepped into the open door, putting his weight against it this time.

"I'm sorry . . . they said it was an emergency. *Emergencia.* . . . Are you all right?" Collin said, looking at Dolores, then at the younger man standing near her. The younger man was holding a gun. "My name's Reeves. Dr. Reeves. May I come in? I was sent by the American Embassy. You can call Ms. Jones, if you would like to check . . . I have the embassy's number." He felt the door against his shoulder as the older one tried to close it on him again.

"I did call for a doctor," Dolores said. She turned and looked at the younger man. He was very slight, in his twenties. Collin felt the pressure release on the door. He took the opportunity and walked by the older one.

"Probably just dysentery," Collin said.

"I'm afraid you'll have to come back," the one by the door said in English. "She's fine. Look at her."

"I've been ill," Dolores said. She looked at Collin but didn't move. "Apparently, I'm under arrest and have to go with these men," she said to him.

"I see. I'll call the embassy, then . . . arrest? What's the charge?" Collin said, looking at the younger one.

The younger one's hair was cut short. He wore a gold crucifix around his neck, above a sweat shirt with a big Nike swish on the front.

"Drugs," the young one said in Spanish. "She'll have a chance to call the embassy as soon as she is down at the station."

"May I see your IDs, please? I'd like to note them. I will have to make a complete report, of course. I was asked to come and see an American citizen with a medical problem, after all. I'm sure you understand," Collin said. He forced a quick smile, the Spanish coming out without his having to think about it.

"Get out, *amigo*," the one by the door said in English. He opened the door wider. Collin didn't move.

"I see. Well, I will. . . ."

"Get out, unless you want to go with her," the older one said. Nike moved towards him. He was whippet-thin. He raised his pistol and pointed it at him, which shocked him. No one had ever pointed a gun at him before. He was stunned.

"Fura pendejo!" Nike said. He came at him and pushed him physically out into the hallway, then threw him to the floor by his coat as if Collin were a child. Collin landed on his medical bag.

The young one stepped on his face with his shoe and looked down at him, holding the pistol against his forehead. He felt a terrible pain in his jaw as the man shifted his weight onto that foot.

"Go," he said in English.

Collin couldn't answer; the pain was horrible. It felt as if the man were standing on his face. He had to close his eyes. Then Nike stepped away. Collin thought he was finished, but he kicked him once, very hard, in the solar plexus. Collin tried to get up but Nike kicked him again, and he collapsed. Suddenly the man stopped kicking him, walked back into the room, and slammed the door closed without even bothering to turn and look back at him.

Collin lay on the floor, gripping his medical bag and coughing. He tried to get up but couldn't, the pain from the kicks too intense and paralyzing.

As the pain receded, he managed to get to his knees. He opened his medical bag and took a scalpel out of its plastic case. The blade was only two millimeters long, but razor sharp. He stood up and went back to the door. He thought for a moment, then moved to the side and knocked.

He heard a gunshot. He pulled back further away from the doorway. The sound of another gunshot filled the hallway. The bullets fired at him had chinked the door and hallway wall across from him.

The door opened, and the thin one stepped out. Collin planted the short blade at the base of Nike's throat, where he knew he'd hit the main artery, and dragged it quickly towards him. The throat muscles and artery cut open. There was an immediate and dramatic loss of blood pressure, and the man sagged to his knees like a doll before he could fire his gun.

Collin tore the pistol out of Nike's jerking hand. The man's dying face turned towards him, horrified, a rain of blood pouring from below his chin. His eyes were already half-dead. He tried to speak to his friend, but it was impossible; only his lips moved.

Collin turned and leaned into the open doorway. He could see Dolores. He fired at the older man, who was drawing his gun. He hit him in the right shoulder and saw him fall back. He stepped back out into the hall and leaned against the wall, well away from the door. He hadn't killed him. He was sure of that.

"*Ay, mierda!. . . Felix?*" On the floor now, the older one called his partner from inside the room. "Felix? *Que te pasa? . . . Puta.*"

The older one was wounded. Collin could hear it in his voice. He crawled over to his bag and took out the alcohol he kept for sterilizing. He tossed it on Nike's still-jerking body in the doorway, then struck the lighter he kept in his medical bag and tossed it onto Nike's jacket. The man's jacket burst into flames, then his hair.

"*Felix? Puta! Madre!*" Collin heard the older one fire, and saw the pockmarks chink the plaster in the hallway above him. The flames from Nike's coat were crawling over his head and growing.

Collin hadn't a clue what to do now. He heard someone scream and looked down the hallway. A mother and her young son were standing in the hall in their nightclothes. Collin motioned them inside with the pistol, and the mother grabbed her boy and pulled him back inside their room.

He took the bottle of alcohol and doused the body again. The flames leapt to the door jamb.

He looked at the pistol. The hammer was back, ready to fire. He'd been a terrible shot in training.

He rolled in front of the burning body. As he did, he saw the wounded man's shoes under the bed. The older one had crawled to the bed and was propped up on it. Half-lying on the bed, he was facing the door, his upper torso protected by the bed, his feet behind him on the floor.

Collin fired at the man's feet and ankles. He saw the bullets strike the man's left foot and heard him scream. He rolled off the bed trying to get out of the line of fire.

Collin crawled over the burning body and heard gunfire. The older one was firing wildly, but hitting the bed, screaming in pain from the wound in his foot. Collin could hear the shots hitting the mattress, making a bizarre smacking-thud sound.

Dolores, pressed against the wall by the window, ran past him. She stumbled over Nike's burning body, knocking it forward, and fell into the hallway.

Collin heard the policeman's gun go empty. He knew how painful injuries to the foot were, and he was counting on that pain to stop the man from standing and reloading.

Dolores lay in the hall, sobbing. Still crouched on his knees, Collin backed out of the door, crawled to Dolores and pulled her out from in front of the doorway, rolling with her. He tried to keep his gun pointed at the room's burning doorway, afraid the wounded man would somehow manage to come out and kill them.

Collin heard him calling again for his partner. He could tell he was in a lot of pain. He thought of all the nerves in the feet and how they'd been damaged, his doctor's brain still working despite the adrenalin.

• • •

The staircase was cold. The plainclothes policeman waved him through the lobby. He'd been told that an important *gringo* was coming, and to let him pass.

Alex went up the stairs alone. He had no idea how he was going to do this without Butch, if he was seriously hurt. All the people he'd started out with in the Company were either dead or retired. He and Butch were the last ones working who'd graduated from The Farm together. It made him feel old.

He heard the sound of his shoes on the concrete. It was late. People were asleep, and it was quiet enough to hear his own footsteps. He heard a baby crying somewhere—in the next building, perhaps.

At the third floor the door was open in front of him, obviously forced. The lights in the apartment blazed, everything on. He walked in.

Butch was sitting on a couch in the living room. He looked pale, his suit coat bloody.

"Are you all right?"

"Yes."

"There was a daughter, wasn't there?" Alex said. He looked down the hallway, thinking he might see her. "Why didn't you send her, too?"

"Those Russians almost got me killed. They don't even know how to clear a room," Butch said, ignoring his question. He was holding a brandy bottle, a small pint bottle. He offered Alex a sip, but Alex shook his head.

"What about the girl?" Alex said.

"She overpowered me. Very strong girl," Butch said.

"Somehow I don't think so," Alex said.

"No. Very, very strong. I didn't have a chance."

"Look, *amigo*. It's late. I'm very tired. I don't want to play this game right now," Alex said. "We have to figure out something we can tell them, whatever happened. Did you let her go?"

"I let her go," Butch said. "Let her walk." He took a drink. He'd bought a pint bottle of brandy, and it was half gone. "I always wanted a daughter. Like yours.. . . There are a lot of things of yours I've wanted."

Butch was drunk. Alex recognized it, and was a little surprised. Butch had always been the sober one, the one who looked after *him* for all these years.

"You can go ahead and report it. I don't really give a shit," Butch said. "Maybe they'll put me in jail. That would be funny, after everything I've done. I mean, for letting someone live. You know what those guys would have done to a young girl."

"What's wrong?" Alex said. He sat down across from him. He felt a hundred years old. He would have had a drink, but he'd promised Helen when he dropped her off at the airport—swore, in fact—that he wouldn't touch anything.

"Everything and nothing. I'm sixty years old, for starters. That's fucked up," Butch said.

Alex looked around the room.

"I asked you what was wrong, Butch. Why did you do it?"

"I just felt like letting her go. She was my daughter for a moment. You know what I mean . . . I had the power to protect her, and I did. She didn't know shit about it. The bomb. And if she did, she can't do anything about it, because she wouldn't know who to contact. Remember? That's the cell system. Like ours. Ours is two-man. One of us dies, the other would be left with a lot of fucking secrets, right? Like Olepango airport. Or certain body bags in Laos."

"You shouldn't have done that—let her go."

"Fuck, Alex, there's a lot of things I shouldn't have done. But I did them anyway," Butch said.

"How's the neck?"

"How's it look? The little fucker nearly killed me."

"Reeves has taken the girl somewhere."

"Well, that's fucked up," Butch said.

"We lost them in traffic. They haven't come back to his apartment. She was supposed to go back to the Gobi and wait. That was our deal," Alex said. "Killed a Mexican policeman and seriously wounded another. They'd come to arrest her. Some kind of screw-up. I shouldn't have gotten Hussein's thugs involved, I suppose."

"Well, shit happens, doesn't it," Butch said. "You were doing your best."

"I've no idea about how to explain this girl you let go. She's in the cable that went off."

"You'll figure it out. You always do, *amigo*. Do you ever worry about the future, Alex?"

"What do you mean? Give me that. I need a drink." He stood up and took a pull from the brandy bottle. He was sorry he'd lied to his wife, but he needed a fucking drink.

"When this is over. When they don't need you anymore," Butch said.

"No, I don't think about it," Alex said.

"What are you going to do?"

"I don't know. Take up something. A hobby, I suppose. Golf."

"That's what I'm afraid of. I don't know. I don't have what you have. Money. A wife and family. I don't got shit. How do you think that makes me feel?" Butch said.

"You know you don't have to worry about money. I've told you that."

"What's it like to have so much, Alex? You've never told me. I've known you how long?"

"A long time," Alex said.

"What's it like?"

"It never mattered to me."

"Is that why you drank?" Butch asked.

"Maybe. I felt like I'd been pushed into this. That my father pushed me into it, and it wasn't what I should have done with my life," Alex said. He took another drink and passed it back. "That's why I drink. I wanted to do something else with my life, but I was too frightened of my father."

"That's it?"

"Yes. More or less."

"That's fucked up. You could have quit. But you didn't."

"No. I didn't," Alex said.

"And now it's too late," Butch said.

"That's right, and now it's too late. You're still bleeding." Alex pointed to his neck. "Just a little."

"What are we going to do about the doctor?" Butch said.

"Find him. . . . Come on." He helped his friend up. "You're getting fat," Alex said.

"She's left me . . . Kwana. The girl," Butch said, looking at him. "I was counting on her not to do that, goddammit." Alex helped him out of the apartment, not bothering to close the door.

24

*L*ike Sargent's "Stairs At Capri," Collin thought, looking at her. She was sitting halfway up the narrow lye-white stairway that went up, from the *pensión's* patio, to their room. He wondered what she was thinking. He always had the sense that she wasn't with him completely.

He was painting a wisteria that grew over a heavy wood trellis along the patio. It was very old and thick, its flowers starting to bud. She'd been quiet since they'd arrived at San Javier. He'd bought her some books at the airport, and she'd brought one out to the patio, but she wasn't reading.

Twice his cell phone had rung and he'd glanced at the screen. It was the embassy calling both times, but he hadn't picked up. He didn't want to think about the embassy, or his life up to this point. He felt for the first time that he had the strength to run away from *everything*.

He paused for a moment and thought about how to render the darkest part of the wisteria, where the bark showed and the wood had turned the color of sand. It was hard to get right, the flowers so soft and ephemeral and the stems fine and completely delicate, the opposite of the woody root.

Where could they go? he wondered. Did she even *really* love him? Would she be worth what she was going to cost him? He decided on the color for the buds and began to mix on his paint box's lid. The colors slid on the white plastic as he sought the color he was after.

"I don't have a swimsuit," Dolores said suddenly, watching him work.

They hadn't talked about what'd happened at the Gobi. He'd taken her back to his place, thrown some things in his suitcase, and they'd taken his car to the airport. Afraid the police might follow him, he'd done everything he could to lose them, driving through a series of red lights. Terrified, she hadn't even asked him where they were going. He told her finally at the airport that they were going to Baja because he thought it would be safe. He doubted it really was, now. Perhaps for a few days, at the most. He'd thought about it a great deal and realized he probably couldn't make it safe for her anywhere in the world.

He put his brush down and turned towards her.

"There's a kind of *bodega*. They may have women's things. Swimsuits," He said.

"The pool is beautiful. It makes me want to swim," she said. "I haven't been swimming in ages."

"We can go take a look if you like," he said. "I can leave my easel set up. No one will care. I think we're the only ones staying here right now, anyway."

He walked to the stairs and looked up at her. She looked so much younger than she'd looked in the city. The sunlight was intense on the stairs, but not too warm, yet.

He felt as if he were seeing her for the first time. Her hair down, she was wearing just jeans and a t-shirt, and was barefoot. He walked up the stairs and sat just below her. His phone rang again; he turned towards it.

"You killed a policeman," she said.

He let it ring. "Yes," he said.

He was facing his easel. The swimming pool reflected the clean blue sky. He looked up toward the mountains above the *pensión's* roof.

"What are you going to do?" she said.

"I haven't a clue," he said. The stairs, like the famous ones in the Sargent painting, were narrow and shaded at the top.

"Thank you," she said, "for what you did." She touched the back of his neck. She put her fingers in his hair.

"Are you going to tell me the truth . . . *are* you married?" he asked.

"Yes," she said. "I'm married."

"Are you in love with him, then? Your husband?"

"I don't know. I don't think so." He turned towards her.

"Do you care for me at all?" He got closer, going up the stairs, and looked into her eyes. The green in them was vivid in the bright sunlight. It was her eyes that he'd noticed first when they'd met.

"Yes. Of course," she said. "Very much."

"Then you have to leave him," he said.

A maid came out from the building below, carrying a stack of towels in her hand, and laid them on a table. She glanced up at them on the stairs, said "Good morning," and left.

"It's beautiful here," Dolores said. "You have to leave me. Leave me here. You should go back to the city. Before you get into any more trouble."

"No, I won't. I won't leave you," he said.

"You have to."

"No, I won't. Why did the police come to your hotel? I don't believe it was about drugs . . . or *was* it? Is that what this is about?"

"No. Of course not," she said.

"Was it about Madani, then?"

"I don't know. Perhaps," she said.

"Sometimes the police in the city are just criminals themselves," he said. "It could have been because you're pretty. They could have simply seen you on the street and followed you to the hotel. It happens all the time to young women here."

"Will you take me to buy a bathing suit, then?" she said.

"Yes, of course."

His phone rang again. He'd left it on the chair where he'd been painting. While it rang, she debated telling him everything, everything that had happened to her since the moment her son was killed, or even before.

Starting with the day Mohammad had come to her house the first time, a complete stranger to her. He'd seemed so dignified and serious. Her father was trying to get his papers in order so he could stay in London for another year. She wanted now to tell someone at last—how she'd been infatuated, about not only the handsome doctor but the idea of Iraq, of going back to what she remembered as a child, Baghdad's tidy quiet streets that lay silently in her memories of childhood.

Her English boyfriend, a clerk in the foreign office, had told her it was over when she'd told him she was pregnant. It had seemed so cruel and unexpected. She'd come through the door very vulnerable that evening, wondering what she was going to do about the baby, feeling dirty for having given herself to the Englishman—at the Green Park Hotel, on sheets that smelled of cigarettes and other women's perfume, and in car parks, because he still lived at home.

Mohammad had smiled at her that evening in a very kind way. His smile made her feel clean again.

He had wanted to stay in London. It had been her idea to go back to Iraq, because she thought they could help make things better. She'd been a fool, and yet he'd agreed to go back.

"*Ana behibak,*" she said. Collin was standing up. It slipped out without her being able to stop it, the Arabic words for "I love you." She slid her arms around Collin's waist and held him. She pressed her face against his chest.

"Are you a terrorist, Dolores? Is that what this is all about?" She didn't answer. "Are you a terrorist? Answer me." He was holding her now tightly, afraid she was going to say yes.

"They think I am," she said, finally.

"Who?"

"The police," she said, holding him.

"Is it three's a crowd?" a man's voice said.

Collin turned around. He saw Alfredo smiling at them.

"*Alfredo*," Collin said. "I was going to call. I'm sorry. I. . . ."

"I don't believe you, not for a moment; but I forgive you. I'd want to be alone with her, too," Alfredo said. He smiled. He had his painting things and looked like he was going out.

"Shall we have lunch later?" Alfredo said.

"Yes. Yes, of course," Collin said.

"Two o'clock? We've just come on the plane, Marita and I and another man. He says he's a painter, too. So it's all artists here," Alfredo said.

"Good," Collin said. "Two o'clock."

Marita walked out onto the patio then behind Alfredo. Dolores recognized her at once and was jealous. Marita was prettier than Dolores had imagined her.

She was going to tell him everything, then: how she hadn't come alone to Mexico, how it all was, how they didn't understand any of it, the man named Tom.

But then she didn't. She found herself again. The thing that had pushed her all this way, the hatred that she'd wanted to lose and never feel again, came back. Even her feelings for the doctor seemed small next to it.

"The pilot said there's going to be a bad storm. So we're stuck for a few days," Alfredo said.

"Yes, I know," Collin said.

"Lunch, then," Alfredo said. Marita waved, but didn't say anything.

"Yes," Collin said.

They walked to the *bodega* in silence. It seemed absurd, given everything that had happened, but she felt jealous in a way she'd never been before.

210

The *bodega* was a dark adobe building with few lights. The wood floor made a sound as they walked to the back. The old woman who ran it said that there were a few bathing suits, but they had to find them. She had no clue where they were.

Everything was on big tables: blankets, gas cans, packages of food stacked next to axe handles. They walked down the center aisle at a loss.

"Is that her? The girl in the painting?" Dolores finally asked.

"Yes," he said.

They'd stopped at one of the tables. He saw men's overalls and Ben Davis shirts, but no women's things at all.

"She's pretty," she said. She looked up and saw a tent hanging from the wall. It seemed odd.

"Yes," he said.

"Do you just have sex with people and then forget them . . . move on?"

He didn't know what to say. He hadn't expected her to be jealous. It was the last thing he'd expected. He moved to another table, further in the back, and found some women's things and called to her. A little girl, maybe four or five, was playing jacks on the floor under the table. She stopped for a moment and looked up at them.

• • •

"And your friend?" Marita said.

They were having lunch at the outdoor tables with the best view of the date palms. The dates had been picked, the flowers gone. Because the town had so few cars or traffic, they could hear all the desert sounds, the sounds of nature as well as the voices of the cook and the waiter in the kitchen.

"We've had a tiff," Collin said. The fact was, they hadn't spoken since they'd gotten back from the *bodega*—except that Dolores had asked him to leave for his own good again, and then she'd begged off lunch.

"Well . . . women, what can you say? They're the biggest, most beautiful problem in the world," Alfredo said. He picked up a piece of melon and cheese and put it on his plate.

"How have you been?" Collin said, looking at Marita. They each both felt guilty for not having called the other, but both had understood that their affair was just that. Something that happened, fun and good, but not meant to last.

"I have a painting of you," Marita said.

"I'm terribly jealous," Alfredo said. "It's a great painting, and I didn't paint it. It makes me mad. She's got you in the buff, old boy. You're lucky I'm not a homosexual. I tried it in grade school but didn't like it. Who wants to kiss someone with a mustache—*really?*"

"You remember I did a sketch of you, by the door in my studio."

"Yes," Collin said. "It was just that—a sketch—when I saw it. Very small."

"Not now, *amigo*. You're seven feet tall and *very* white," Alfredo said.

"I've titled it 'The Good Physician'," Marita said. She smiled. "You know—Science is Mankind's brother and all that . . . the Enlightenment. How can we go backwards?"

"You mean sacking Darwin?" Collin said.

"Exactly. That, too," she said. "How dare they?"

"You mean, *before* the Americans went crazy and elected that asshole," Alfredo said. They all laughed. "He's a complete Torquemada."

"I'm going back to Germany," Marita said. "Soon."

"I told her it was a bad idea," Alfredo said. "Maybe you can convince her, Collin. She won't like it anymore."

"I'm a *German*," she said. "It's my home."

"Yes, yes. But you've been infected by all *this*," Alfredo said. "The freedom of Mexico." He held up his hands. "What is so important back there?" Alfredo asked.

Collin wondered if Alfredo was in fact in love with her. It surprised him. He assumed Alfredo was in love with himself, not in an ugly way, but in a way that some artists are in love with themselves. The way Gauguin was in love with himself, Collin thought.

"I'm painting the stairs at Capri," Collin said. "Well, my version of it, anyway. I've added a wisteria, though."

"He's a modernist," Alfredo said.

"I was wrong about you. I said you weren't one of us," Marita said. "I was wrong. Would you give me a painting before I leave?"

"Of course," Collin said. He was truly flattered.

"That does it. She doesn't give a shit about my work," Alfredo said. "Not one shit, and she apparently *loves* yours."

They heard a chair dragged across the floor behind them. Collin turned casually to see who it was. He saw a tall man in his early forties, a Greek or perhaps a Latin, with a horribly scarred face. The man's right hand was missing and he had used a prosthetic metal one, slightly old-fashioned looking, to pull his chair back. He had the chair gripped in his metal claw. He nodded a hello to them.

Collin noticed that one eye was gone, replaced by a glass one. The man looked at him with his one good eye for a moment. He thought it a strange look, as if they might know each other.

Alfredo stood up and introduced them. They'd met the man on the plane. His name, Alfredo said, was Byron Petros.

Collin stood up as they were introduced. There was an awkward moment as the man held out his metal claw for Collin to shake.

He noticed Dolores, then. She'd come up the stairs to the restaurant and was staring at them.

213

25

Collin had gone to paint at the church with his friends. Dolores had told him she'd rather read by the pool.

She'd gone to the desk, rung and asked for Petros' room number. The owner of the *pensión*, part Chinese, had been smitten with her the moment she and Collin had checked in. He immediately gave her the man's room number.

"Is Mr. Petros a friend of yours?" the man asked in English, looking at her in that way that men did. She didn't bother to answer him, but walked out of the office and into the corridor. The corridors were painted green. The hotel in Cyprus where she and Mohammad had gone for their honeymoon had had similar corridors.

It had been an awkward honeymoon. She'd been experienced sexually, and he hadn't been with many women. He seemed sorry that he couldn't please her. He'd understood that much about her. It was really in Cyprus that they'd gotten to know each other. It was there that she realized that she could never really love him that way, the way she'd expected to be able to. It just wouldn't happen. She knew that instinctively after they'd made love. She'd kept waiting for it to happen, but it hadn't. It was like a long-anticipated vacation that had turned out to be ordinary.

But he was a good man, and he did love her. She felt a very modern bitch, raised on women's magazines and television shows

214

and Oprah confessions. He seemed to belong to a different world, where sex and its rapture had been banished. His lovemaking had been clean and neat and somehow a sideshow to life. She'd simply wanted to have an orgasm. It all seemed silly now, given what had happened. She walked down the corridor. It was open to the desert. It seemed very fitting, the desertscape.

She'd sat in the window of the room after Collin had gone up to lunch and looked out at the view, trying to decide how much her hate would control her. She sought a kind of message from nature. Hadn't nature sinned against her and her husband? Didn't *it* owe her an explanation for how it could murder her child? How could the world, and people, *be* this way? There had to be a reason.

She'd scanned the barrel cactus like a woman searching for some sign, some message that could make her believe in anything but revenge. She wondered if she herself, and her hate—that physical thing that had been left after her son's murder—wasn't in fact the natural way of things. Wasn't a mother to hate her child's murderer? Didn't nature give her that hate? Wasn't it natural? As natural as the hawk she'd seen with the serpent in its claws, on the way here from the plane. The bird had picked up the serpent as she'd watched, swooping in from a cactus top. She'd wondered why it dove the way it had, but then in a moment, as it made its way back to the cactus top, she'd seen it: the snake trapped in the hawk's talons. That perhaps was nature's message to her.

"Who is it?"

"It's me . . . Fatima," she said through the door.

It had started to rain. The heat pushed out from the desert, and a breeze blew against her back as she waited for the door to open. She could smell the rain.

"Fatima?"

"Yes."

Her husband pulled the door open. He looked out to make sure she was alone. Then he stepped back and she entered the room.

It was dark. He'd been lying down on the couch. She could see a book on the pillow. It seemed such an innocent thing, so normal, just a man reading a book in the afternoon. The door closed behind her, and then she was standing in the penumbra. She went immediately to the couch and turned on the light.

"I told you not to come here. It's dangerous," she said.

She hadn't turned around yet. She was afraid to. She was afraid to face her husband; their connection was so strong now that she wouldn't probably be able to break it again. Their son, and their hate, held them together like lovers.

"I was afraid you weren't . . . I was afraid that you weren't going to come back," he said.

She turned around. It was still hard to look at his face and his hand. He'd been holding their son's hand when the rocket went off. He'd been maimed, but had survived.

"I heard you were sick," he said.

"Yes. After we got to the city."

"Why didn't you call me?"

"I was told not to," she said, "and I was afraid, too. I don't want you to be caught because of me."

"I've missed you terribly," he said. "I don't know why we couldn't have waited together."

"You know why," she said. "In case one of us is caught, the other can go on."

"Yes. I suppose so," he said.

"We are dead already," she said.

"Don't talk that way," he said.

"We are. What difference does it make? Any of it. Whether we get sick or not. Whether we see each other or not."

"Why are you here?" Petros said.

He came across the room and put his metal hand on her shoulder. She touched it. That was part of her hatred. He'd been a surgeon, and they'd taken that away from him, too. No amount of wailing and crying and hitting walls, all of which she'd done, would bring back her son or her husband's hand, or any of it. It had all been spoilt in an instant—in one long horrible moment, when she'd seen through the window of the shop, as she picked up her silly bottle of wine, her husband and their son being lifted in a horrible way, her son's body hurtling out into the street as if she were watching it all in some monstrous movie-nightmare.

The darkness came then, a strange darkness, as the blast lifted dust from the street, clouding the sky; behind that, the flashes of fire as the cars in the street burst into flames, their occupants becoming death-candles. The concussion had blown out the shop's front window; incredibly, she'd been untouched but mercifully knocked unconscious so that she wasn't there to see her son when they found his broken body.

The women had shrieked when he was picked up because they were mothers and their shriek belonged to all mothers everywhere. And everyone knew and understood the meaning of that sound. It meant the world had gone mad again. Everyone talking about their God. But their Gods were mad, she thought now, turning and looking at her husband.

"I had to leave the city. The police . . . they came to the Gobi. They were going to arrest me."

"The American. He brought you?"

"Yes. He saved me. He had to kill one of the policemen."

"You can't stay in the same room with him."

"Why?"

"Because—because—it's wrong."

"We're dead, remember? No one will care if it's wrong or right."

"I care."

"Why?"

"You're my wife," he said. He sat down on the couch and put his metal hand on his lap. "Are you . . . are you sleeping with him?"

217

"Yes," she said. "But I'm dead. Your wife is dead. I'm someone else now. Dolores, they call me."

"Who?"

"I don't know. Just a woman. She's inside the other woman who has to die. That's all I know," she said.

She'd called him from the airport, to warn him, but asked him to let her go—not to follow her. He'd asked where she was going and she told him, believing he wouldn't follow her.

"Fatima, I love you. Please come back to the city with me."

"No. I'll come back, but not right away. I've got to get him to leave me. I'll meet you at your hotel in a day or two, at the most. We can wait there together."

She sat down next to him. The room seemed cold. They sat in silence. She could hear the rain hitting the roof. It was a beautiful sound. He took her hand in his good one. *They were dead,* he thought. She was right. They would go to heaven now, and all the hours since that moment when he'd been lifted by the force of the explosion were compressed into one moment. *Dead,* he thought, *dead.*

He started to weep, and she let him. She'd cried all the tears she would ever cry. She had no tears left. There had come a moment when she couldn't cry any more and all she was left with was hate. Just hate, and that was all.

"Do you know where they are sending us?" she asked finally.

"No," he said. "What difference does it make?"

"None," she said. "None."

"Do you love this man?"

"Yes. Yes, very much. I love him."

"I'm glad for you," he said.

"Thank you," she said. "Thank you. I'll meet you at your hotel. I promise. Wait there, Mohammad."

She got up to leave, but turned for a moment and looked at him. "Do you know, I don't believe in heaven," she said. "I don't believe in anything. But I hope you believe in it. Do you? Do you truly believe? I want to know."

"Yes," he said. "I do."

"Good," she said. "Good. I'm happy for you, then."

• • •

"They're always smarter than we think," Alex said "That's our problem with Mr. bin Laden. Everyone thinks he's not quite right in the head. But he is, you see. He's not mad at all. Well—he's mad, but you know what I mean. He's a very clever little boy."

"How's Helen?" Butch said. He was looking at the paintings on the wall as he spoke. He liked the one of a girl sitting by a pool.

"She's coming home in few days," Alex said.

"Early, isn't it?"

"Well, no. They've done the deed," Alex said.

"The deed?"

"Double mastectomy. Necessary, the hacks say. Things were in a bad way. Did it the day after she got there."

Butch didn't answer him. The last he'd heard, she was fine.

They'd gone to the doctor's digs to see if they might get some kind of clue of where the hell he'd gone.

"I'm sorry," Butch said.

"Yes, well. Everyone is. My daughter is calling me every few hours, too."

"It was for the best. I mean, otherwise. I mean.. . ."

"Yes. Can we change the subject, old boy? I'd rather not talk about it," Alex said.

"Okay. I'd like to call her. I want to say hello," Butch said. "Wish her well."

"She'd like that, of course. I'll give you the number," Alex said. "My dad is with her. She likes him. I think that's good—that he was there, if I couldn't be. But then I've always been busy, haven't I?

219

"So where is our doctor, Butchie? Huh?" Alex went and stood by the closet. "He's taken his suitcase. The watchers say they lost him. He was driving like a bat out of hell, running stop lights. So he was trying to get away from them. He's hiding and he's got her, and we need her very badly."

"Gone home perhaps?" Butch said.

"She has a passport now," Alex said. "We'll know if she tries to use it."

"Good. If they try to cross, we'll know it," Butch said.

"Right . . . and if she decides to give the good doctor the slip. She may, you know, despite our having her mother and sisters. If she's a real *believer*," Alex said.

"I don't think she is," Butch said. "She's not even a Muslim."

"Okay then, it's a question of finding two love birds. Lost in the woods," Alex said. He seemed a million miles away, and angry.

"He's taken her somewhere he's been. Somewhere he knows," Butch said.

"It's a bloody big country, Butch. And I don't have much time."

"He killed that cop. That surprised me," Butch said.

"Why?"

"I don't know. I didn't think he had that kind of stones."

"Grow up, man. He's in love. Put yourself in his place. He wants to protect her."

"I like him now. I didn't really before. But I like him now," Butch said.

"Well, I don't give a damn. How's that? I like him too, for that matter. But we have to find him."

"We'll sit on his phone. He'll use it, sooner or later," Butch said.

"Let's hope so. I'm going home for a few hours. Do we have anyone that's worth a damn to watch this place?"

"No. Not really. I'll see what I can get."

"Get rid of the uniformed people, for a start. I don't want to scare them if they come back."

"If we told him what we know, he'd bring her himself, I think," Butch said.

"We could leave a message on his phone," Alex said.

"Why not?" Butch said. "It's worth a try."

Alex smiled suddenly. It was an old smile; Butch remembered seeing it years before in Africa when everyone thought Alex was too young for the job they'd given him.

"Well, well. You mean, a simple phone call? All this money we spend on satellites and smart bombs and pilotless drones . . . and you just want to leave him a message."

"Yeah," Butch said.

"I'd kiss you, but you're far too ugly. Why not? Even if you thought of it, it's worth a try. I'm going to go visit Hussein's brother on the way home. They're taking him out of the country tonight—Guantanamo."

"There's a man here, quite interesting looking," Collin said. It was after lunch and he'd come back to the room. "You really have to see him. Maybe tonight at dinner. He'll probably be there in the restaurant. There's nowhere else in town to eat at night."

She came and kissed him. He hadn't expected it. The curtains were closed, and the room was deliciously bathed in a half-light that was struggling against the dark red curtains across the one window.

"I took a nap," she said. "I missed you." She kissed him again, and they moved towards the bed. He pulled her t-shirt off and looked at her for a moment. Something about looking at her like that, half-naked in the middle of the day, was incredibly exciting.

They made love in a way they hadn't before. It was athletic and innocent, as if they were two different people.

26

The clouds had gathered over the mountains. The temperature
had fallen quickly; it was almost cold when they stepped out
of their room. They'd lain in bed and talked a long time. She
was going to have to leave and was looking for the right way to
tell him. Every time Collin went on about what they should do,
she'd let him. It was as if she were listening to a small child talk
about his future. She didn't have the heart to stop him.

He'd decided to leave Mexico and go to Europe. He asked her
to come with him. He did it leaning on his elbow, his blue eyes
clear and full of the moment. He confessed that he wanted to be
an artist; he'd been afraid to admit it, but now he could.

There was a wonderful closeness to the room—the feeling of
his body, the fact that they seemed to be so alone. The world
turned without them. As she played with his hair, she realized her
anger was absent, as if she were another woman. The promise
she'd made to her husband—to die with him—seemed, if not
absurd, then oddly unimportant. For the moments she was alone
with the doctor she felt free of her grief and was not guilty about
it.

"He seems a queer man, Petros. Did you see him stare at us
over lunch? He seems out of some Russian novel," Collin said.

"Does he?"

"Yes. Some grim Russian novel about the gulag or being exiled in Siberia. I'd like to paint him. I almost asked him, but I don't have the nerve."

She looked at him. She wished he hadn't brought him up. She looked away to the window near the bathroom. The bright sunlight that had lent intensity to their lovemaking was gone. She'd lain in the sun for the first time in years and felt its warmth, felt it in her sex when she thought about Collin. She wished the sun were still out. It seemed to cover things up, make it possible to be that other woman.

"I can't imagine what he's doing here," Collin said. He sat up in bed.

He seemed so beautiful, she thought. Like some kind of god who walks among men and never suffers as men are made to suffer. Lying there, he seemed above all that. His intellect, the fact that he was an American, the fact that he was a man, the fact that he'd been given a car—so many things about him seemed godlike.

"Certainly he's odd," Collin continued. "I mean, not his poor hand, but he's so . . . so. . . ."

"What?" she said.

"Dramatic. Mysterious. Like the Italians in a Sherlock Holmes story."

"He's just a man," she said quickly. Perhaps too quickly.

"Well, he isn't a painter. Or if he is, he hasn't gone to the Church. The three of us were there all afternoon thinking he would show, but he didn't. That's the only reason people come here, for God's sake—to paint the church, or at least to *see* it."

She looked at him a long time. Perhaps if he'd never brought up Mohammad, she would have gone with him. Perhaps she could have forgotten the pact, forgotten her life before she'd met him. But talking about it spoiled the dream. It made her see Mohammad, see his wretchedness. See him following her here and waiting for her. Was it that her husband didn't have the strength? Was that it? Was he incapable of going through with it? Did he need her to be close?

For the first time she realized that she had been the strong one, not Mohammad. He didn't need her as a wife; that had all died on the street with their child. They had barely touched after their son died, much less made love. She'd been willing, but something had happened to her husband. Something had left him. Anger had blotted out all of his healthy human appetites: food, companionship, love, sex. She'd understood that.

But hers, she found after a few months, were not dead, and it had surprised her. She wanted to live again. But he hadn't. He'd died on the street with their son.

"Maybe he's taken ill," she said. She rolled away, not able to look at him now. Guilty again for lying in this bed, guilty because she wanted to be there, guilty because her husband was sitting in that cold room waiting for the wife who would never come back to him. *I'm not a martyr.* She bit her lip. She was a whore, she thought, a whore who had no love for her son or her husband or respect for anything.

There was a knock on the door. Loud. It startled her.

"Señor doctor. Por favor. Por favor, Doctor." It was the *pensión's* owner. Collin had heard that tone a hundred times. Something was terribly wrong.

"It's the manager." Collin moved off the bed. He stepped into his underwear and walked to the door.

"Doctor. *Hay que venir.*" The manager was standing at the door. He looked terrified.

"What's wrong?"

"Oye! Doctor! El huspede en el quince. Alacranes. Piso en el mero nido."

"Bark scorpions?" Collin asked.

"What, *Señor?*"

"Speak in English, man! The man. Was he bitten by the white ones?"

"I think so. *Sí. Alacranes blancos,*" the man said.

"Call a doctor!" Collin said. "Someone with the antidote. And *hurry.*"

"What doctor, señor? We have no doctor here."

"What?"

"No doctor, señor. There's a doctor in Loreto. He has to come by plane."

"Jesus. I've got no medicine," Collin said. "You must have anti-venin here. If someone is bit."

"No, señor."

"But you *must*. Scorpions are everywhere here."

"No, señor," the man said stupidly.

Collin had already moved away from the door. The manager looked at Dolores. She was sitting up in the bed. He turned away out of decency.

"It must be Petros. He's in 15. Alfredo is in 2. It has to be him, Petros. He's been bitten by a scorpion. I'll have to go see. Stepped in the nest.. . ." He was hopping into his pants and picking up his t-shirt from the floor. "It's life-threatening if they're bark scor-pions," he said.

And then he was gone. She was still there, looking at the open door and the rain. It had just started to rain so hard that she couldn't see the mountains.

"My name is Reeves. I'm a doctor," Collin said. He put his hand on Petros' forehead. It was burning. Collin could see the man was in shock. Naked except for a towel, Petros gripped the edge of the couch, his eyes rolling into the back of his head.

Collin looked down at the man's foot. He could see multiple bites. *"Shit."* He said it out loud. He was helpless. The man would die without the antidote. He didn't even have his medical bag. He'd left it at the Gobi, in the hallway.

"Call the doctor in Loreto and tell him to come *immediately,*" Collin said. He turned and looked at the manager. He had stepped into the bathroom and was looking at the hole in the tile where Petros had stepped through the floor. His foot had broken through the rotten floorboards. He'd stepped into a nest and been bitten several times before he could pull his foot out. "Did you hear me?" The man came out from the bathroom.

"I . . . I don't understand," the manager said.

"Don't worry about that, for God's sake! Call the doctor or he's going to die. Do you understand me?"

"Yes, *Señor.*"

"Help me get him over to the bed first."

They were carrying Petros to the bed when they heard the scream. It was surreal. At first Collin didn't understand where it was coming from. He looked up just as they laid Petros on the bed. Dolores was standing in the doorway, screaming. It was as if the world had stopped for a moment and all he could hear was her screaming and the wall of rain behind her.

"I said, call the fucking doctor," Collin said over her screaming. "Do you understand me? *Now!*"

The manager, who'd been staring at Dolores, ran out of the room. Collin looked down at Petros' foot. It was swelling badly.

"Shut up." He went to the doorway. "Shut up, Dolores!" He slapped her, and she stopped screaming. "What is it? Do you know him?"

"It's my husband," she said. She was stunned by the slap. He'd hit her harder than he'd intended to.

"Collin, what the hell is going on?" Collin turned around and saw Marita and Alfredo coming down the corridor. The rain was splashing the corridor. The clouds had come in from the Pacific and were dark and ominous, unleashing rain, finally.

"Alfredo, go make sure the manager has called someone with bark scorpion antivenin." He looked at Dolores for a moment, then turned and went into the room.

He didn't expect Petros to be alive, but he was. His breathing was shallow. A few more minutes, and his heart would stop. It would have been different if it had been one or two bites, but several were fatal without the antivenin. Collin doubted the man would live even if they'd had antivenin.

Collin stripped off his belt, put it on the thigh of Petros' bitten leg and cinched it down as hard as he could. He looked at his watch. A six-foot man. The lymph system would protect him for a few minutes, the swelling, but the poison was going to the heart. *Right to the heart,* he thought. He looked at Petros, whose eyes were roving now. The classic symptom.

"God damn it." Collin said it out loud. He cinched the tourniquet harder, so that he could see the flesh trapped by the buckle turn white. Petros seemed to be looking around, but not able to speak.

"I'm a doctor," Collin said. "I'm here to help you. Can you understand me? I need to know how long ago you were bitten. Can you understand me?"

Petros looked at him. It seemed he wanted to answer, but he began to jerk. A series of muscle spasms twisted his body as if he were being electrocuted, loosening the belt. Collin had to use his knee to keep it cinched down tight.

"I've got to shock his heart. When it stops." Dolores was standing behind Marita. "You'll have to hold him down if he moves. We don't have much time. It could stop any minute. Do you understand me? It's his only chance." They were both looking at Petros.

"Are you sure he'll die?" Dolores asked.

"He'll die for sure if we don't *do* something," Collin said. Alfredo ran in.

"They can't fly. He won't come. The doctor's afraid to land. I spoke to him myself—the doctor," Alfredo said.

"You'll have to help hold him down," Collin said. "When it stops, I'm going to beat on his chest. I'll try to keep his heart beating." Alfredo looked at him and nodded.

"With *what?*" Alfredo said.

227

"My fist," Collin said. They watched Petros start to buckle again. "You have to hold him down."

Alfredo hadn't moved. "Come on, man! For God's sake; we don't have much time."

Alfredo moved expressionless to Petros' side.

"Now you take the shoulder. Keep him down as best you can. Marita, you hold his other shoulder. Dolores, hold his legs. You're going to have to grab him by the ankles. Do you understand me?"

They all looked at him—the women looking terrified. Alfredo stepped up and grabbed Petros by the shoulder. Collin looked at Marita. She followed Alfredo's lead. Dolores was looking at her husband.

"Dolores. Grab his feet!" She did as she was told. The manager came back into the room.

"Call *Señor* Hidalgo at the airport in Cabo. He'll come. I'm sure he'll come. Tell him what's happened. If you get him on the phone, let me talk to him," Collin said to the manager. "We'll need to get him out to a hospital if he lives."

There was a moment in the quiet, after the manager had left the room, when Collin heard Petros' heart stop.

Collin stopped breathing suddenly. He'd been listening, keeping his ear on Petros' chest, when the heartbeat just stopped.

He stood up and began to beat on Petros' chest with his fist. Again and again he beat him on the sternum. Hard. He heard Dolores scream for him to stop, saying that he was killing him. But he didn't stop until Petros' began to breathe again.

Señor Hidalgo had come, even with the bad weather. He'd asked to speak to Collin on the manager's cell phone. Collin had told him that he might be able to keep Petros alive if someone could bring the antivenin and some epinephrine.

"I come," Hidalgo had said. "I come myself. I try and get what you need and I come."

"You sure? The weather is very bad." Collin had felt suddenly guilty. He was asking the man to risk his life for what could turn out to be a dead body by the time he got there.

He'd had to restart Petros' heart twice, in the most brutal fashion, with just his fist. They were sitting up in the *pensión's* restaurant now. Hidalgo had brought the antivenin and the epinephrine.

"You'd make a good pilot, *cojones* like yours," Hidalgo said. "I'm glad I came."

"I don't see how you landed," Collin said.

"I don't, either," Hidalgo said. They laughed. "You injected the epinephrine straight *into* the heart, doctor?"

"Yes," Collin said. He was having a coffee. It tasted like metal. He was exhausted but happy; Petros had lived.

"You can do that?" Hidalgo asked.

"You can do that," Collin said.

"*Amigo,* I couldn't do it." Hidalgo had put his cane on the table. "Technically, I'm not supposed to fly anymore. But I didn't bother to stop and ask permission."

It was still raining, the sound of it steady on the metal roof above them. Collin could still feel the moment in his fist, the blow that had brought him back. Life had come back each time with a gasp. Then it went on, and he stopped. They'd all looked at him and he nodded to himself. And they'd realized what he'd done, that he'd saved Petros in such a rude way.

"I'm sorry in a way that I asked you to come," Collin said.

"My pleasure. At my age, I look forward to dying," Hidalgo said. "My planes are all paid off. My son doesn't need me. I'm in the way now because of my leg. I just tell people what to do all day. I don't like it that much." He was drinking brandy. "What I liked was being your age. My dick was stiff all the time and I had a future. It's the small things. I wanted to own a plane and have a small company. I was nobody, believe me, when I went to Spain to learn to fly. Now I have three planes, but I can't fly them." He reached over the table and touched Collin's hand.

"You just pound on the chest until the heart starts again? That fascinates me," Hidalgo said. "That's like God. Did you feel like God?"

"It's science," Collin said. "That's all. It's no more mysterious than that plane of yours. Science."

"Maybe. But to a Mexican it seems like magic. *Tu eres un magico,*" Hidalgo said. He finished his drink in one swallow. "Would you like a drink? You look tired, doctor."

"Yes. I would."

Hidalgo poured some brandy into his coffee cup. "Do you want to leave tonight? We can," Hidalgo said.

"If we can. It's still raining quite hard. Won't that matter?"

"No. It's the wind that matters. We can leave if you want. You're the doctor. We should leave at midnight. I called my son; he says the winds will calm after eleven. Can he fly? Your patient."

"Yes. A few hours shouldn't matter now," Collin said. "If his heart stops again, I have the epinephrine."

"We go after the winds calm; it would be a shame to lose him in a crash!" Hidalgo laughed.

27

Dolores was sitting with Petros when Collin came in to check on him.

"He's asleep," she said. She was holding Petros' good hand. The sight of her touching him made Collin wince slightly. He hadn't had time to let the fact that he'd saved her husband sink in. When he'd thought of it upstairs with Hidalgo, he'd pushed it away, too tired to deal with it.

"We'll leave in a few hours. When the weather's better," Collin said. "How long have you been married?" Collin asked. He went to her side and took Petros' pulse. It seemed normal, but he wasn't out of danger yet. The antivenin had come too late to stop the allergic shock to so much poison.

He was angry in a way he'd never been angry before. Not jealous, but angry; Petros was in their way, here. Collin had wanted to leave Mexico and take her with him.

"Three years," she said.

"I see," he said.

"He's a doctor, too," Dolores said. Collin turned and looked at her.

"Petros?"

"Yes," she said. "I met him in London."

"We can leave him in Cabo. There's a good hospital there. He'll be fine," Collin said.

"I can't," she said. "Not like he is."

231

"Why not? He'll be fine once we get him there."

"I can't, that's all."

"Then you're still in love with him."

"No. Not like that. It's not what you think."

"Well, I'm in love with you, and I want you to leave with me. I have to leave. I can't stay here. Do you understand? I can't stay in Mexico. Not after what happened at the Gobi, with the police."

"No, I don't understand. Not really," she said. "Thank you for what you did. For him, I mean."

"No reason to thank me. That's what I do. He would have done it for me—if it were different."

"He would have," she said. "It's true."

"I'm leaving the country and I want you to come with me," Collin said again.

"I can't. Not right now. He's my husband. I told you." He didn't say anything, then. He just looked at her.

"He will be fine," Collin said. "If that's what you're worried about."

"I'm his wife, for god's sake. I can't just leave him."

Collin's cell phone rang; he looked and recognized the number. It was Law. He didn't answer. He knew if he did that they would find him, and he didn't want to be found. Not now. He felt finished with all that. All their horrible rationales, their great patriotic mumbo jumbo. He didn't care. They could go hang. He hadn't made their world, and he wanted no part of it, now. It was over. He broke the phone in two, walked to the coffee table and put it down, not knowing what else to do with it.

"I'm not an American. And he's not a Greek," she said.

He turned and looked at her. "I never thought you were," he said.

"We came together from Saudi Arabia," she said.

"Stop right there. I don't want to know."

"No. I want to tell you," she said. "I have to tell someone."

"You don't understand," he said. "I'm not who you think."

"I don't care. I trust you," she said. "If I tell you, then you'll understand why I can't go with you.

"We came here to take a bomb and walk into the U.S. embassy and blow it up. We had a martyr's pact," she said.

He looked at her a moment as if he'd heard something that he'd understood on some level but had refused to listen to or believe.

"We're martyrs. Do you understand? I was already dead when you met me. Can you understand that?"

"No. I can't," he said. "Not at all. Those people . . . they're innocent."

"What about my son? Was he guilty when you killed him? He was just a baby. Was he guilty? Was the woman standing next to my husband when the American rocket exploded guilty? Tell me—*was* she?"

"I don't know what you're talking about," he said.

"I'm talking about my son. He's dead, and you killed him."

"I didn't kill anyone," Collin said.

"People like you. Blond people. Americans who are so proud of themselves and their country and their religion. You killed him. Mohammad was a surgeon. Now look at him. Was he guilty because he tried to save people's lives? It's a war, isn't it? Isn't that your side's excuse for killing women and children and bombing hospitals and burning cities? It's a war. And if Mohammad and I blow up the embassy? What is that? Isn't that war?"

"Whatever happened to you and your husband and child doesn't justify blowing up people. That's madness. They're just innocent people. Clerks and secretaries who haven't done any-thing to you."

"And what about the ones who aren't clerks and secretaries? The ones who give the orders and take the orders? The ones who murdered Madani? What about them?" she said.

"Then you'll have to kill me, too," he said.

"What are you talking about?"

"I was there when they took Madani away. I'm one of them. I'm one of those who give the orders."

She looked at him, not understanding at all. "You're a doctor."

"Am I? I'm a CIA officer. I'm afraid I don't have a card or a pin or anything. You'll just have to believe me," he said.

"You're lying."

"No. I wish I were." He turned and saw that Petros was awake and staring at him. Petros said something in Arabic. His voice was so soft that he couldn't make it out at first.

"Fatima?" Petros said.

"Yes."

"Is it true?" Petros said.

"I don't know," she said.

"It's true," Collin said. "I'm the policeman you were running from all along. And now I know."

Petros tried to slide himself up on the bed, but winced in pain and stopped. His chest and ribs were bruised.

"I wouldn't move too much yet," Collin said. "Fatima. Is that your real name, then?"

"Yes," she said.

"I like Dolores. It suits you better," Collin said. "Well . . . now what?"

"Let us leave. I'll take him home. Back to Baghdad."

"What about your little errand?"

"No," she said. "I can't. I couldn't the day you met me. And I can't do it now. I don't want to kill anyone. I want to be left alone; that's all."

"I didn't think so. I thought you might be a terrorist, but I knew from the moment I saw you that you weren't capable of killing anyone. That isn't you—Fatima or Dolores, or whatever your name really is," he said. "Maybe your husband, but not you."

"I'll take him home. I promise you," she said.

"And what if he doesn't want to go home? What if he's determined to go to Allah and take some people with him?"

"Can't you see? Look at him. He's of no use to them now."

"Do you know where the bomb is?" Collin said.

"No. We were to wait at the hotel and they were to come and get us," she said. "That's all we knew, just to go to the Gobi and ask for Madani. They would come to us. He kept us in separate rooms."

"How do I know you're telling me the truth?" Collin said.

"Why would I tell you any of it, Collin?"

"How did your husband know to come here?" he said.

"I told him. I told him I was leaving him. I called him from the airport. I told him I couldn't do it. That I'd fallen in love with you."

"So he followed you."

"Yes. As a husband, not a terrorist."

"I love her," Petros said. It was the first thing he'd said to him. His English was perfect, and somehow Collin wasn't surprised.

"I'm sure you do. That's why you were going to let her die like that," Collin said. "If you *are* a doctor, how could you do that?"

Petros lifted up his metal claw. "I *was* a doctor," he said.

"Bullshit. You still are, in my book. You took the oath, didn't you? First, do no harm. What did you think that meant, only when it was easy?"

"You don't understand," Petros said.

"Oh, yes I do. You're all mad. You're as crazy as the ones on my side. With their beautiful explanations of why they have a license to be cruel and put hoods on people and send them away to be tortured. You're *all* mad. I understand that now. *All of you*. The boys on the top floor of the embassy and men like you. You're all the same. Can't you see that?

"I'm taking Dolores with me. I'm going to leave you in Cabo San Lucas. They're after her by now. And when they catch her, they won't let her go. Do you understand *that*—what they'll do to her if they catch her? Men just like you, Mohammad, who

235

believe it will be justice. I'm not going to have it. Do you know why? Because I *do* love her. And the rest of you madmen can go to hell and burn the world down in the name of God or Democracy or whatever shitty excuse that sounds pretty enough on CNN or Al Jazeera."

"He's right, Fatima. They'll catch us," Petros said. "You have to go with him. Leave me."

"You see? He does understand. He knows what it's about," Collin said.

"Thank you, Doctor," Petros said.

"For what? I probably shouldn't have done it. You see, I don't believe your wife. I think you're going to do it. Not now, maybe, but later. If not here, somewhere else. In some market in Jerusalem or Chicago or Paris. That's what I think. So don't thank me. I'm a doctor; I don't have a choice. That's my job."

Dolores said something in Arabic. Petros looked at her but didn't answer.

"I'd prefer if you spoke in English," Collin said.

"I told him I can't just leave him," Dolores said. "Not like this."

"The plane is leaving at midnight. He has to be on it. His heart could stop at any time, still. He got a tremendous amount of venom. He needs to be in a hospital. And if he's really a doctor, he knows that as well as I do."

Collin walked out of the room and closed the door. A sheet of rain poured off the roof of the corridor, in front of him. He was a little high from the brandy, perhaps; it had made him more angry than he would have been otherwise.

He stood for a moment looking at the rain and the desert beyond. He could just leave, he thought. He didn't have to care about her. He could still go back to Mexico City and pretend this hadn't happened. He'd tell Law he'd taken her here, and then he'd left her. He went to the edge of the corridor and held his hand out to where the rain was pouring off the roof. Cupping his hand, he splashed the water on his face. It was cool.

He'd never been so tired. He walked down the hallway to his room and went in and lay on the bed. He thought of calling his father and asking him what he should do. As he drifted off to sleep, he saw his father standing at the dining room table with the carving knife, looking at him in that disappointed way. But he fell asleep before he remembered any more.

"You wake up." He heard the voice from a distance. He had no dreams in him but was in the most silent deep sleep. He heard the voice again and felt something. And then, like a man who had been held under water, he came rushing to the surface.

"You wake up." There were two men standing in his room. One of them was holding a pistol and pointing it at him. At first he thought he was dreaming. The one with the pistol hadn't shaved and was tall and thin.

"Get up," the tall one said. "Get up now." He spoke with a thick accent. The room was dark. He'd slept for an hour or more. He could see the clock on the bed; it was just 8:00 P.M.

"What's going on?" Collin said. The other one had a gun, too. The other one was heavier-looking, wearing a suit and no tie, and was maybe forty or older. The one in the suit said something to the other one in Arabic. There was a knock on the door and the heavier one went to the door and opened it. A third man, who Collin couldn't see, said something and then left again.

"Who are you?" Collin said.

"Never mind," the one pointing the gun at him said. "You get up. Come with me." The tall one who'd woken him up stepped closer and pointed the gun directly at his face. He stood up.

"All right," he said.

The man pushed him towards the door. "Lobby," the tall one said. The other one opened the door. They walked down the corridor. It was still raining. As they neared the lobby, Collin saw an old Green Land Rover parked in the lot. *So they'd driven in from Loreto.* Had Mohammad called them—or Dolores?

Collin walked through the lobby door and saw Jimmy Hidalgo sitting on a couch with Marita and Alfredo.

"They've killed the bloody manager," Alfredo said.

"Shut up," one of the Arabs said. Collin couldn't see who as they were all standing behind him. He walked toward the couch and sat in one of the chairs. He and Alfredo exchanged a look.

"Which one fly the plane?" the tall one said.

"Don't answer him," Collin said. He waited to be shot, but the shot didn't come. Petros walked in, helped by Dolores. He was leaning on her. He'd dressed.

"You. Come with me," the one who'd woken him said.

"No," Petros said. "No. We have to find out which one is the pilot."

"I don't think he is," the shorter man said, pointing at Collin. "I kill him."

"My colleagues would like to know which one of you is the pilot," Petros said. He was in pain from his bruised ribs.

Dolores looked at him. *She damn well knows who the pilot is,* Collin thought; *why didn't she tell them?*

"This man needs to get to a hospital," Collin said. "I'm a doctor. He'll die if he doesn't get there, and soon."

"It's not him, then," the tall one said. The tall one wanted to kill Collin now. It was obvious.

"You murdering swine," Alfredo said. "He's the one who killed the manager. He just shot him in the face."

"Are you the pilot?" the tall one asked Alfredo.

"No. I'm an artist, you piece of shit."

The tall one fired almost immediately. He hit Alfredo in the chest. He fired again before Collin realized what was happening. Petros moved to stop him.

Collin looked at Alfredo. He was dead, his mouth still open, his eyes fixed still on the man who'd shot him. Marita screamed, looking at the tall one, then stood up and went to Alfredo. The blood began pouring out of the exit wound in his back.

"He's the pilot," Dolores said. She pointed at Jimmy Hidalgo, who was standing by the bar. "Please don't kill them," she said.

Marita was still screaming, hysterical.

"How much fuel you have?" the tall one asked Hidalgo.

"Enough to get back," Hidalgo said.

"How much?" the tall one said again.

"About 500 pounds."

The skinny one smiled then, and Collin saw it. The man looked at Petros and the other one, and said something in Arabic that Collin didn't understand.

"DC-7?" Petros asked.

"No," Hidalgo said. "A DC-5."

"Never heard of it," Petros said.

"Does that mean you're going to shoot me?" Hidalgo said. "They only built a few of them."

"How many miles can it fly?" the tall one asked.

Hidalgo looked at Collin quickly, then back at the tall one.

"How many miles?"

"About sixteen hundred," Hidalgo said.

"Okay," the tall one said. "We go to San Diego."

"I can't fly into the United States, asshole," Hidalgo said. "It's against the law."

28

T he bar's over there. I'm getting up and having a drink," Collin said, looking at the man they'd left to guard them. Petros and the tall one had taken Hidalgo to the plane. "Tell him that . . . the son of a bitch."

Dolores translated.

"He says you should stay seated," Dolores said.

"You can tell him I'm going to stand up. He can kill me if he wants. I don't care anymore," Collin said. "They're going to shoot Hidalgo, aren't they? As soon as he shows them what they want to know. Is it your husband? Is he a pilot?"

"Yes. The Iraqi air force. They sent him to London, to medical school," Dolores said.

Collin got up. Their guard barked something at him but he kept walking, not sure what would happen. Collin turned and saw that Dolores was standing between him and the guard. She was speaking in Arabic, very deliberately. Whatever she said seemed to work; the gunshot he'd expected didn't come, and he kept walking.

He went to the small bar that the manager ran for the guests in the evening. It was tidy, a few wine glasses neatly stacked on a bar towel. He found a bottle of red wine and poured himself a glass. He looked at the guard, smiled fatuously, and raised his glass.

"I told him you were the doctor," Dolores said. "That if something happened to Mohammed, they would need you."

"Well, great. I'm so glad. I hope the son of a bitch dies. That's what I get for helping him." He took a drink.

"I didn't know," she said. "I didn't know they were here. The cell is in Tijuana. The ones who came; that's where they've been."

"How wonderful for them," Collin said.

"Don't worry; he can't understand English," Dolores said.

"What is this about?" Marita said. She was pale and hadn't said a word since they'd shot Alfredo.

"Let's see. These men are going to try and use that plane the way their friends did in New York, I suppose. Just a guess. There never was a bomb, was there? Quite smart of them to make us think it was about that. Waste of time . . . even you, I suppose. Did you know the truth?"

"I didn't know about the plane. They always said a bomb," Dolores said.

"That was if you were caught. Then you wouldn't know, would you? Or maybe they just decided it now. Clever boys."

"Are you all mad?" Marita said. "You're all *mad*. What are you talking about?"

"Perhaps we are," Collin said.

He leaned on the bar. He was thinking about the AK-47 their guard had pointed at him. If he opened fire with that, he could kill them all in a few seconds. If Collin attacked him? Perhaps he might be able to do something. Or he could simply get them killed for nothing.

He had another sip of wine. He could taste it and was surprised. He looked casually around the bar but saw nothing he might use as a weapon.

"This son of a bitch might speak German, so I'd stick to English," Collin said. "Half of these bastards are from Hamburg, from what I've read." He looked at Marita. "They're *al Qaeda*, or something close to it. Holy warriors."

Marita turned and looked at the man with the gun.

"*Sprechen sie Deutsch?*" Marita said

241

"*Ja. Germanie,*" the man said. She called him a name in German, and the man smiled at her as if they were all children in a playground.

"You see?" Collin said. "It was his dark suit in the desert. Something European about that. I bet he drove a taxi . . . was very polite to everyone, helpful with the luggage."

"Stop it!" Dolores said. "Stop it!"

"I'd like to. But you see, he has a very big gun and I've got nothing here but a corkscrew," Collin said.

"No. I mean that tone of voice," she said. "It's awful."

"Terribly sorry; I didn't know you were the sensitive type," Collin said. The rain got louder then. It beat against the roof. "Under the circumstances."

"Are they going to kill us?" Marita said.

"I think so," Collin said. "Would you like a drink?"

"Yes," she said. He poured one, brought it to her, and sat down next to her. They'd thrown a blanket over Alfredo's body.

"And we're just here for the painting," Collin said. He put his hand on her knee. Dolores looked at him.

"Ask him if he's going to kill us," Collin said.

"Stop it," she said.

"Tell him she's just a painter. That she's nothing to do with this. She isn't even an American. Why doesn't he let her go? Let her walk out. Go on—before that tall ugly bastard comes back, because he *is* a killer. I don't think our taxi driver is. Not a real one. Not like that other bastard," Collin said.

Dolores told the man. She tried to sound reasonable, and he wasn't surprised when the man said no in Arabic. That Collin did understand.

"He says he can't. He has orders."

"Yes, orders. I'm sure he does," Collin said. He looked at Marita. She was holding the glass of wine he'd given her, but she hadn't taken a drink.

"I'm frightened," she said. The sound of her voice; the tone went through him and for the first time he was frightened, too. Not for himself, but because he couldn't do anything to stop it. He might stop this man in a struggle, but not the plane. Not them leaving on the *plane.*

"We'll have a drink," Collin said. "It will make you feel better." He tried to sound kind. The sardonic tone had suddenly left him. The rain picked up again. For a moment, the sound of it on the metal roof was maddening, a hysterical sound. "Ask him if he has a family. A sister. A mother. Go on. Ask him." Dolores asked him. The man nodded. He had a family, he said.

"And if they were here, in her place?" Collin asked. "Wouldn't you want me to show them mercy?" The man didn't answer this time. "You see, I'm right. I've shaken him up. . . . What's your name?" Collin asked the man in Arabic.

He was surprised that Collin spoke Arabic. "Mustafa," the man said, looking at him differently.

"Well, Mustafa. I've got to go to the restroom." Mustafa looked at Dolores. "I don't want to piss myself." The man took a pistol out of his belt, walked over to Dolores and handed it to her. He said something in Arabic. It felt as if the air had been drained out of the room for a moment. Collin was afraid to move.

"Get up," Dolores said. She pointed the gun at Collin. The man said something to her.

"He says I should shoot you if you try and run away. I'm to let you go outside. Just outside."

"I don't want to piss outside. There's a bathroom in the back, by the office," Collin said.

"Collin, for God's sake," she said.

"Tell him that!" he told her. She lifted the pistol and roughly pushed Collin, berating him. He took the cue and walked towards the office.

He walked into the pension's office and put his hands down. He put his fingers to his mouth. She came into his arms, and he held her.

243

"I love you so much," she said. "Please hold me."

He held her for a moment and felt her trembling.

"You have to kill him. And then go," she said. "Should I kill him when we go back out? That's better."

"No," he said. "I need him."

"*What?*" She was still holding him.

"I've got to stop them. The plane."

"How?"

"There's no time to explain, but I need him."

"No," she said. "No. I'll kill him."

He pulled her off him.

"Dolores, I'm a doctor. Do you understand? I took an oath. I can't stand by and let them do this. Do you understand that? If you love me, you have to let me go."

"But *why?*"

"Because. Until now I didn't really understand . . . I thought. I thought it was about other things, but it's not. It's about people like me and you not doing what we should. They're all crazy . . . both sides. They're all the same. But we can't let them run the world."

"But I want to be with you. Since the moment that I saw you, since the moment you put your hand on my head that day in the hotel room. It was the first time since my son died that I felt human. That's all I want now." She held his hand and put it against her face. "For us to be together. I'll go with you."

"Did you love your son more than yourself?"

"Yes, of course," she said.

"Then love me that way now . . . and help me. Please?"

She held him again. "All right," she said finally, "but I will be dead again without you."

He'd been in London at the same time as she. Perhaps they'd walked by each other or sat in the same restaurant and missed each other, until now. It seemed strange that they hadn't gotten their chance at life—an accident, a chance meeting somewhere in that city. They'd been close, he thought.

"I love you," he said. Then he said it in Arabic.

"How? How can you stop them?"

"I just can, I think."

When they walked back into the little lobby they could see the headlights from the Land Rover as it turned into the parking lot.

Petros and the tall one came through the door. Petros looked terrible. Hidalgo hadn't come back with them. It was what Collin had expected; they'd had to kill him.

"Where's the pilot?" Marita asked. "Where's Hidalgo?"

"He's not coming back," Collin said. "He's out there somewhere. Isn't he, Mohammad?"

"We eat something . . . then we go," Petros said, ignoring him.

"Last supper, then," Collin said. "Right?"

"Shut up," the tall one said.

Petros was holding his chest.

"How are you feeling, old boy? Did I hit you too hard? Hope so."

The tall one raised his pistol to kill Collin, but Petros stopped him again, shoving his metal hand and knocking the pistol's barrel down.

"Just wondering," Collin said. Suddenly he wasn't afraid. He was looking at something in a test tube: a virus. He examined it now with his doctor's eye: the barrel, Petros staring at him in a strange way, the tall one with his murderous expression. He felt as he had in Africa, when he was about to enter a dark hut and the juju men were inside, and everyone was waiting for the patient to die, hardly expecting their incantations and filthy fetishes to make a difference. So he set himself now with his intelligence, the way he had against the virus. Perhaps Petros recognized the doctor's clinical look; he looked away and spoke to Dolores in Arabic.

"You see, he needs me. Doesn't want you to shoot the doctor

in case I have to use the epinephrine. He knows his heart could still stop on him." Collin said to the tall one.

"I'm going to kill you," the tall one said. "You see. Short time now."

"I'm sure you will. Just not right now," Collin said.

"Take the body outside," the tall one said. Then he pointed at Marita and told her to help.

"I can do it myself," Collin said.

"Hurry up, then," Petros said.

They watched Collin strip off the blanket. Marita looked away. He had to drag Alfredo from the couch and across the floor by his feet. Marita wanted to help, but he told her not to.

He dragged the body out the lobby door and down the empty green corridor. Collin looked behind him once; the one in the suit had stepped out, and was watching him. Collin looked out into the night at the heavy rain and then down at Alfredo's body sliding on the tile floor behind him, and thought about his plan.

The one in the suit said something in Arabic. Collin let Alfredo's shoes slip from under his arms. He knelt down and shut his friend's eyes. The day they'd met, Alfredo had said that if there was a God, he was a painter and just wanted to be left alone to work. Collin remembered that day now and smiled to himself. He supposed Alfredo would see this all as some kind of terrible joke the universe had played on him.

Everyone runs out of luck somewhere, Collin thought, and went back inside.

They'd been led into the room, which was lit with the soft and beautiful light of old-fashioned propane lamps. There was a dining room table the *pensión's* manager had used for himself at the back of the lobby, in a separate room. The walls were decorated with paintings that down-and-out artists had used to help pay their bills, or just left as gifts over the years. They were all scenes of the town and the church. Collin had never seen the collection before. He saw two of Alfredo's paintings: one of the date palms with pickers at work up in the trees, and one of the church at night. He stood in front of it a moment.

Petros had gotten the women to fix them a meal. The men sat at the table, drank lemonade, and spoke in Arabic. From what Collin could make out of the conversation, it had to do with Petros' ability to fly the plane without Jimmy Hidalgo.

Collin had been told to sit with them. The smell of the food being prepared seemed strange under the circumstances. The men were discussing their plans for mass murder and, Collin imagined, the chances of getting through to San Diego. Petros was sweating as he spoke, his body still fighting the venom, the allergic reaction not finished. Collin hoped it killed him, but it might not be soon enough.

Marita and Dolores brought their food to the table. They'd made sandwiches. Petros didn't pick one up.

"Sit down," Petros said. He spoke to Dolores in a kind voice. "What's your name?" he asked Marita.

"Marita."

"Sit down and eat, Marita," Petros said.

"You're very gracious for a dying man," Collin said. He reached over and picked up a sandwich from the platter. Petros looked at him.

"Do you want to die? Is that it?" Petros said. "We can oblige you, doctor."

"No, not particularly," Collin said. He put the sandwich on a napkin and poured himself a glass of lemonade from the pitcher at the table.

"You saved my life. I'm grateful," Petros said.

"Are you?"

"Yes. That's why you're still with us."

"I think we should kill him," the tall one said. He took a bite of his sandwich and looked at Collin. "Anyway, he has to die; they both do. We can't leave them here."

247

"No," Dolores said. "No." Then she said something in Arabic that Collin couldn't understand.

"Shut up," the tall one said to her. "You have nothing to do with it. Men decide this."

The simple one with the suit was eating. He seemed to know that it was his last meal, and he wasn't paying much attention to what else was happening. There was a bang from a clap of thunder, the sound rolling over the *pensión* as if someone had dropped something very heavy on the mountain behind them.

"You'll be all right," Dolores said, looking at Marita. "I promise you."

"Is that true then, Mohammad?" Collin said. The sweat was pouring down Petros' face now.

"Perhaps," he said.

Dolores looked at her husband. "No! You promised me," she said.

"He can't promise that. He knows we'll get a message off some-how. Someone in the village will have a phone. And then what? They'll shoot him down before he gets to the border. He has to kill us," Collin said. He had a bite of his sandwich and watched Petros' face. "Anyway, it won't matter. The allergic reaction is going to kill you before you get too far."

"Shut up, doctor. I'll be fine.. . . It's not far I have to go."

"Eight-hundred miles. But you know as well as I do that your heart could stop at any time. Plenty of poison in you still."

Petros looked at him.

"You see, *amigos*, he doesn't want to tell you the truth. The truth is, he might get you up there and then crash before he gets to the border. You die for nothing. How does that sound?" Collin said.

The one with a suit asked the tall one to translate. The one in the suit looked over at Petros. It was the first time he'd taken notice of the conversation. He was obviously a frightened martyr, and the thought that he might be going to die for nothing didn't seem to go down too well.

"I'm *fine*. We will be in the air a little over an hour. If that," Petros said.

"Is that true?" the tall one said. "That you won't be able to fly?"

"No, it isn't," Petros said. "I'm fine. I'm over it now."

"Does he look fine, *amigos?*"

The one in the suit asked for a translation again, and the tall one gave it to him. Petros looked at his watch.

"You don't have much time . . . if you want to eat," Collin said to him.

"Do you want me to kill him?" the tall one said. His face was greasy from eating. The one in the suit had stopped eating.

"Are they going to kill us, Collin?" Marita asked. She was terrified, doing everything she could not to panic.

"Yes," Collin said.

"You're like Hitler," Marita said. She spoke directly to Petros. "That's what you are. You're mad, like the Nazis."

"No. I'm a soldier," Petros said. "That's all. It's a war."

"No. You're just like they were." She was shaking with fear.

"Hitler killed Jews," the tall one said. "What's so wrong with that?"

"You see!" Marita said. She bolted from the table and ran for the lobby door. The tall one picked up his pistol, but Dolores stopped him. Marita disappeared into the night.

"Go get her," Petros said. "Take her to my room and wait for me there . . . hurry up, man, before she gets away!" The tall one got up and hurried from the room. The lobby door slammed behind him.

"You can't kill them. We'll lock them up in one of the rooms," Dolores said.

"You love him, don't you?" Petros said. He seemed hurt by it. "We had a pact, you and I."

"We still do. I'm just begging you not to hurt them."

"No. He can't promise that. It's too dangerous, isn't it, doctor?" Collin said. "He's a smart fellow. He knows that if I am able to, I'll warn them. You have to kill me, Mohammad. Go ahead and tell her the truth." Petros didn't say anything. "I've got a deal for you," Collin continued. "Let Dolores and the German girl stay. And I'll go with you. She'll keep the girl from calling anyone—and I'll keep you alive. I've got the epinephrine. I'll give you a shot right away if it gets bad.

"You don't want Dolores—excuse me, Fatima—to die. I know you don't. You love her as much as I do. You only want her to come because you're not sure if you're man enough to do it, but if you have her, you know you will be. She will remind you of why you're here. Otherwise, you're not so sure you can do it—because somewhere inside of you is still a little bit of humanity. But you have to do it, because my guess is that you're the only one that can fly that plane."

"No. I'll go," Dolores said.

"Shut up," Petros said.

"I'll let the girl go if you leave me here," Dolores said. "I don't want Collin to go."

"The office has a lock you can lock from the outside. It has no windows. Put them in there tonight. By the time the staff finds them in the morning, you'll be long gone," Collin said. "Take me. That makes sense . . . doesn't it?"

29

Petros had tried to eat—Collin had watched him pick up a sandwich—but he couldn't. He'd put it down almost immediately.

"You have more epinephrine?" Petros asked. "Is that true?"

"Yes. I had him bring two vials. In case something happened and we couldn't take off—because of the weather," Collin said.

Petros looked at him a moment. "I would have done the same," he said. "We're a lot alike."

"Not at all. I took an oath to do no harm," Collin said.

"I did, too."

"Then *don't*."

"Tell that to your President," Petros said.

"He's not a doctor," Collin said.

"No. *He's* the Hitler. He killed my son. Why?"

"It was wrong," Collin said.

"He took my hand," Petros said.

"I'm sorry for that. But it doesn't give you the right to murder people."

"It's a *war*. We just want them out of our country. We don't have anything to do with bin Laden and his bunch. We aren't religious," Petros said.

"Don't kill civilians, and I'll believe you," Collin said.

"What do you want us to do? We don't have an air force or an army anymore. All we have is ourselves," Petros said. "Your side kills civilians every day."

"Are you trying to convince me you're not a murderer?" Collin said. "You can convince me by leaving in the jeep and not doing this."

"You're so sure of yourself," Petros said.

"Yes, well. I'm not mad," Collin said.

"You really think I'm mad?"

"Absolutely," Collin said.

"And killing civilians. How many do you think have died in Iraq?"

"It's madness. All of it," Collin said. "None of it's right. I see that now."

"Mohammad, you can't take him," Dolores said.

"Yes, I can. He's right. I don't want you to go. He's right about that."

"Good," Collin said. "Good. I'll get my things. And I'd like to write a note to my family. I'd like to do it in peace. You know I won't try to run away." He stood up. "I'll be back in twenty minutes."

"Do you really love her?" Petros asked.

"Yes, I love her."

"She won't have either one of us if you go."

"That's right," Collin said. "We missed our chance . . . like your son missed his. It happens. You've seen it, as a doctor. Bad things happen to people that shouldn't, and sometimes there's nothing we can do about it."

The tall one came back into the lobby. He had Marita by the shirt. He'd slapped her, her nose was bloody.

"He's going to his room," Petros said. "Leave him be."

"You can't let him just walk out," the tall one said.

"Shut up, fool, and do as I say. Put the girl in the office," Petros said. "I'll kill the girl if you aren't back here in twenty minutes," he told Collin. "And you're right, we're not at all alike."

Collin closed the door to his room. The rain had slowed for a moment, and he leaned against the door and listened to it. It sounded beautiful.

He'd been around death since medical school, but he'd never thought about his own death. It was a strange feeling. He was frightened. He'd seen other people, countless people, face death. It was always worse if they were afraid. He tried not to be now.

He wanted to write a note to his mother and father, something that would make them feel better about it. He went to the desk and took out a piece of stationery from the drawer. He looked and found a pen, but it was dry and skipped. It took a minute for the ink to start to flow.

He wrote in his neat hand that he loved them, that he'd done what he had because he was a doctor and had a responsibility to fight to save people, even like this. It was all very simple and clear to him. He hoped they would understand. He signed it. It seemed too short, but he had no more time.

He looked at his watch. He began to fold the note, then suddenly unfolded it and put a PS at the bottom. He left the paintings in his apartment to his sister, he said. Then he put "Mexico" at the top, for some reason. Satisfied, he folded it up, put it in the envelope, and sealed it. *I'll give it to Dolores and she'll see they get it,* he thought.

He looked around the room. He got his coat. He went to his painting things and picked them up. He should never have been a doctor, he thought. That was a mistake. It hurt a little, because he couldn't go back and start again. That was the problem with life; you could never go back and start over and do it right.

"Why are you doing this?" Dolores had followed him to the room and came in while he'd been standing there.

"I told you," he said. He put his coat on.

"Do you love me?"

"Very much," he said.

253

"Then how can you leave me?"

"I told you why," he said.

"I can't lose you," she said. "Do I have to *beg* you?"

"I have to go," he said. "There's a man called Alex Law. He'll come soon, once he hears what's happened. You have to leave before he gets here."

"The one called Tom?" she asked.

"Is that what he said his name was?"

"Yes. He thinks you're involved with this. He's a policeman, too."

"Yes." He wanted to explain to her, tell her the whole story. But there was no time.

"He's arrested my mother and sisters," she said.

"I'm sorry." Collin said.

The door swung open; it was Petros. "I want to see the epinephrine," he said. He was sweating and looked terrible.

"You won't make it, Mohammad." she said. "Why go at all? Collin is right; they're all mad."

"I'm a soldier. I have to go," Petros said. "Let me see the epinephrine."

He thought he could kill Petros, but what about the tall one? If they could fly, he'd never stop them. "Do either of the other ones fly?" Collin asked as he lifted the vial out of the makeshift medical bag Hidalgo had brought him. He handed it to Petros.

"Yes. The one in the suit, he's had a little training. But probably not enough to take off. I was in the Iraqi air force. They sent me to medical school. I know what I'm doing." Petros looked at the vial's label carefully as he spoke. "You give me the shot, then, if I need it. I'm going to have to trust you. To give it to me. . . .."

"Yes," Collin said.

"I'm not a monster," Petros said to him. He was looking at both of them now. He handed the vial back.

"Give us a moment, Mohammad, please." Dolores kissed her

husband. He held her with his bad hand. They hugged and didn't speak. Then he was gone.

"I have a letter for my mother and father," Collin said, holding it out.

She took it. "I thought, that first day you came to see me at the Gobi, you were too young to really be a doctor," she said.

"You'll make sure the postage is right? They always get it wrong," he said.

"I'll make sure," she said.

"Where will you go?" he asked.

"I don't know," she said.

"I would have asked you to. . . .."

"I would have said yes," she said.

"Good," he said. "Thank you for understanding." They kissed. "I wish I'd known you in London," he said. "That would have been good." Then he walked out, and she let him go.

He and Petros sat in the back seat, the tall one next to the driver. They drove through the town. The streets were empty, the night sky clear now. He could see the stars. It was just past midnight. The passing of the storm left a peaceful feeling.

"Did you know all the time about her?" Petros asked. They drove by the church. Collin realized he'd never gotten a good painting of the church or even gone inside, and he wondered what it was like.

"No," Collin said. He didn't feel like talking. They passed a few houses that, for one reason or another, had been abandoned over the years, as if the town couldn't grow beyond the church. He remembered how happy he'd been that morning, coming back from the Rancho. Alfredo had showed his painting off at lunch and told Collin he should be a painter. *Sometimes*, he realized, *you're as happy as you're going to get and don't even realize it.*

They drove into the palm trees. He closed his eyes. In his imagination the sun was beginning to rise over the mountain, and it was flashing though the trees. Collin heard Petros talking, but he didn't bother to pay attention. He just wanted to watch the morning unfold as it had when he'd come here to paint the palms.

He remembered the way the bottoms of the palm trees were dark from the rain, almost black in places. His mind started to fashion a painting with the sharp moments of glare dropping under the fronds and hitting the desert floor, making light pools, magical looking.

He opened his eyes and saw Jimmy Hidalgo's body as they drove by it. It startled him. In a moment they were out onto the muddy dark airstrip.

They got out of the Jeep. Petros looked at him. It was surprisingly cold out. Collin looked at the airstrip as he climbed out of the car. It was muddy and badly puddled. "Go on. Get in," Petros said. Collin followed the tall one up into the cargo door. Petros made an inspection of the plane. They watched him walk around it, his shoes sinking in the mud.

Collin put his improvised medical bag on the pile of webbing. The tall one sat in the co-pilot's seat. He knew enough to turn on the engines; the port side coughed and started, then the starboard. The sound was queerly beautiful, even now.

Petros came to the cargo bay door and tried to pull himself up, but he couldn't. He looked at Collin and held his hand out for help. They stared at each other a moment; then Collin gave him a hand, and he was in.

"Give me the injection if something happens," Petros said. Collin turned around; the one in the suit was pointing a pistol at him. "He'll shoot you if you don't. Do you understand?" Petros said. "If you do anything wrong, he'll kill you."

"Yes," Collin said. "I understand."

Petros went forward and got in the pilot's seat. Collin looked out at the palm trees lining the bottom of the runway. He could see the town, its metal roofs in the starlight. He saw the ailerons being tested. They'd be taking off soon, and he thought for a moment of jumping. *The problem is that no one wants to die,* he thought. He knew that. *But there's always a place where it happens.* He knew that, too. *What difference does it make where?*

He slid down and sat on the stack of webbing. He touched where the webbing was bolted to the fuselage, looking at the bolts. Satisfied, he clutched his bag. The plane started to move, the engines getting louder.

They taxied down toward the base of the mountain. Collin watched through the cargo door as they turned back around and were finally pointed west. The engines went hard; suddenly they were bouncing down the runway, picking up speed.

Collin stood up. The one with the suit was standing, holding onto a strap. They looked at each other. Collin glanced towards the cargo door and saw the desert floor rushing by, quicker now. He could see the tree line and then he felt that moment when they were airborne, and everything changed inside of him.

He'd been afraid all his life. He understood that as he turned and looked at the man with the suit. He glanced into the cockpit. Petros was fighting to bring the plane's nose up, fighting to clear the palm trees. Collin remembered his own father in the cockpit: in control, so sure of himself. How he'd admired his father like that. He closed his eyes and felt that joy again, a child's joy, and felt safe—the way he had always felt flying with his father as a boy.

Collin reached down then and grabbed the webbing, bringing it up with him. He wondered if there would be enough; Hidalgo had said six feet. He was hoping it was enough. The one with the suit didn't understand at first, just looked at Collin as he stood up and started to walk towards the cargo door. Then he understood, and fired twice.

The doctor didn't hear the bullets. The first one missed, but he fell forward, looked down and saw the tops of the palm trees. Six feet; Hidalgo had been right, he thought. The second bullet hit him in the back; and when he spilled out of the cargo door, the webbing went, too. It didn't catch the first palm, or the second, but it caught the fourth one and held.

They heard the explosion in the town. People came out into the street and saw the fire in the tops of the palm trees—a bright yellow, just like the sun coming over the mountain.

30

From the helicopter, the *pensión* looked quite beautiful and quaint, Alex thought.

It had already been over twenty-four hours since the "accident" at San Javier, as the Mexico City newspapers were calling it. The Mexican Navy helicopter had landed in the *pensión's* parking lot. The sky was clear blue. The storm had passed and moved back out over the Pacific. The FBI was already there, two of their own helicopters parked nearby. A body was lying out in the corridor as Alex walked in. It was still a little cold, and he buttoned his coat as he passed it.

The activity inside the lobby was heated. Beefy types from the San Diego office with blue nylon jackets—the letters FBI announcing them to the world—were going over the room, trying to lift prints and find shell casings, in short, Alex thought, losing themselves in the minutiae of a "crime scene." It was just what he wanted. Like any good intelligence officer, he had a natural reluctance to engage with these police types because of their hopeless naiveté about what was and was not important. Here he welcomed them, as their notorious bungling would help him begin the long process of obfuscating what had really happened.

"My name's Tom," Alex said to the team's leader, who came up to him. The man looked a little overwhelmed.

"*Al Qaeda,*" the man said right away. "Maybe the dead one in the hallway, too."

"I see," Alex said.

"You from the embassy?" the man asked. "They said they were sending someone."

"Yes," Alex said. "From the embassy. Tom." He shook the agent's hand.

"Well, Tom. The bad guys are all out on the airstrip, burnt to a crisp—except for a white guy hung up in the trees. I think the Mexicans are pulling him down. These Mexican cops don't know their ass from their elbow." The man smiled at what was supposed to be a shared off-color joke, but Alex ignored it.

"Right," Alex said, looking around. The man went on about the *pensión* being a headquarters of the "cell," and that they were sure to find all kinds of things that would help them track their friends down.

Alex looked around the room. He doubted it but smiled when the man said he expected this to lead to a major breakthrough against *al Qaeda.*

"They aren't supermen," the agent said. "Couldn't even fly the goddamned plane well enough to get out of here. Dumb bastards."

• • •

"I want to thank the nice doctor. His father was wonderful to me," Helen had said to Alex that morning as he was getting dressed.

He didn't want to tell her. She still looked weak, and the doctors had told him that they weren't out of the woods yet. She'd had to give up both breasts, but that hadn't been enough to satisfy God, or whoever was in charge of the planet.

He looked at her in the mirror when she came into the bathroom. She was wearing a white robe. She pulled it tight around her waist; he saw that they were gone, and that she was changed by it. It had hurt her badly. He wanted to say something but didn't know what he could say that would help.

"How about we go up to Acapulco this weekend?" he said, looking away. "I'm in the mood to be out of the loop."

"I don't know . . . I mean, I'm not exactly feeling like Cindy Crawford right now, Alex," she said.

"I promise no marathon sex or cliff diving. I would just like to be alone with you," he said. "No telephones."

"All right," she said. "Could you be a dear and see if Dr. Reeves can come for dinner sometime soon?"

"Of course," he said. "I'll call him."

"Can you do something for him? His career," Helen said. "A push, perhaps?" She came and sat down on the bench she used for her make-up mirror and held his hand for a moment. "Do you hate it? The way I look?" The question frightened him. He'd dreaded this moment, but he'd known she would ask.

"It's the most unimportant thing in the world. All that doesn't matter a whit," he said. "I love *you*." She squeezed his hand.

"Can you help him? Send him to Paris or something. God knows Paris is a good place to be young. Better than Mexico, I'd have to think," she said. "I never had much luck here."

"Yes. Why not? Paris. I'll see what I can do," Alex said.

"His father is very proud of him," Helen said. "I'm going to get dressed."

"Listen. They're picking me up in a helicopter. The office," he said.

"Then I'll see you for dinner," she said.

"Yes. Dinner," Alex said. "I should be back by then."

"Don't forget to tell the doctor," she said.

"Butch is going to Washington," Alex said, wanting to change the subject.

"Why, for heaven's sake?"

"Some woman at the embassy is accusing him of sexual harassment."

"You're kidding," she said. She was standing in the doorway to the bathroom and smiled. "Is it serious?"

"I don't know yet," Alex said. He kissed her. "He's being forced to go home and wait for some kind of investigation. It's out of my hands."

"I don't believe it," Helen said. They heard the helicopter then, and he had to go.

• • •

"How many were there?" Alex asked the man.

"Don't know, Tom. Can't say yet. There were three in the plane, we think, and the guy in the tree."

So the German girl was gone, Alex thought. And they hadn't found the pilot, whom he'd already been told was dead.

He already knew how many people were here, of course. They had gotten an immediate report from the local Mexican intelligence officer, a very thorough man who had sent an email to the embassy with a flash report. The Mexican officer's team had found the makeshift medical bag near the plane, and Alex heard then that the doctor was probably dead.

They'd arrested two women. Alex had called the man personally and told him to let both of the women go. He called his friend at Homeland Security and told some lies; DHS had sent the FBI.

"Well. I've just been sent to kick the tires," Alex told the FBI agent. "Formality, really." They hadn't found Fatima, and he knew she'd been here. He wasn't about to tell the FBI, as they would arrest her, and he didn't want that. He'd decided that in the helicopter as it had flown over Mexico City and he'd seen the enormity of the city, all gray and huge and messy. He was going to do the doctor a last favor. It wasn't much, but he wanted to do it.

"They say there was some kind of Arab girl here," the man said. "One of the maids we interviewed. But I think she was probably just a Mexican."

"Probably," Alex said. "Good luck, then."

"Thanks, Tom," the man said, giving him one of those hearty male handshakes Alex loathed.

He was about to leave, but he noticed the paintings in the dining room. Plates were still on the table, smudged now where the FBI had painstakingly dusted for finger prints.

Alex went to the wall and studied the paintings. He'd seen the church from the air, its small tile dome shining in the sunlight, a few palm trees planted around it. He turned to go and noticed a watercolor on the floor with a pile of evidence. He stopped and looked at it while a woman slipped it into a plastic bag. It was of a stairway, with a girl on it.

He walked outside. It was a little warmer now. He could see the palm trees in the distance. The air smelled very clean and fresh. Alex told his bodyguard and the pilot of the helicopter that were waiting for him that he wanted to go see the church while he was here, and that he would go alone.

The church steps were made of granite. He wondered how the padres had managed to quarry the rock, and where it might have come from. He stopped for a moment and looked behind him. He could see the landing strip and the date palm grove. It was absolutely still. He'd gotten so used to the sound of the city that to hear the silence was almost magical. He turned then and walked through the big seventeenth-century doors and into the church.

He saw her then, sitting near the altar. He'd known she'd be here—or at least, he'd hoped she would be. She turned and looked at him, then turned away again.

The Indians who'd lived at the church with the padres had painted murals on the walls, scenes from the cross. The girl was

263

sitting by the scene from Calvary with Jesus on the cross next to the thieves. Alex looked up at it a moment. The sun streamed through the big stained glass window over the altar, a crusader's cross burning red.

"Hello," he said.

"Hello, Tom," she said.

"I thought you might be here."

"He said the church. That I should wait here. That you'd find me," she said.

"Well, it's over," Alex said. "I've had your mother and sisters released. They're back home."

Dolores looked at him. She'd been crying; her eyes were red.

"I thought. I thought . . . I wanted you to find me. Collin said you'd come."

"I have," Alex said.

"He worked for you?" she asked.

"Yes," Alex said. She nodded her head. "It was all an accident, you see. He didn't know when he met you. He had no idea."

"I know," she said.

"Odd how things work."

"Yes," she said.

"So he went with them?" Alex asked.

"Yes," she said. "He convinced them to leave me and take him."

"Couldn't have been easy," Alex said, looking at the purple sheet that had been laid over the altar. He hadn't been in a church in years.

"He stopped them," she said. "I wanted you to know that. It was he alone who stopped them. Collin."

"I know . . . not surprised, really," Alex said. "Does anyone know you came to the Gobi with your husband—besides Madani?"

"No. He split us up. He put Mohammad in another room. I never saw him again until he came here."

"Good. No one knows you came together to Mexico, then."

"You know?" she said. "That we were martyrs."

"Do I?" Alex said. "I'm getting old, and I forget things now. Small things. People's names. When I've met them. It's quite shocking, the things I forget. Here. You'll need this. It's English." He slid an envelope towards her. "There's a plane ticket at the Lufthansa office in the capital for the holder of this passport. Tomorrow. For London. You shouldn't have any problems."

"Why, Tom?" she said. "Why are you doing this?"

"Well . . . why not? It's done, isn't it? I'm hoping you'll go home and start over. That's what he would have wanted." Alex stood up. "Cold in here. Odd. I mean it's the desert, isn't it?" he said. "Have a good trip."

"Thank you," she said. "Tom. . . ." Alex stopped, turned, and looked at her. "He was a good man, the doctor."

"Yes. There are still a few out there . . . thank God. A plane's coming from Cabo in a few hours," he said. "They'll be looking for you."

"Would you see that they get this—his parents?" she said, and handed him the letter.

He nodded and took it from her; then he turned and left.

She heard him close the door, and she was alone again. She picked up the envelope and opened it. Inside were an English passport with her photo, travelers' checks, and a postcard of the *Zócalo* in Mexico City.

• • •

The movers were bringing boxes up. The apartment was in Virginia Beach. It was one of those new condominium complexes, with the multi-colored flags out in front. Butch had bought a rear unit because the sales lady essentially told him to. He didn't really care that much one way or the other. The whole time she'd been prattling on about the place—*"It's got radiant heating. . . . And there's a pool you haven't seen—"* Did she really think he was going to go down to the pool? Butch wondered.

He'd had a drink already. He remembered a pool in Saigon that he'd liked. Alex and he had gone there and picked up stewardesses from the French airlines. When he was a little drunk, it was harder to turn off the past.

A black kid walked by him with a box. Butch told him to put it in the bedroom.

"I'll have to go down and see," he'd told the realtor.

"They have a tenants' association, and they have a welcome committee—" He'd turned and looked out the window and seen the expressway. Why was it that the one thing he'd feared in life had somehow come true? He didn't understand. He wanted to understand, but he couldn't.

He'd tried to call Alex at the embassy the other day from the bar, but his call had been flagged by some flunky. He had none of his direct numbers now, and couldn't get through. It was over.

"I'll take it." Butch had told the saleslady, suddenly.

They'd drummed him out a week later, after so many years. Alex had called him just afterwards saying he'd done everything he could, but things had changed. Ironically, the accusation had been directed at Butch's "legend," created years before, as an AID official, and not as a CIA officer. But it barred him from government work of any kind nonetheless.

They had had an awkward moment then, with nothing left to say. Helen had passed away that fall, and he couldn't bring himself to ask Alex how he was coping. Butch already knew what it had to have been like for him. He'd gone to the funeral in San Francisco. He'd felt a little strange there; it had been nothing but rich people, no one from the agency. He was glad in a way that he didn't have to be there with his friend now. It might have been too much.

"I've asked to go to Bangkok," Alex had said on the phone. "I don't know why, just want the hell out of Mexico. I've only got a year left, then I get the boot. They've agreed. Come if you like. When I'm settled," Alex told him. "I'd like that."

"Okay. Okay," Butch said.

The hours after that call were very long. The days seemed indistinguishable. At the health club he joined, he picked up an old *Time* magazine and thumbed through it in the sauna. *"Homeland security reports today that Mexican intelligence officials have uncovered a plot by terrorists to fly a. . . ."* There was no mention of the doctor.

He put the magazine down and left it. He had no idea where he would go as he walked out of the place later. He ended up at a park, sitting on a swing.

Time seemed dead now, like the winter he was walking out into. The past thirty years had all been a dream. A long winter to get through, and all he had left were the names of places he'd been: Saigon, Laos, Guatemala, Philippines, Iran, Beirut, Panama. . . .

The Good Physician by Kent Harrington: An Appreciation

This is a book that fights the good fight. This is a book that has courage and wit and style. I first read this story as a favor, as part of a commitment to a fellow writer I have long admired and to an editor I have long put up with—all right, and also admired. Both are artists of a kind. One puts the words together beautifully, and one packages them just as beautifully. My sympathies lie first with the writer, of course, and so I promised I would read his book. Out of this commitment the reading was first a chore—finding the time to make good on the promise. But once I was there, the chore became an obsession. I read this book page for page in one sitting. No longer because I had agreed to, but because I had to. It is that rare story that inexorably drags the reader into a world of intrigue and danger that is so fully realized that you feel it. You can hear the bullets buzz past your ear in the night. You can taste the blood on your split lip. That is the experience of *The Good Physician* by Kent Harrington. The book has got a painter's soul and a terrorist's conscience. It is muscled with both politics and humanity, both love and betrayal. With an unflinching eye it tells us about the world we live in. At center is a man who has done many bad things on a path that leads him to doing the right thing. Dr. Collin Reeves is that man. But don't we wish we all had the same journey, to a place where one choice could vanquish all the wrong we have done before it? This is the universal desire, I believe, and that makes this the universal story. There is a quality of redemption in anything that is art. Who said that first? Chandler? Twain? I can't remember, but it rings hard and true to me after reading this book. Harrington has taken one man's journey to the righteous land and made it our collective journey. That to me is art.

— Michael Connelly